THE
TURNAROUND

GEORGE PELECANOS

PHOENIX

A PHOENIX PAPERBACK

First published in Great Britain in 2008
by Orion Books
This paperback edition published in 2009
by Phoenix,
an imprint of Orion Books Ltd,
Orion House, 5 Upper St Martin's Lane,
London WC2H 9EA

An Hachette UK company

1 3 5 7 9 10 8 6 4 2

A CIP catalogue record for this book
is available from the British Library.

ISBN 978-0-7538-2660-7

Printed and bound in Great Britain by CPI Mackays,
Chatham ME5 8TD

The Orion Publishing Group's policy is to use papers
that are natural, renewable and recyclable products and
made from wood grown in sustainable forests. The logging
and manufacturing processes are expected to conform to
the environmental regulations of the country of origin.

www.orionbooks.co.uk

'Pelecanos transcends the elements of formula because his grasp of the nuances of his characters' lives is sure, and his writing reflects fine details without false sentiment' *Spectator*

'Perhaps the greatest living American crime writer'

Stephen King

George Pelecanos was born in Washington, DC in 1957. He worked as a line cook, dishwasher, bartender, shoe salesman, electronics salesman, construction worker, and retail general manager before publishing his first novel in 1992.

He is the author of 15 crime novels set in and around Washington, DC. *The Big Blowdown* was the recipient of the International Crime Novel of the Year award in both Germany and Japan and *King Suckerman* was shortlisted for the Gold Dagger award in the UK. He is also an award-winning journalist and pop-culture essayist who has written for the *Washington Post*.

Pelecanos served as producer on several feature films, and is a writer and producer on the acclaimed HBO series *The Wire*, for which he was nominated for an Emmy.

He lives in Silver Spring, Maryland, with his wife and three children.

In Memoriam

Lance Cpl. Philip A. Johnson
3rd Battalion, 2nd Marine Regiment
2nd Marine Division
2nd Marine Expeditionary Force

ACKNOWLEDGMENTS

Many thanks to Gail Moore of the Army Wounded Warrior Program (AW2) and the staff and patients of Walter Reed Army Medical Center. Sushant Sagar, Mark Tavlarides, and Henry Allen added to my memories of the Stones at RFK. In addition, thanks go out to Reagan Arthur, Michael Pietsch, Marlena Bittner, Betsy Uhrig, Sophie Cottrell, Heather Rizzo, Karen Torres, Tracy Williams, and all my other friends at Little, Brown; Jon Wood, Gaby Young, and the rest of the staff at Orion in the UK; Sloan Harris and Alicia Gordon; and my parents, Pete and Ruby Pelecanos. As always, love to Emily and my crew.

PART ONE

ONE

H**E CALLED** the place Pappas and Sons Coffee Shop. His boys were only eight and six when he opened in 1964, but he was thinking that one of them would take over when he got old. Like any father who wasn't a *malaka*, he wanted his sons to do better than he had done. He wanted them to go to college. But what the hell, you never knew how things would go. One of them might be cut out for college, the other one might not. Or maybe they'd both go to college and decide to take over the business together. Anyway, he hedged his bet and added them to the sign. It let the customers know what kind of man he was. It said, This is a guy who is devoted to his family. John Pappas is thinking about the future of his boys.

The sign was nice: black images against a pearly gray, with "Pappas" twice as big as "and Sons," in big block letters, along with a drawing of a cup of coffee in a saucer, steam rising off its surface. The guy who'd made the sign put a fancy *P* on the side of the cup, in script, and John liked it so much that he had the real coffee cups for the shop made the same way. Like snappy dressers got their initials sewn on the cuffs of a nice shirt.

John Pappas owned no such shirts. He had a couple of blue

GEORGE PELECANOS

cotton oxfords for church, but most of his shirts were white button-downs. All were wash-and-wear, to avoid the dry-cleaning expense. Also, his wife, Calliope, didn't care to iron. Five short-sleeves for spring and summer and five long-sleeves for fall and winter, hanging in rows on the clothesline he had strung in the basement of their split-level. He didn't know why he bothered with the variety. It was always warm in the store, especially standing over the grill, and even in winter he wore his sleeves rolled up above the elbow. White shirt, khaki pants, black oilskin work shoes from Montgomery Ward. An apron over the pants, a pen holder in the breast pocket of the shirt. His uniform.

He was handsome in his way, with a prominent nose. He had turned forty-eight in the late spring of 1972. He wore his black hair high up top and swept back on the sides, a little bit over the ears, longish, like the kids. He had been going with the dry look the past few years. His temples had grayed. Like many men who had seen action in World War II, he had not done a sit-up or a push-up since his discharge, twenty-seven years ago. A marine who had come out of the Pacific campaign had nothing in the way of manhood to prove. He smoked, a habit he had picked up courtesy of the Corps, which had added cigarettes to his K rations, and his wind was not very good. But the physical nature of his work kept him in pretty fair shape. His stomach was almost flat. He was especially proud of his chest.

He arrived at the store at five a.m., two hours before opening time, which meant he rose each morning at four fifteen. He had to meet the iceman and the food brokers, and he had to make the coffee and do some prep. He could have asked for the deliveries to come later so that he could catch another hour of sleep, but he liked this time of his workday better than any other. Matter of fact, he always woke up wide-eyed and ready, without an alarm clock to prompt him. Stepping softly down the stairs so as not to wake his wife and sons, driving his Electra deuce-and-a-quarter down 16th Street, headlights on, one cigaretted hand dangling out the window, the road clear of traffic. And then the quiet time, just him and the Motorola radio in the store, listening to the smooth-voiced announcers on WWDC, men his age who had the same kind of life experience he had, not those fast-talkers on the rock-and-roll stations or the *mavres* on WOL or WOOK. Drinking the first of many coffees, always in a go-cup, making small talk with the delivery guys who dribbled in, a kinship there because all of them had grown fond of that time between night and dawn.

It was a diner, not a coffee shop, but coffee shop sounded better, "more high-class," Calliope said. Around the family, John just called the store the *magazi*. It sat on N Street, below Dupont Circle, just in from Connecticut Avenue, at the entrance to an alley. Inside were a dozen stools spaced around a horseshoe-shaped Formica-topped counter, and a couple of four-top booths along the large plate glass window that gave onto a generous view of Connecticut and N. The dominant colors, as in many Greek-owned establishments, were blue and white. The maximum seating was for twenty. There was a short breakfast flurry and a two-hour lunch rush and plenty of dead space, when the four employees, all blacks, talked, horsed around, brooded, and smoked. And his older son, Alex, if he was working. The dreamer.

There was no kitchen "in the back." The grill, the sandwich board, the refrigerated dessert case, the ice cream cooler, the soda bar, and the coffee urns, even the dishwasher, everything was behind the counter for the customers to see. Though the space was small and the seating limited, Pappas had cultivated a large carryout and delivery business that represented a significant portion of the daily take. He grossed about three, three hundred and twenty-five a day.

At three o'clock, he stopped ringing the register and cut its tape. The grill was turned down and bricked at four. There was little walk-in traffic after two thirty, but he kept the place open until five, to allow for cleanup, ordering, and to serve anyone who happened to drop in for a cold sandwich. From the time he arrived to the time he closed, twelve hours, on his feet.

And yet, he didn't mind. Never really wished he could make a living doing anything else. *The best part of it*, he thought as he approached the store, the night sky beginning to lighten, *is now:* bending down to pick up the bread and buns left outside by the Ottenberg's man, then fitting the key to the lock of his front door.

I am my own man. This is mine.

Pappas and Sons.

ALEX PAPPAS had had his thumb out for only a few minutes, standing on the shoulder of University Boulevard in Wheaton, before a VW Squareback pulled over to pick him up. Alex jogged to the passenger door, scoping out the driver as he neared the car. He looked through the half-open window, saw a young dude, long hair, handlebar mustache. Probably a head, which was all right with Alex. He got in and dropped onto the seat.

"Hey," said Alex. "Thanks for stoppin, man."

"Sure thing," said the dude, pulling off the shoulder, catching second gear, going up toward the business district of Wheaton. "Where you headed?"

"All the way down Connecticut, to Dupont Circle. You going that far?"

"I'm going as far as Calvert Street. I work down there at the Sheraton Park."

"That's cool," said Alex with enthusiasm. It was only a mile and a half or so down to the Circle from there, all downhill. He could huff it on foot. It was rare to get one ride all the way downtown.

An eight-track player had been mounted on a bracket under the dash. The live Humble Pie, *Rockin' the Fillmore*, was in the deck, "I Walk on Gilded Splinters" playing in the car. Music came trebly through cheap speakers on the floorboard, the wiring running up to the player. Alex was careful not to get his feet tangled in the wire. The car smelled of marijuana. Alex could see yellowed roaches heaped in the open ashtray, along with butted cigarettes.

"You're not a narc, are you?" said the dude, watching Alex survey the landscape.

"Me?" said Alex with a chuckle. "Nah, man, I'm cool."

How could he be a cop? He was only sixteen. But it was common knowledge that if you asked a narc if he was one, he had to reply honestly. Otherwise, a bust would always be thrown out of court. At least that was what Alex's friends Pete and Billy maintained. This guy was just being cautious.

"You wanna get high?"

"I would," said Alex, "but I'm on my way to my father's store. He's got a lunch place downtown."

"You'd get paranoid in front of Pops, huh."

"Yeah," said Alex. He didn't want to tell this stranger that he never got high while working at his dad's place. The coffee shop was sacred, like his father's personal church. It wouldn't be right.

"You mind if I do?"

"Go ahead."

"Righteous," said the dude, with a shake of his hair, as he reached into the tray and found the biggest roach among the cigarette butts and ashes.

It was a good ride. Alex had the Pie album at home, knew the songs, liked Steve Marriott's crazy voice and Marriott's and Frampton's guitars. The dude asked Alex to roll up his window while he smoked, but the day was not hot, so that was fine, too. Thankfully this guy did not have a change of personality after he had gotten his head up. He was just as pleasant as he had been before.

As a hitchhiker, Alex had a fairly easy time of it. He was a thin kid with a wispy mustache and curly shoulder-length hair. A long-haired teenager wearing jeans and a pocket T was not an unusual sight for motorists, young and middle-aged alike. He did not have a mean face or an imposing physique. He could have taken the bus downtown, but he preferred the adventure of hitching. All kinds of people picked him up. Freaks, straights, housepainters, plumbers, young dudes and chicks, even people the age of his parents. He hardly ever had to wait long for a ride.

There had been only a few bad ones that summer. Once, around Military Road, when he was trying to catch his second ride, a car full of St. John's boys had picked him up. The car stank of reefer and they smelled strongly of beer. Some of them began to ridicule him immediately. When he said he was on the way to work at his dad's place, they talked about his stupid job and his stupid old man. The mention of his father brought color to his face, and one of them said, "Aw, look at him, he's getting mad." They asked him if he had ever fucked a girl. They asked him if he had fucked a guy. The driver was the worst of them. He said they were going to pull over on a side street and see if Alex knew how to take a punch. Alex said, "Just let me out at that stoplight," and a couple of the other boys laughed as the driver blew the red. "Pull over," said Alex more firmly, and the driver said, "Okay. And then we're gonna fuck you up." But the boy beside Alex, who had kind eyes, said, "Pull over and let him out, Pat," and the driver did it, to the silence of the others in the car. Alex thanked the boy, obviously the leader of the group and the strongest, before getting out of the vehicle, a GTO with a decal that read "The Boss." Alex was sure that the car had been purchased by the boy's parents.

Where University became Connecticut, in Kensington, the dude with the handlebar mustache began to talk about some chant he knew, how if you repeated it to yourself over and over, you were sure to have a good day. Said he did it often, working in the laundry room at the Sheraton Park, and it had brought him "positive vibes."

"Nam-myo-ho-rengay-kyo," said the dude, dropping Alex off at the Taft Bridge spanning Rock Creek Park. "Remember it, okay?"

"I will," said Alex as he closed the door of the VW Square-back. "Thanks, man. Thanks for the ride."

Alex jogged across the bridge. If he ran all the way to the store, he wouldn't be late. As he ran, he said the chant. It couldn't hurt, like believing in God. He kept his pace, going down the long hill, passing restaurants and bars, running straight through Dupont Circle, around the center fountain, past the remnants of the hippies, who were beginning to look unhip and out of time, past secretaries, attorneys, and other office workers down along the Dupont Theater and Bialek's, where he often bought his hard-to-find records and walked the wood floors, browsing the stacks of books, wondering, *Who are these people whose names are on the spines?* By the time he reached the machinists' union building, on the 1300 block of Connecticut, he had forgotten the chant. He crossed the street and headed toward the coffee shop.

Two evergreen bushes in concrete pots outside the store

bookended a three-foot-high ledge. Alex could have walked around the ledge, as all the adults did, but he always jumped over it upon his arrival. And so he did today, landing squarely on the soles of his black high Chucks, looking through the plate glass to see his father, standing behind the counter, a pen lodged behind his ear, his arms folded, looking at Alex with a mixture of impatience and amusement in his eyes.

"TALKING LOUD and Saying Nothing, Part 1," was playing on the radio as Alex entered the store. It was just past eleven. Alex didn't need to look at the Coca-Cola clock, mounted on the wall above the D.C. Vending cigarette machine, to know what time it was. His father let the help switch to their soul stations at eleven. He also knew it was WOL, rather than WOOK, because Inez, who at thirty-five was the senior member of the staff, had first pick, and she preferred OL. Inez, the alcoholic Viceroy smoker, dark skin, red-rimmed eyes, straightened hair, leaning against the sandwich board, still in recovery from a bout with St. George scotch the night before, languidly enjoying a cigarette. She would rally, as she always did, come rush time.

"*Epitelos*," said John Pappas as Alex breezed in, having a seat immediately on a blue-topped stool. It meant something like "It's about time."

"What, I'm not late."

"If you call ten minutes late not late."

"I'm here," said Alex. "Everything's all right now. So you don't have to worry, Pop. The business is saved."

"You," said John Pappas, which was as effusive as his father got. He made a small wave of his hand. Get out of here. You bother me. I love you.

Alex was hungry. He never woke up in time to have breakfast

at home, and he never made it down here in time to make the breakfast cut. The grill was turned up for lunch at ten thirty, and then it was too hot to cook eggs. Alex would have to find something on his own.

He went around the counter to the break at the right side. He said hello to Darryl "Junior" Wilson, whose father, Darryl Sr., was the superintendent of the office building above them. Junior stood behind a heavy clear plastic curtain meant to shield the customers' view of the dishwashing, and also to keep the attendant humidity and heat contained. He was seventeen, tall and lanky, quiet, given to elaborate caps, patch-pocket bells, and Flagg Brothers stacks. He kept a cigarette fitted behind his ear. Alex had never seen him remove one from a pack.

"Hey, Junior," said Alex.

"What's goin on, big man?" said Junior, his usual greeting, though he was twice Alex's size.

"Ain't nothin to it," said Alex, his idea of jive.

"All right, then," said Junior, his shoulders shaking, laughing at some private joke. "All right."

Alex turned the corner from behind the curtain and came upon Darlene, precooking burgers on the grill. She spun halfway around as he approached, holding her spatula upright. She looked him over and gave him a crooked smile.

"What's up, sugar?" she said.

"Hi, Darlene," said Alex, wondering if she caught the hitch in his voice.

She was a dropout from Eastern High. Sixteen, like him. The female help wore dowdy restaurant uniform shifts, but the one she wore hung differently on her. She had curvaceous hips, big breasts, and a shelf-top ass that was glove tight. She had a blowout Afro and pretty brown eyes that smiled.

She unnerved him. She made his mouth dry. He told himself

that he had a girlfriend, and that he was true to her, so anything that might happen between him and Darlene would never happen. In the back of his mind he knew this was a lie and that he was simply afraid. Afraid because she had to be more experienced than he was. Afraid because she was black. Black girls demanded to be satisfied. They were like wildcats when they got tuned up. That's what Billy and Pete said.

"You want somethin to eat, *don't* you?"

"Yes."

"Go on down and talk to your father," she said, with a head motion to the register area. "I'll fix you something nice."

"Thanks."

"I get hungry, too." Darlene chuckled. "And I would just . . ."

Alex blushed and, unable to speak, moved along. He passed Inez, who was bagging up a rack of delivery orders, preparing to move them over to "the shelf," where Alex would get his marching orders. Inez did not greet him.

Farther down the line, he said hello to Paulette, the counter girl who served the in-house customers. She was twenty-five, heavy everywhere, large featured, and very religious. After lunch she commandeered the radio for the gospel hour, which everyone endured, since she was so sweet. With her high-pitched, soft-as-mouse-steps voice, she was nearly invisible in the store.

Paulette was filling the Heinz ketchup bottles with Town-house ketchup, the inexpensive house brand from Safeway. Alex's father shopped at the Safeway every night for certain items that were cheaper than the offerings from the food brokers.

"Morning, Mr. Alex," she said.

"Morning, Miss Paulette."

Alex met his father down by the register. Only John Pappas and his son rang on the machine. A D.C. tax schedule was fixed to the front of it, beside two keys rowed by dollars and cents. If the tab hit twenty dollars, which it rarely did, the ten-dollar key would be punched twice. On the sides of the register were Scotch-taped pieces of paper on which Alex had handwritten bits of song lyrics that he found poetic or profound. One of the customers, a pipe-smoking attorney with a fat ass and an overbite, assumed that Alex had written the lyrics himself, and jokingly told John Pappas that as a writer, his son "made a good counterman." Pappas replied, with a smile that was not a smile, "You don't need to worry about my boy. He's gonna do fine." Alex would always remember his father for that, and love him for it.

John handed his son some ones and fives. He pushed rolls of quarters, dimes, nickels, and pennies along the Formica.

"Here's your bank, Alexander. You've got a couple of early orders."

"I'm ready. First I'm gonna grab a bite to eat."

"When those orders hit the shelf, I want you outta here. I don't want you to get behind."

"Darlene's makin me a sandwich."

"Quit screwin around."

"Huh?"

"I got eyes. I told you before: don't get too familiar with the help."

"I was just talking to her."

"Do what I tell you." John Pappas looked toward the shelf over the dishwashing unit, where Junior was pulling down a drop hose with a power nozzle, preparing to hand-clean a pot. Inez was nudging him aside, placing a couple of tagged brown paper bags on the shelf. "You got orders up."

"Can't I eat first?"

"Eat while you're walkin."

"But Dad—"

John Pappas jerked his thumb toward the back of the store. "Get on your horse, boy."

ALEX PAPPAS wolfed down a BLT back by Junior's station, then grabbed two bags off the shelf. A light green guest check was stapled to the front of each. On the top line was written, in Inez's florid, lucid script, the delivery address. Below was the detailed order, itemed out, with prices, taxes, and grand total circled. Alex liked to guess the tax based on the subtotal. It wasn't easy, as the D.C. tax was always a percentage and a fraction, never a whole number. But he had figured out a way to do it by stages of multiplication and addition. He had struggled all his life with school math, but he had taught himself percentages by working the register.

Working here was more beneficial than school in many respects. He learned practical math. He learned how to get along with adults. He met people he would otherwise never have met. Most important was what he learned from watching his father. Work was what men did. Not gambling or freeloading or screwing off. Work.

Alex took the back door to a hallway that held a utility closet and a janitor's bathroom that the help used (he and his father used the bathrooms in the office building above them). He went up a short flight of stairs to the back exit and stepped out into an alley. The alley was fashioned as a T and had three outs: N Street to the north, Jefferson Place to the south, and 19th Street to the west. Alex's first stop was the Brown Building, a boxy structure so called because of its color, housing government workers, at 1220 19th.

The money was good. It was better than any buck-sixty-an-hour minimum-wage thing he could have gotten on his own. His father paid him fifteen dollars a day. He cleared another fifteen, twenty in tips. As he did with the other employees, his father paid him weekly in a small brown envelope, in cash. Alex paid no taxes. Unlike his friends, he had walking-around dollars in his pocket all the time.

After all these summers, he knew every alley, every crack in the sidewalk in the blocks south of Dupont. He had been working as a delivery boy for his father for six summers. He had started when he was eleven. His father had insisted on it, though Alex's mother felt he was too young. He had surprised himself when he found that after a few shaky days, he could do the work. His father was never easy on him. When he came up short on cash a couple of times in the first few weeks, his father took the shortfall out of his pay. Alex was mindful after that to carefully count out the customer's change.

At eleven he had been a typical head-in-the-clouds kid. He was distracted easily, stopped to look in store windows on the Avenue, and often fell behind. He was naive to the ways of the city and its predators. That first summer, as he made a delivery up by the Circle, an older man had pinched him on the ass, and when Alex turned around to see who had done this thing to him, the man winked. Alex was perplexed, thinking, *Why did that man touch me like that?* But he knew enough not to tell his father about the incident when he returned to the store. His father would have found the man out on the street and, Alex was certain, beaten him half to death.

Many major law firms were situated around the shop. Arnold and Porter, Steptoe and Johnson, and others. Alex didn't like the way some of the attorneys, men and women alike, talked down to his father. Didn't they know he was a marine and a veteran? Didn't they know he could kick their soft asses around the block? Some of them clearly thought they were better than his father, which placed a longtime blue-collar chip on Alex's shoulder. But just as many were kind. Often they nursed coffees at the counter just as an excuse to talk to his old man. John Pappas was more than quiet; he was a good listener.

These law firms needed secretaries and mail room eccentrics to make them run, and Alex grew friendly with the girls and the oddballs, bearded guys wearing shorts and *Transformer* T-shirts, along with the garage attendants who watched their employers' cars. On Jefferson Place, a narrow street of residential row homes converted to commercial, were smaller firms and associations that took on causes like Native American rights and higher wages for grape pickers. Fancy hippies, his dad called them. But they were not like the hippies, those few who remained, up at the Circle. These people wore shirts and ties. And the women who worked on this street seemed to be on equal footing with the men. Braless with short skirts, but still.

In the earlier years, Alex had been in his own dreamlike state, but as his hormones kicked in, he began to notice the young workingwomen, just about the time that rock and roll and soul music began to mean something to him. He knew elementally that all of it was connected in some way. He would sing the songs he heard on the soul stations while walking his deliveries, and sometimes would sing them in empty elevators, learning through experimentation which ones had the best acoustics. "Groove Me." "In the Rain." "Oh Girl." And he plotted his routes so he would spot particular young women he liked, knowing just where they might be at certain times of day. Most of them thought of him as a kid, but sometimes he would smile at them and get a smile in return that implied something else: You are young but you have something. Be patient, Alex. This will come to you. You are not that far away.

Everything was in front of him and new.

TWO

TWO BROTHERS walked up a slightly graded rise toward a small market and general store called Nunzio's. They had just finished playing one-on-one at the outdoor court of a recreation center that adjoined an African Methodist Episcopal church. The older of the two, eighteen-year-old James Monroe, held a worn basketball under his arm.

Both James and his younger brother, Raymond, were long and thin, cut in the solar plexus and flat of chest, with good definition in the shoulders and arms. Both wore their hair in blowouts. James, a recent high school graduate, was good-looking and fully formed, and stood over six feet. At fifteen years old, Raymond was just as tall as James. As they walked, Raymond used a fist-topped pick to upcomb his hair.

"James," said Raymond, "you seen Rodney's new stereo yet?"

"Seen it? I was with him when he bought it."

"He got some big-ass Bozay speakers, man."

"Call it *Bose*. You sayin it like it's French or somethin."

"However you say it, those speakers is bad."

"They *are* some nice boxes."

"Man, he played me this record by this new group, EWF?"

"They ain't all that new. Uncle William got their first two records."

"They're new to me," said Raymond. "Rodney put on this one song, 'Power'? Starts off with a weird instrument—"

"That's a kalimba, Ray. An African instrument."

"After that, the music kicks in hard. Ain't no words in this song, either. When Rodney turned it up . . . I'm telling you, man, I was *trippin*."

"You shoulda heard those speakers at the stereo store we went to," said James. "Down on Connecticut? They got this sound room in the back, all closed up in glass. Call it the World of Audio. The salesman, long-haired white dude, puts Wilson Pickett on the platter. 'Engine Number Nine,' the long jam. Got to be the one record he spins when he trying to sell a stereo system to the black folk. Anyway, Rodney, you know he don't play that. So he says to the dude, 'Don't you have any rock records I can hear?'"

"Messin with the white dude's head."

"Right. So the salesman puts on a Led Zeppelin. That song with all the weird shit in the middle of it, music flyin back and forth between the speakers? One where the singer's talking about, 'Gonna give you every inch of my love.'"

"Yeah, Led Zeppelin . . . he's *bad*."

"It's a group, stupid. Not just one dude."

"Why you always tryin to teach me?"

"You shoulda heard it, Ray. Those speakers liked to blow us out the room. I mean, Rodney couldn't pull his wallet out fast enough. Fifteen minutes later, the stock boy is cramming a couple of Bozay Five-Oh-Ones into Rodney's trunk."

"Thought it was Bose."

James reached out and tapped his brother's head with affection. "I'm just playin with you, son."

"I'd like to have me a stereo like that one."

"Yeah," said James Monroe. "Rodney got the baddest stereo in Heathrow Heights."

Heathrow Heights was a small community of about seventy houses and apartments, bordered by railroad tracks to the south, woods to the west, parkland to the north, and a large boulevard and commercial strip to the east. It was an all-black neighborhood, founded by former slaves from southern Maryland on land deeded to them by the government.

By geography, some said by design, Heathrow Heights was both self-enclosed and cut off from the white middle- and upper-class neighborhoods around it. There were several traditionally black communities, most of them larger in area and population, like this one in Montgomery County. None seemed as secluded and segregated as Heathrow. The people who grew up here generally stayed here and passed on their properties, if they had managed to retain ownership of them, to their heirs. The residents were proud of their heritage and generally preferred to stay with their own.

The living conditions were far from utopian, though, and there certainly had been challenges and struggles. The early residents had owned their properties through deeds, but many houses had been sold to land speculators during the Depression. The properties were bought by a group of white businessmen who razed them, then built minimally sound, cheap houses on the lots and became absentee landlords. The majority of these homes had no hot water or indoor bathrooms. Heat was provided by wood-burning kitchen stoves.

Children had attended a one-room schoolhouse, later a

two-room, on the grounds of an AME church. Elementary-age kids were educated there until the big change of 1954. Residents shopped at a local market, Nunzio's, founded by an Italian immigrant and eventually passed on to his son, Salvatore. Consequently, many grew up without much contact with whites.

Most of the roads in Heathrow had remained unpaved by the county until the 1950s. By the '60s, community activists had petitioned the government to force landlords to make improvements to their properties. Officials did so reluctantly. A women's association in one of the neighboring white communities had joined Heathrow's residents in forcing the government's hand, but by '72, the neighborhood was blighted still. Ramshackle houses, improperly constructed and "improved," were in disrepair. Rusting cars sat on cinder blocks in backyards among broken toys and other debris.

To liberals, it made for dinner conversation, the stuff of slow head shakes and momentary concern between the serving of the roast beef and the pour of the second glass of cabernet. To some of the middle- and working-class white teenagers of the surrounding area, who learned insecurity from their fathers, Heathrow Heights was the subject of ridicule, slurs, and pranks. They called it "Negro Heights." To James and Raymond Monroe, and to their mother, a part-time domestic, and their father, a D.C. Transit bus mechanic, Heathrow was home. Of them, only James had dreams of moving out and on.

James and Raymond came up on a couple of young men, Larry Wilson and Charles Baker, sitting on the curb in front of Nunzio's. Both were shirtless in the summer heat. Larry was smoking a Salem, drawing on it so hard and rapidly that its paper had creased. Both of them were drinking

Carling Black Label beer from cans. A brown bag sat between them.

Baker had a wild head of hair that was matted in spots. He looked over Raymond with hazel eyes prematurely drained of life. Baker's face had been scarred by a young man with a box cutter who had casually questioned his manhood. Several people had gathered to witness the fight, the subject of rumors for days. Charles, bleeding profusely from the slice but visibly unfazed, had downed his opponent, kicked aside his weapon, and broken his arm by snapping it over his knee. The crowd had parted as a laughing, wounded Charles Baker had walked away, the boy on the ground convulsing in shock.

"Y'all been ballin?" said Larry.

"Down at the hoop," said James. It was the only one in the neighborhood, and he didn't have to elaborate.

"Who won?" said Larry.

"I did," said Raymond. "I took him to the hole like Clyde."

"You let him win?" said Larry, with a nod to James.

"He won square," said James.

Larry hotboxed his cigarette down to the filter and pitched it out into the street.

"What you all gonna do today?" said Raymond.

"Drink this brew before it gets too hot," said Charles. "Ain't nothin else *to* do."

Of them, only James had a job, a twenty-hour-a-week thing. He pumped gas at the Esso up on the boulevard and was hoping to move up from there. He planned to take a mechanics class. His father, who occasionally let him work on the family's Impala, changing the belts, replacing the water pump, and the like, said he had skills. James was hoping to hook Raymond up with an entry-level position at the station when he turned sixteen.

"You hear Rodney's new system?" said Raymond, looking

at Charles and not Larry. Raymond, being young, admired Charles for his violent rep and courted his favor.

"Heard *of* it," said Charles. "Hard not to hear of it, the way Rodney be braggin on it."

"He got a right to brag," said James. "Rod earned that money; he can spend it how he wants to."

"He ain't got to boast on it all the livelong day," said Larry.

"Actin superior," said Charles.

"Man's got a job," said James, defending his friend Rodney and making a point to his kid brother. "No reason to cut on him for that."

"You sayin I can't hold a job?" said Charles.

"I ain't never known you to hold one," said James.

"Fuck all a y'all," said Charles, looking past them and addressing the world. He drank from his can of beer.

"Yeah, okay," said James tiredly. "Let's go, Ray."

James tugged on Raymond's belt. They walked up the steps to Nunzio's market. On the wooden porch fronting the store, they stopped to say hello to a Heathrow elder who was retrieving her small terrier mix from where she had tied his leash to a crossbeam, used often as a hitching post.

"Hello, Miss Anna," said James.

"James," she said. "Raymond."

They entered the store and went to a refrigerated bin, where James found some Budding pressed luncheon meat that sold for sixty-nine cents. He grabbed two packages, beef and ham. Raymond got himself a bag of Wise potato chips and two bottles of Nehi, grape for him and orange for James. They stood on the porch and ate the meat straight out of the package. They shared the chips and drank their sweet sodas as they looked down at the street, where Larry and Charles now stood, having risen off the curb but still inert.

"What you gonna do now?" said Raymond.

"Go home and get ready for work. I got my shift at the station this afternoon."

"Rodney home, right?"

"Should be. He's off today."

"I'm 'a see if Charles and Larry wanna go over to Rodney's and check out his stereo. They ain't seen it yet. Maybe if Charles get to know Rodney, he won't be so, I don't know . . ."

"Charles gonna be what he is no matter who he gets to know," said James. "I don't want you runnin with him."

"Better than bein out here alone."

"I'm here."

"Not all the time."

Raymond had been stressing about recent incidents in the neighborhood, cars of white boys driving through, yelling "nigger" out their open windows, leaving rubber on the street and then speeding back up to the boulevard. It had happened more often in the past year. In one way or another, it had been going on for generations. Their mother had been the recipient of such a taunt a few weeks earlier, and the thought of someone calling their mother that name had cut James and Raymond to the heart. The only white people with reason to be in this neighborhood were meter men, mailmen, Bible and encyclopedia salesmen, police, bondsmen, or process servers. When it was drunken white boys coming through in their jacked-up vehicles, you knew what they were about. Always driving in quietly and turning around at the dead end, then speeding up around the market, where folks tended to hang in groups. Yelling that stuff and driving away fast. *Cowards*, thought James, 'cause they never did get out their cars.

James handed Raymond the bag of chips. "Do what you

want. Just remember: Charles and Larry, they ain't headed no place good. You and me, we weren't raised that way."

"I hear you, James."

"Go on, then. Mind the time, too."

James stayed on the porch of Nunzio's as Raymond went down to where Larry and Charles still stood, the bag of Carlings under Charles's arm. They talked for a little bit, Charles nodding as Larry lit another smoke. Then the three of them walked slowly down the block, turning right at the next intersection.

James kept his eyes on his brother. When he could see him no longer, he dropped the empty soda can in a bin and headed home.

RODNEY DRAPER stayed with his mother in their old house on the other east–west-running street of Heathrow Heights. This street, too, dead-ended down by the woods.

Rodney lived in the basement of the house, which was small and boxy, with asbestos siding. The basement took in water when it rained and got damp at the threat of rain. It always smelled of mold. He had a double bed and a particleboard chest of drawers and an exposed toilet that he and his uncle, a handyman and odd-jobber, had plumbed in themselves back by the hot-water heater. His mother and sister lived upstairs. Rodney's setup was not luxurious, but his mother did not charge him rent the way many parents did when their children turned eighteen.

Rodney, nineteen, had a thin nose with a small hump in the bridge. He was skinny, bucktoothed, and had knobby wrists and large feet. His nickname was the Rooster. He worked at Record City, on the 700 block of 13th Street. He loved music and thought he could combine his passion with work. He spent most of his earnings on albums, receiving a small employee discount. The new stereo had been bought "on time," a revolving-credit thing, a small-print contract he would be paying off for years.

Rodney was showing off his stereo to Larry, Charles, and Raymond. Larry and Charles were sitting on the edge of his bed, drinking beer, watching without apparent interest as Rodney pointed to the components the way the white, long-haired salesman had done, presenting them piece by piece.

"BSR turntable," said Rodney, "belt drive. Got the Shure magnetic cartridge on the tone arm. Marantz receiver, two hundred watts, driving these bad boys right here, the Bose Five-Oh-Ones."

"Bama, we don't give a fuck about all that," said Larry. "Put on some music."

"All that gobbledy-goop don't mean a motherfuckin thing," said Charles, "if it don't sound good."

"Tryin to educate you, is all," said Rodney. "You drink a fine wine, don't you want to read the label?"

"Black Label," said Larry, holding up his can, grinning stupidly at Charles. "That's all I got to know."

"Stereo looks real nice, Rodney," said Raymond with a smile. "Let's hear how it sounds."

He put *America Eats Its Young*, the new double album from Funkadelic, on the platter and dropped the needle on track 3, "Everybody Is Going to Make It This Time." It was a number that started off slowly and built to a kind of gospel-like fervor, and it got Larry and Charles to bobbing their heads. Larry studied the album cover, which was a takeoff on a dollar bill, with a zombied-out Statue of Liberty, her mouth a bloody mess, cannibalizing babies.

"This shit is wild," said Larry.

"Paul Weldon drew that cover," said Rodney.

"Who?" said Larry.

"He's an artist. Black artists making their mark in this country, and not just on record covers. We had a woman living here in the nineteen twenties whose work got showed at a gallery downtown."

"Man, *fuck* a history lesson, all right?"

"I'm sayin, we got a rich past in this neighborhood."

"We don't care about that," said Charles. "Just turn the music up."

"Sounds good, right?" said Rodney.

"I heard better," said Charles, unable to give Rodney full respect. "My cousin got a stereo make this one be ashamed."

Later, Larry, Charles, and Raymond sat on the government fence, a barrier painted yellow and white at the end of the street. Rodney had politely asked them to leave, saying he planned to meet a girl he knew, a customer he had met at the record store. Raymond suspected that Rodney just wanted Larry and Charles out of his basement and had made up the date.

Larry and Charles had grown more belligerent behind the alcohol. Larry got louder, and Charles had become quiet, a bad sign. Raymond had taken them up on their offer to join them and was drinking a beer. He was three quarters done with it and could feel its effect. He had never had more than one, and he didn't really care for the taste. But it made him feel older to drink with these two. He kept an eye out for anyone who might tell his parents that they had seen him drinking beer in the afternoon.

They talked about girls they'd like to have. They talked about the new Mach 1. As Larry had done many times, he asked if James and Raymond were related to Earl Monroe, and Raymond said, "Not that I know."

There was a lull in the conversation while they swigged beer. Then Larry said, "Heard some white boys came through, couple weeks back."

"White *bitches*," said Charles.

"Heard they talked some shit to your mom," said Larry.

"She was walking home from the bus stop," said Raymond. "They weren't sayin it *to* her, exactly. She was passing by the market when they were callin out, is what it was."

"So it *was* to her," said Larry.

It wasn't a question, so Raymond did not reply. His face grew warm with shame.

"Anyone did that to my mother," said Charles, "they'd wake up in a grave."

"My father say you got to be strong and shake it off," said Raymond.

"Hmph," said Larry.

"It was my mother, I'd go ahead and shoot the motherfuckers," said Charles.

"Well," said Raymond, hoping to put an end to the embarrassment of the conversation, "I got no gun."

"Your brother got one," said Charles.

"Huh?" said Raymond. "Go ahead, man, you know *that* ain't right."

"I heard it from the man who sold it to him," said Charles. "A revolver, like the kind the police carry."

"James got no gun," said Raymond.

"I guess I'm lyin, then," said Charles, staring straight ahead. Larry chuckled.

"I ain't sayin that," said Raymond. "I guess what I'm sayin is, I didn't know."

Larry lit a cigarette and tossed the match out into the street.

"He got one," said Charles, looking into his beer can, shaking it to see what was left inside. "You can believe that."

JAMES MONROE liked to keep a clean red rag hanging from his back pocket when he worked the full-service pumps up at the Esso. Once he got the gas going into the car, he'd wash the windows, using the long-handled double-edged tool that sat in a bucket filled with diluted cleaning fluid. When he was done scraping the excess fluid off the windshield and rear window, he pulled that rag and wiped softly at any smudges or residue. Didn't matter if it needed to be done or not. The act showed the customer that he took pride in his job and cared about the appearance of their automobile. Because of this one little thing he did, what he liked to call his "finishing touch," he would occasionally receive a tip, sometimes a quarter and sometimes, around the holidays, fifty cents. Didn't matter if it was only a dime, really, or even just a look in someone's eye that said, That young man cares about his job. When you got down to it, it was about respect.

James had been the first black, to his knowledge, to be hired at the station. In his mind, he was not breaking a racial barrier but rather changing a tradition they had up at this particular Esso. In the past, the proprietor had always hired neighborhood white boys and their friends. James had been persistent, going back many times to talk to Mr. George Anthony, the station owner, a stocky, bearded man whose eyes crinkled around the sides when he smiled. Mr. Anthony had not hired him straightaway, but James's persistence had paid off one day when Mr. Anthony said, almost as an aside, "All right, James. Come on in at eight tomorrow morning. I'll give you a try."

Later, when Mr. Anthony had seen what James could do, how conscientious he was about reporting for work on time, never calling in sick, even when he *was* sick, Mr. Anthony said, "You know why I hired you, James? You kept on asking me for the job. You didn't give up."

James did good work, but he could only get part-time hours up at the station. Mr. Anthony tried to be fair to all the young men he employed and give them the equal opportunity to earn some coin. James took home about forty-two dollars a week. Not enough to move out of his parents' house or buy a car on credit. But he did have a plan: he wanted to be a mechanic, like his father, Ernest Monroe. James thinking, *Maybe I'll have my own gas station someday, make real money. Enough to buy a house for myself in the city, and help my mother and father find one near me, too. Live in a place where redneck white boys don't drive by my mother when she's walking home from the bus stop up on the boulevard after getting off work. Calling my mother a nigger after she's been on her feet all day, wearing that cleaning uniform of hers. She who has never judged anyone.*

He felt his blood quicken, thinking of his mother taking that abuse. He had recently bought something, something to show in case that kind of thing happened again. Just to scare those punks, was all it was. To see the looks on their faces when it was them eating dirt.

He didn't like to feel this angry. He moved the image of his mom from his mind.

As far as the ownership thing went, James realized he was dreaming, but there wasn't anything wrong with thinking ahead. He had to concentrate and work to get to where he needed to be. He had signed up for the mechanic classes through Esso. They had a kind of training program set up for their employees, the ones they thought could cut it. Mr. Anthony had urged him to do it and agreed to pay for half the course fee. Working on cars was not a bad way to make a living. When you fixed something, you made someone happy. A car came in broke and it left out of there in running condition. You had accomplished something.

A career as an auto mechanic would separate him from boys like Larry and Charles, who he felt were already done. He'd get Raymond up here, too, teach him how to work, to get along with people outside their neighborhood, the way he, James, got along with the white customers and the white boys who worked at the station. Raymond had been in a little trouble lately, a shoplifting thing up at Monkey Wards and, more serious, getting caught for throwing a rock through the window of a house in that high-class neighborhood near Heathrow. Mr. Nicholson, the man who owned the place, had paid Ray less than they had agreed for yard work, saying Raymond had not done a thorough job, and Raymond had gone over there one night for some get-back. The police, sent by Nicholson, had come to their house straightaway, and Raymond had admitted what he'd done. They gave him an FI for that, meaning no arrest or court if he paid for the damages, but now he had something on his record. One more thing like that, the police said, and he'd be in some real trouble. Ernest had given James the task of keeping Ray on the straight, looking out for him, reining in his violent impulses. He was just a kid, jacked up with too much energy, was all it was. The boy did have anger inside him.

James had been like that himself when he was younger, with big resentment and distrust, mainly of whites. That feeling had softened, somewhat, when he and the other kids from his neighborhood had been bused to the white junior high and then the high school on the rich side of the county. He didn't run with those white kids at all, but at least they weren't any kind of mystery to him, as they had been before. And most of these white boys he worked with at the station, he found them to be all right. Not that he hung with them outside the job. They were what they were, and he was from Heathrow Heights. But at work they were all young men, dark blue pants and light blue shirts, their first names written in script on oval sew-on patches. You could be the best of them or you could be average. He wanted to be the best. He wanted respect.

"Yes, ma'am?" said James, approaching the open window of a white-on-white Cougar, an oldish blond lady under the wheel.

"Fill it up," she said, not looking him in the eye. "High-test."

"Right away," said James, pulling the nozzle out of its holster in the pump. "I'll go ahead and get those windows for you, too."

THE MONROE home was, at a glance, as modest as the other homes in Heathrow Heights. The house was a two-bedroom with wood siding, a storm cellar, and a front porch. Ernest Monroe, being a mechanic, was handy, and he kept the place maintained and right. He had taught his sons the smooth stroke of a paintbrush, the proper swing of a hammer, and the use of glazier points and putty in the replacement of broken windows, a frequent occurrence when boys and baseballs were around. Ernest knew that a fresh coat of paint every two years was the difference between a shabby-looking home and one that told others that a steady workingman lived here and cared about what was his. Didn't take money to achieve that impression, but rather a little bit of sweat and pride.

Ernest worked hard, but he also looked forward to his

relaxation time. After dinner, his nights were all about sitting in his recliner, watching his bought-on-time twenty-five-inch Sylvania console color TV, drinking a few beers, and smoking his menthol Tiparillo cigars. Once he got in that chair, the late edition of the *Washington Post* in his lap, he didn't move except to make trips to the home's sole bathroom. Ernest would watch his CBS action shows, occasionally reading aloud from the newspaper when something got his attention or amused him, sometimes getting a response from his wife, Almeda, or his sons if they were around and listening. This was entertainment, to him.

"Y'all keep your voices down for a minute," said Ernest. "I want to hear the song."

Mannix, his favorite detective show, was about to come on. He enjoyed the opening, where they played the music over split-screen shots of Joe Mannix running, drawing his pistol, and rolling over the hoods of cars.

"Da-dant-de-da, da-dant-de-da-daaaaah," sang James and Raymond in unison, cracking up and giving each other skin.

"Quiet," said Ernest. "I'm not playin."

Ernest Monroe was a medium-sized man with ropy forearms built from years of turning wrenches. His thick mustache and modified Afro were flecked with gray. In the evenings his hands smelled of cigar smoke and Lava soap.

"Da-dant-de-da, da-dant-de-da-daaaaah," sang James and Raymond, now almost in a whisper, and Ernest grinned. When the music did come on, they stopped the game and let their father hear the song.

"Work good today, Jimmy?" said Almeda, a thin woman, once pretty, now handsome, in a sleeveless housedress. She was seated between her sons on a worn couch that she had worked on with needle and thread to keep nice. She was fanning herself with a *Jet* magazine. The house had no air-conditioning and stayed hot in the summer. It didn't even seem to cool down much at night.

"Work was all right," said James.

"He was pumping Ethyl," said Raymond.

"*Raymond*," said his father.

"And where were you this afternoon?" she said to Raymond, pointedly ignoring his off-color comment.

"Just around," he said. Raymond had been chewing on wintergreen Life Savers up until dinner, hoping his mother and father would not smell beer on his breath. It had been hours since he'd had it, but, being inexperienced as a drinker, he did not know how long the stench of alcohol lingered.

The opening credits ended, and the network went to a commercial. Something caught Ernest's eye in the newspaper and made him smile.

"Listen to this right here," said Ernest. "Congresswoman Shirley Chisholm visited George Wallace in the hospital today . . ."

"He still over at Holy Cross?" said James.

"They did some operation," said Almeda, "trying to get the bullet fragments out of his spine."

"See if they can get that cracker to walk again," said Raymond.

"That's not very Christian of you, Ray," said his mother.

"Anyway," said Ernest. "Shirley Chisholm is walking out the hospital, and some reporter asks her why she is visiting this man. Does this mean that she would support him in a presidential election if he moderated his views? You know how Shirley Chisholm responded? All she said was, 'Jesus Christ!'"

"Heard Wallace gonna get the sympathy vote if he runs again," said James.

"From who?" said Ernest.

The show came back on. The boys chuckled at the story line, which had Mannix being blinded by the powder of a close-to-the-face gunshot, then, still sightless, spending the rest of the hour going after the man who did it.

"How he gonna find the dude if he blind?" said Raymond.

"Peggy gonna help him out," said Ernest, cigar smoke streaming from the side of his mouth.

"Your father likes that Gail Fisher," said Almeda.

"I don't like her like I like you," said Ernest.

"I remember when she did that commercial for All detergent." Almeda liked to follow the careers of black actors and actresses, whom she read about in her magazines.

"She was fine in that, too," said Ernest.

They talked through most of the show. It was predictable, and it was also a repeat of a show their father had seen the previous fall. As he did many times, Ernest mentioned that the actor playing Mannix wasn't a white guy, exactly, but some kind of Arab. "Romenian, or some such thing," he said.

"*Ar*menian," said Almeda. "And they are Christian people. Orthodox Christian, matter of fact. Not Muslim. The ones I know are, anyway."

Almeda cleaned the house of an Armenian family up in Wheaton, out there by Glenmont. It was one of two daylong jobs she'd held on to since the riots of '68. Many of the domestics she knew had stopped doing maid work after the fires of April. She had continued to work part-time because her family needed the money, but she had given notice to those she didn't care for and stayed with the people she liked. The cutback in hours hadn't even hurt her much. The homeowners who employed her, the Armenians and a Protestant couple out in

Bethesda, had given her raises after Dr. King was assassinated. She hadn't even asked.

"One of you boys," said Ernest, "go get your father a cold beer." James got up off the couch.

Ernest read from the paper. "Redd Foxx and Slappy White coming to Shady Grove. Since the Howard got messed up, they're having all the good shows out in farmer country. Who's gonna go all the way out there?"

James returned with a can of Pabst and pulled the ring off its top. He dropped the ring into the hole and handed the beer to his father.

"You tryin to choke me?" said Ernest. "Throw the tab away next time."

"That's how I see other guys do it," said James, who had only drunk beer a couple of times.

"Those other guys are fools, then. I ain't about to swallow a twisted piece of metal."

"I can get you another one," said Raymond.

"That's all right. Now that it's open I'm gonna drink it. Shoot, I paid for it."

"Barely," said Raymond.

"Watch your mouth, boy."

PBR was only a dollar and change for a six-pack up at the Dart. The Tiparillos that Ernest smoked were fifty for one ninety-nine at the same store. Ernest Monroe had habits, but they were cheap ones. Almeda never complained about his smoking or his drinking. The man worked hard and came home every night.

James and Ernest began to talk about the difference between small- and big-block engines. Raymond said he was tired, kissed his mother on her cheek, and touched a hand to the shoulder of his father, who grunted by way of acknowledgment.

Raymond went to the back bedroom, which he and James had always shared. There were two single beds placed against opposite walls. The beds had become too small for them as they had grown, and now their feet hung off the ends. At the foot of each bed was a dresser, previously owned, that their father had brought home, having found them or bought them for next to nothing. Ernest had strengthened the dressers with nails and fortified them with carpenter's glue and vises. He had then refinished them, making them better than fine. One closet held shirts and church trousers that needed to be hung.

On the wall was tacked a team photo of the 1971 Washington Redskins, who had reached the playoffs for the first time in twenty-six years. The man who ran Nunzio's had given Raymond the photo, having obtained it in a Coca-Cola promotion, saying he had no use for it. Raymond suspected the man was just being kind. Raymond was into the Skins, but his first love was basketball. The Knicks were his team. He was a Clyde Frazier fan, and James was partial to Earl Monroe. Some folks called Earl Monroe the Pearl, and some called him Black Jesus. James and his friends just called him Jesus, but not around Almeda, who said that this was blasphemous.

James had a white T-shirt on the back of which he had Magic Markered the name Monroe, with Earl's number, 15, carefully written below. He'd put the number on the front as well. Raymond Monroe had decorated a T-shirt in the same way, with Frazier's jersey number hand-printed on the front and back, along with the single name Clyde.

Raymond picked up James's Earl Monroe T-shirt off the wood floor and smelled it to see if it was clean. It didn't stink much, so he folded it and went to James's dresser, opening a drawer and placing the shirt inside. His hand lingered on top of the shirts, and he looked over his shoulder at the open door.

He didn't hear footsteps. There were the sounds coming from the television and the muffled voices of James and their father, still talking.

He ran his hand under the T-shirts and felt nothing. He closed the drawer and pulled on the one below it, which housed jeans and shorts. Beneath the shorts, Raymond found steel. A short barrel, a crenellated cylinder, and a checkered grip.

It was as if a match had been struck inside him. Strength and manhood could come to a boy at once with the touch of a gun.

Charles was about bullshit most times. But this time, Charles had spoken true.

THREE

ALEX PAPPAS had the ticket stub from the Rolling Stones concert up on the bulletin board in his room. The Stones had played RFK Stadium on July 4, a few weeks earlier, and Alex and his friends Billy Cachoris and Pete Whitten had been there. Alex had spent hours in line at the Ticketron outlet at Sears in White Oak, waiting with the other heads to score seats, but it had been worth it. Alex did not think he would ever forget that day, not even when he got to be as ancient as his old man.

Also on the board were tickets from Baltimore Bullets games he had attended with his father, who had generously driven him and his friends up to the Baltimore Civic Center. Earl the Pearl, Alex's player, had been traded to the Knicks this midseason past, and with him had gone some of the attraction of the Bullets. It wasn't the same, rooting for Dave Stallworth and Mike Riordan instead of Monroe.

Alex was in his bedroom, waiting for his girlfriend to call. The record by that new group Blue Öyster Cult was playing on his compact stereo system, an eighty-watt Webcor home entertainment unit that included two air suspension speakers,

38

an AM/FM radio, a record changer and dust cover, and a built-in eight-track deck. He had saved up his tip money and bought it with cash up at the Dalmo store in Wheaton. By the unit were some eight-tracks, *Manassas*, *Thick as a Brick*, and *Broken Barricades*, but Alex preferred records, which sounded better than tape and didn't have channel breaks in the middle of the songs. Plus, he liked to take the shrink-wrap off a new album, read the credits and liner notes, and study the artwork as he listened to the music.

He was looking at the Blue Öyster Cult art now, while "Then Came the Last Days of May" played in the room. The song was about the end of something, its tone both ominous and mysterious, and it troubled Alex and excited him. The cover of the record was a black-and-white drawing of a building that stretched out to infinity, stars and a sliver of moon in a black sky above it, and, hovering over the building, a symbol that looked like a hooked cross. The images were unsettling, in keeping with the music, which was heavy, dark, dangerous, and beautiful. This was Alex's favorite new group. They were due to open for Quicksilver Messenger Service at Constitution Hall, and Alex planned to go.

The phone on the floor rang, and Alex picked it up. From the tremor in her voice he knew Karen had been crying.

"What's wrong?" said Alex.

"My stepmother is *such* a bitch."

"What she do?"

"She won't let me go out tonight," said Karen. "She says I've got to stay and babysit my sister. She says she told me about this last week. But she never told me anything."

Karen's sister was her half sister. The baby, no longer an infant, was the result of the union between Karen's father and his youngish second wife. Karen's mother had died of breast cancer. Karen's father was a prick. Everything was wrong in their home.

"Can you sneak out later?" said Alex.

"Alex, the baby's only two years old. I can't leave her."

"Just for, like, fifteen minutes."

"Alex!"

"Look, okay, I'll come over. After your folks go out."

"What are we going to do?"

"You know, just talk," said Alex. He was thinking of Karen's pink nipples and black bush.

"We better not," said Karen. "You know what happened last time."

Her parents had come home early and surprised them during a make-out session on Karen's bed. Alex had emerged from Karen's bedroom with a bone protruding from under the fabric of his Levi's and some excuse about having gone in there to try and fix her stereo. Her father had stood there red-faced, unable to speak. He was a class-A jagoff who had been lousy to Karen since the new wife had come into the family.

"I guess you're right," said Alex. "I'll just go out with Billy and Pete."

"Maybe tomorrow?" said Karen.

"Maybe," said Alex.

He hung up and found his friends. Pete could get the family's Olds that night, and Billy was ready to go. Alex put on jeans with a thick belt, a shirt with snap buttons, and Jarman two-tone shoes with three-inch heels. He shut down the stereo and left the room.

His brother, Matthew, fourteen, was in his bedroom down the hall. Matthew was close to Alex's size and excelled on the football field, the baseball diamond, and in class. He was more competent than Alex in every way except the one way that counted between boys. Alex could still take him in a fight. It wouldn't be that way for much longer, but for now, it defined their relationship.

Alex stopped in the doorway. Matthew was lying atop his bed, tossing a baseball up in the air and catching it with his glove. He had thick, wavy hair and a big beak, like the old man. Alex's hair was curly, like their mom's.

"Pussy," said Alex.

"Fag," said Matthew.

"I'm headin out."

"Later."

Alex went along the hall, past his parents' bedroom, and stopped at the bathroom door, which was slightly ajar. The air drifting out smelled like soapy water, cigarettes, and farts. His father was in there, taking one of his half-hour baths, something he did every night.

"I'm goin out, Dad," said Alex through the break in the door. "With Billy and Pete."

"The three geniuses. What're you gonna do?"

"Knock down old ladies and steal their purses."

"You." Alex didn't have to look in the bathroom to see the small wave of his father's hand.

"I won't be late," said Alex, anticipating the next question.

"Who's drivin?"

"Pete's got his father's car."

"Idiots," muttered his father, and Alex continued down the hall.

His mother, Calliope "Callie" Pappas, sat in the kitchen at the oval eating table, talking on the phone while she smoked a Silva Thin Gold 100. Her eyebrows were tweezed into two black strips, her face carefully made up, as always. Her hair

41

had recently been frosted at Vincent et Vincent. She wore a shift from Lord and Taylor and thick-heeled sandals. Second generation, she cared about fashion and movie stars, and was less Greek than her husband. Their house was always clean, and a hot dinner was always served promptly. John Pappas was the workhorse; Callie kept the stable clean.

"Goin out, Ma," said Alex.

She put her hand over the speaker of the phone and tapped ash into a tray. "To do what?"

"Nothin," said Alex.

"Who's driving?"

"Pete."

"Don't drink beer," she said, as a horn honked from outside. She gave him an air kiss, and he headed for the door.

Alex left the house, a small brick affair with white shutters on a street of houses that looked just like it.

BILLY AND Pete had bought a couple of sixes of Schlitz up at Country Boy in Wheaton. They held open cans between their legs as Alex got into the backseat of the Olds. Billy reached into the bag at his feet and handed a can of beer to Alex.

"We're way ahead of you, Pappas," said Pete, lean, blond, agile, and tall, a Protestant white boy among ethnics in the mostly working-to-middle-class area of southeastern Montgomery County. His father was a lawyer. The fathers of his friends worked service and retail jobs. Many of them were World War II veterans. Their sons would grow up in a futile, unspoken attempt to be as tough as their old men.

"Drink up, bitch," said Billy, broad of shoulder and chest. He carried a shadow of a beard, though he was only seventeen years old.

Billy and Pete usually swung by Alex's last, so they could

commandeer the front seat. It was understood that Alex was not the lead dog in this particular pack. He was somewhat smaller than they were, less physically aggressive, and often the butt of their jokes. They were not cruel to him, exactly, but they were often condescending. Alex accepted the arrangement, as it had been this way since junior high.

Alex pulled the ring on the Schlitz and dropped it into the hole in the top of the can. He drank the beer, still cold from the coolers of the store they called Country Kill.

"You guys got any reefer?" said Alex.

"Bone dry," said Pete.

"We're gettin some tomorrow morning," said Billy. "You in?"

"How much?"

"Forty for an OZ."

"*Forty?*"

"It's Lumbo, man," said Pete. "My guy says it's prime."

"Not like that Mexican ragweed you buy from Ronnie Leibowitz."

"Hebe-owitz," said Billy, and Pete laughed.

"I'm in," said Alex. "But, look, pull over soon as you get off my street."

Pete curbed the Olds and let it idle. Alex produced a film canister that held a thimble-sized portion of pot. "I found this in my drawer. It's a little stale . . ."

"Gimme that shit," said Billy, who took the canister, looked into it, and shook it. "We can't even roll a J with this."

Pete pushed the lighter in on the dash. When it popped back out, he pulled it and Billy immediately dumped the small amount of reefer onto the lighter's orange coils. They took turns snorting the smoke that rose off the hot surface. It was only enough for a headache, but they liked the smell.

"Where we goin?" said Alex.

"Downtown," said Pete, turning the car onto Colesville Road and driving south for the District line.

Billy pulled a Marlboro from a pack he had slipped behind the sun visor and fired it up. The windows were down and the warm night air flowed into the car, blowing back their hair. They all wore it long.

The car was a white-over-blue Cutlass Supreme. Because of the color scheme, and because it was not the 442, Billy often needled Pete about the vehicle, saying it was a car for "housewives and homos."

"What," said Billy, "did your mother pick this out while your father was at work?"

"Least we own it," said Pete. Billy's father, a Ford salesman at the Hill and Sanders showroom in Wheaton, brought home loaners. Pete's father was an attorney for the UAW, a "professional," which Pete never tired of mentioning to his friends. Pete got good grades and had recently scored well on the SATs. Billy and Alex were C students and had no special plans. They had gotten high and drunk the night before the test.

The boys argued over the choice of radio stations all the way down 16th Street. Alex wanted to listen to WGTB, the progressive FM station coming out of Georgetown U's campus, but Billy blew that idea off.

"He's hoping they play Vomit Rooster," said Billy.

"*Atomic* Rooster," said Alex.

"Nights in White Satin" came on the radio, but Billy switched it because they weren't stoned. He switched off another station that was playing that Lobo song about the dog and stayed with another one only long enough to change the words of the Roberta Flack hit to "The first time ever I sat on your face." Billy found a station that was spinning music with guitars and let it ride. They listened to singles by T-Rex, Argent, and Alice Cooper, and when "Day After Day" came on, Billy turned it all the way up. They were down near Foggy Bottom by the time the song had finished. Pete found a place to park.

They walked to a nightclub owned by Blackie Auger. They weren't old enough to drink, but all of them had draft cards they had bought from older guys in the neighborhood. The doorman had a look at them, saw three guys in jeans from the working-class side of the suburbs, and balked at letting them in. But Alex talked them through the door by saying he knew Blackie, the legendary Greek restaurateur and bar owner. Alex did not know Auger and neither did his parents. In fact, he was in an entirely different class of Greek American and had never come in contact with him. Alex's family attended "the immigrant church" on 16th Street, while Auger and others of his standing were members of the "uptown" cathedral at 36th and Mass.

The doorman let them pass. The chance that the kid might be telling the truth was their ticket in.

They knew they were out of place as soon as they entered the club. The men were in their twenties and wore stacks and tight double-knit trousers, with rayon big-collared shirts opened to expose chest hair, medallions, crucifixes, and gold anchors. The women wore dresses and did not look their way. Those on the dance floor seemed to know the current steps. Alex, Billy, and Pete could do stuff they'd seen on the *Soul Train* dance line, but that was all. Their stay was cut short when a guy with a dollar sign for a belt buckle said something to Billy about being "in the wrong club," and Billy, who was smoking a Marlboro at the time, said, "Yeah, I didn't know this was a fag bar," and flicked his live cigarette off the dude's chest. The same doorman who had let them in told the boys to get out and "don't never" come back.

"Don't never," said Pete, out on the sidewalk. "Dumbass used a double negative."

Billy and Alex didn't know what Pete meant, but they figured it was something about Pete being smarter than the bouncer. Being tossed had been momentarily embarrassing, but none of them felt bad about it for long. It had been fun watching the sparks fly off that dude's chest, hearing Billy's cackle of a laugh as the guy balled his fists but didn't step forward, Billy not giving a good fuck about anything, which was his way.

They drove around some more and drank beer. They thought about going to the Silver Slipper, but the club had a drink minimum and enforced it, and anyway, the Slipper featured burlesque dancers, and burlesque to them meant the ladies didn't show snatch and took their time about showing bare tit. They ended up buying tickets to a movie called *The Teachers*, down at 9th and F, at a theater called the Art, which was the wrong name for the place because it was just a stroke house. In the auditorium, which smelled of tobacco, perspiration, and damp newspapers, they sat apart from one another so no one would think they were like that and watched the movie and the older guys in the audience who moaned while they jacked off. Alex got an erection but nothing like the strong one he got while making out with Karen, and thinking of her made him lonely and sad to be where he was. The other guys must have been feeling something like that, too, since they mutually decided to leave before the end of the film. On the way to the car they joked about the fact that all the girl characters were named Uta.

They drove over to Shaw. The beer was warm now, but they

continued to drink it. At 14th and S they talked about the time they had bought a whore on that corner for Pete's sixteenth birthday, a rite of passage for boys in the D.C. area, and joked with Pete about how he had shot off the second he got inside her. In fact, he had blown his load on the dirty sheets of the bed in a tiny third-floor row house room before he had the opportunity to insert his pecker, but he hadn't related this to his friends. It was bad enough that he had lost his cherry to a black hooker named Shyleen. These guys were the only ones who knew that he had done this thing, and the story would die with their friendship. He would be gone in a year, off to college and a new life. It couldn't come fast enough.

"Remember when we gave her the fifteen dollars?" said Billy. "Right out on the street? She said, 'Put that money away; you tryin to get me 'rested?'"

Alex had been there. The girl had said "arrested," not "'rested."

"What do you expect from a boofer?" said Billy.

"Don't talk about your mama like that," said Pete.

At U Street, they started up the long hill, going north. From U up to Park Road, the commercial and residential district had been burned and virtually destroyed in the riots. What was left was boarded and charred. Many businesses that had managed to remain standing had closed and moved on.

"Man, did they fuck this up," said Pete.

"Wonder where the people who lived here went," said Alex.

"They all out in Nee-grow Heights," said Billy.

"How do you know, you been out there?" said Pete.

"Your daddy has," said Billy.

"'Cause you're always talking about it," said Pete. "When you gonna stop talking and do it?"

Billy, Pete, and Alex lived a few miles from Heathrow Heights, but they knew of it only by reputation and had not come into contact with its residents. The black kids who lived there were bused to a high school in the wealthier section of Montgomery County whose white students were bound for college, while the boys who went to the high school in down-county Silver Spring were known to be an unpolished mixture of stoners, greasers, and jocks, with a few closet academics in the mix.

"What, you think I'm afraid to go there?" said Billy. "*I'm* not afraid."

Billy *was* afraid. Of this Alex was certain. Like Billy's old man, who told nigger jokes on the steps of their church, where everyone gathered after the liturgy. Mr. Cachoris was afraid of black people, too. That's all it was: fear turned into hate. Billy wasn't a bad guy, not really. His father had taught him to be ignorant. With Pete it was something different. He always had to look down on someone. Alex wasn't very book smart, but these were things he knew.

"I just wanna go home."

"Alex got himself a nig girlfriend down at his father's coffee shop," said Billy. "He doesn't like it when I talk bad about his peoples."

Billy and Pete gave each other skin and laughed. Alex got small in his seat. Wondering, as he often did when he was coming down at the end of the night, why he hung with these guys.

"I'm tired," said Alex.

"Pappas wanna go night-night," said Pete.

Pete Whitten tipped his head back to kill his beer, his long blond hair catching the wind.

The boys grew quiet on the ride home.

*   *   *

RAYMOND WAS in his bed, listening to the crickets making their sounds out in the yard. He and James kept the windows open in their room three seasons of the year. Their father had made wood-frame screens that slid apart like wings to fit the space and hold up the sash windows, which no longer stayed up on their own, as their tracked ropes had long since torn. Ernest Monroe could fix most anything with his hands.

Raymond, wearing only briefs, lay atop the sheets, wide awake. He was excited by what he'd found and also feeling a bit guilty for going through his brother's dresser drawers. James had come in a while ago, said he was tired, and flopped down on his bed. That would have been the time to talk about the gun, but Raymond had been hesitant. He had been wrong to do what he'd done. He'd have to admit that his interest had been stirred by Charles and Larry, and Raymond knew that James didn't think much of them. It was complicated, trying to find the best way to start the conversation. By the time he'd gotten up the courage to do it, a stillness had fallen in the room that told Raymond he had waited too long.

"Hey, James," said Raymond.

The crickets rubbed their legs together. A little dog barked from the backyard of the tiny house down the street where Miss Anna lived.

Softly, Raymond said, "James."

FOUR

THREE TEENAGE boys cruised the streets in a Gran Torino, drinking beer, smoking weed, and listening to the radio. Three Dog Night's "Black and White" came from the dash speaker. The vocalist sang, "The world is black, the world is white / Together we learn to read and write." Billy sang along but changed the words to "Your daddy's black, your mama's white / Your daddy likes his poontang tight." They had heard Billy sing this one many times, but they were laughing as if it were new to them. The three of them had just blown a fat bone. Though the temperature was in the upper eighties, they had rolled up the windows to keep the high in the car.

Billy sat under the wheel of the Torino, a green-over-green two-door with a 351 Cleveland under the hood, his dad's latest loaner. He wore a red bandanna over his thick black hair. He looked like a heavy pirate.

"Pin this piece," said Alex from the backseat.

Billy gave the Ford gas. Beneath them, dual pipes rumbled pleasantly as they headed up a long rise on an east–west residential thruway. They were nearing the small commercial district not far from their neighborhood.

"Mach One," said Billy, reverently. "Hear it roar."

"It's a Torino," said Pete, riding shotgun.

"Same engine as the Mach," said Billy. "That's all I'm sayin."

"To-*ree*-no," said Pete.

"Least I'm drivin a car," said Billy.

"It's off your dad's lot," said Pete. "It's like a rental."

"Still, I'm *drivin* it. Wasn't for me, you'd be walkin."

"To your mother's house," said Pete.

Billy's wide shoulders shook. He laughed easily, the way big guys did, even when a friend was cracking on his mother.

"Your baby sister, too," said Pete, holding his hand palm up so that Alex could slap him five. Alex did it sharply, and the action made Pete's straight shoulder-length hair move about his face.

Pete killed his Schlitz and tossed the can over the seat. It hit the other ones they had drained that day, now in a heap on the floorboard, and made a dull sound.

"I need cigarettes," said Billy.

"Pull into the Seven-Ereven," said Pete, like he was a Chinese trying to talk American.

They parked and got out of the car. They wore 501 straight-leg Levi's, rolled up at the cuffs, and pocket T-shirts. Pete wore Adidas Superstars, and Billy sported a pair of denim Hanover wedges. Alex wore his Chucks. The boys weren't stylish, but they had down-county style.

The store was not a 7-Eleven, but it had been one for a time, and the three boys still identified it as such. Now run by a family of Asians, its primary offerings were beer and wine. As the boys entered, Climax's "Precious and Few" played through a cheap sound system from behind the counter. One of the Asians was singing along softly, and when he came to "precious," he sang "pwecious." When Alex heard this he chuckled. He found these things funny when he was high. Alex went to the candy aisle and stared at its display.

Pete and Billy had a brief conversation that ended with a bit of laughter. Then Pete went to a spinning rack and tried on a hat with a hooked-bass patch stitched on its front while Billy bought cigarettes, Hostess cherry pies, and beer. They never carded Billy here or anywhere else. He looked like a man.

Outside, Billy broke the cellophane on a hardpack of Marlboro Reds, tore out the foil, and extracted a cigarette. He fired it up with a Zippo lighter that had an eight ball inlaid on it. He had lifted it at the Cue Club after some greaser had left it lying on a rail.

"What do you girls wanna do now?" said Pete.

They were standing by the car in the direct sun. The heat was coming up in waves off the sidewalk. Billy held the bag of beer and cherry pies under his arm.

"Drink this brew before it gets too hot to drink it," said Billy.

"Who don't know that?" said Alex.

Pete watched Billy smoke. Pete didn't use cigarettes himself. His father said his friends came from uneducated people and that was why they had stupid habits. Pete took mild offense at this and expressed it vocally, but he felt in his heart that his father was right.

"Y'all ready to get torched?" said Billy.

Alex shrugged a Why not? There was nothing to do on this Saturday afternoon but get higher than they were now.

Billy finished smoking. He flicked his cigarette out into the parking lot with practiced nonchalance.

"Let's roll, Clitoris," said Pete to Billy Cachoris.

They got back into the Ford.

*   *   *

THEY DRANK six more beers and smoked another joint of Colombian, scored that morning, and got stoned and reckless behind the alcohol they had been pouring on empty stomachs. "Tumbling Dice" was finishing up on the radio, and Pete had cranked it up. In front, Billy and Pete were heatedly discussing the Fourth of July Stones concert, which had included good bud, a party ball of sour mash whiskey, and a girl in a halter top.

"God made halters," said Billy, "so blind guys can grab tit."

"Jenny Maloney," said Pete, naming the pom-pom girl at their high school whom the boys called the Hole. "She's got this one halter top, boy . . ."

Alex remembered the girl in the halter top and Peanut jeans who had danced in front of him during the concert. He could recall the details of the entire day. He, Billy, and Pete had gone down to RFK Stadium on the morning of the Fourth in the Whitten family Oldsmobile and parked in the main lot, where the Dead and the Who were blasting from the open windows of cars and vans. They had brought sandwiches, packed by Alex's mom, and a dude in a wheelchair traded them a small piece of hash for a ham-and-Swiss. They smoked it, got up immediately, and went to join the crowds moving toward the venue. When the gates opened, the expected chaotic surge ensued, caused by the festival seating policy, which had thousands trying to enter the stadium at once. Coolers holding bottles of beer and liquor were being smashed by security guards, and at one point Alex was pinned against a chain-link fence, only to be rescued by Billy, who yelled, "Jerry Kramer!" with joy as he body-blocked a big man to the ground and set Alex free. Alex, Billy, and Pete found seats behind the dugout, where Alex had sat with his father at baseball games before the

Nats left town, and commenced smoking one of the many joints they had rolled that morning with Top papers. Martha Reeves and the Vandellas came on first, played "Dancing in the Street," and when they sang the phrase "Baltimore and D.C.," the audience lit up. The girl in the halter top danced before them, her hips alive, and the boys imagined her in the act, all of them transfixed. Stevie Wonder appeared next, oddly opening with "Rockin' Robin," a hit for Michael Jackson earlier that year, and then got the throngs going when he moved into his own material. During "Signed, Sealed, Delivered (I'm Yours)," a handler came out and turned Stevie around, as he was inadvertently singing to the empty, obstructed-view portion of the stands. After a dead period during which people got more inebriated, more unruly, and more high, the Stones walked onto the stage, and Mick Jagger, cocaine skinny in a white jumpsuit and red silk scarf, shouted, "Hello, campers!" launching the band into "Brown Sugar." Forty thousand were up on their feet, fueled by alcohol, speed, acid, pot, and youth. A police officer twirled his nightstick in unison with the rhythm section. The band played cuts from *Exile on Main Street*, which had recently been released. Mick Taylor's guitar solo on "You Can't Always Get What You Want" was epic. Jagger pranced, pirouetted, and whipped the stage with a leather belt during "Midnight Rambler." Jagger toasted the crowd with a bottle of Jack, saying, "I drink to your independence." Tear gas drifted in from police action outside the stadium. The boys' eyes burned, but they didn't care. Girls who tried to climb onstage were thrown off or hauled away by security and had their hands cut by nails driven up through the stage's edge. Near the end of the concert, during a violent "Jumpin' Jack Flash," the houselights were turned on, and the smoke in the air was industrial as it moved up into the night sky. Alex could not remember being happier. He had never experienced anything like this and doubted that anything in his life would ever top it.

"The Hole must wear a halter top down there, too," said Billy. " 'Cause she likes to allow that easy access."

"For real," said Pete.

Billy and Pete were still talking about Jenny Maloney. Alex wondered how long they had been discussing her. He wondered if he had blacked out.

"I know you had your fingers in it," said Billy, setting Pete up.

"I had my *arm* in it, man," said Pete. "In the stairwell up at the HoJo hotel? Her parents were giving her a sweet sixteen party and shit. While they were passing out party favors, me and Jenny were up there on the landing, making out, and she put one foot up on this step and took my hand and kinda guided it up there. I didn't need no petroleum jelly, either, no lie. . . ."

As Pete went on, Alex Pappas tuned him out. Billy and Pete always sat together up front, and at some point when they were partying, they forgot he was in the car. He didn't mind. The things they said when they were high, he had heard them all before. Pete, elbow deep in Jenny Maloney's pussy at her sweet sixteen party, in the stairwell of the HoJo hotel up in Wheaton while her parents passed out birthday hats in the rented room . . . no shit, he knew it by heart.

Alex looked out the window. The world outside was tilted a bit and moving, and he blinked to stop the spin. He could feel the sweat dripping down his chest under his T. They were at the red light at the Boulevard. They were in the middle lane, which meant straight only. He had never been "over there" to Heathrow Heights, and as far as he knew, neither had his friends. He vaguely wondered why Billy was in this lane. He remembered the conversation between Billy and Pete the night before, and he thought: *Now Billy is going to show us that he is not afraid.*

PGC was playing "Rocket Man." The song reminded Alex of his girlfriend, Karen. Karen lived on a street called Lovejoy. Billy called the street "Lovejew" because the neighborhood was heavy with the Tribe. In the spring, Alex and Karen had cut school and gone out to Great Falls in Karen's eggplant-colored Valiant. They swam in a natural pool and drank warm Buds, sunning themselves on the rocks. On the way home, Karen let Alex drive her car. "Rocket Man" was on the radio, and Karen sat beside him smoking a cigarette, shivering in her bikini top and damp jeans, tapping ash into the tray as she sang along to the song and sometimes smiled at him with strands of black hair stuck to her face. Karen's cold father and hateful stepmother made him want to protect her. He pondered if this was what it meant to love someone and he guessed that he did love Karen. He thought, *I should be with her right now.*

"What are we gonna do when we get in there?" said Pete.

"Just fuck with 'em," said Billy. "Raise a little hell."

Alex wanted to say, "Let me out here." But his friends would call him a pussy and a faggot if he did.

Alex looked through the windshield as Billy caught the green.

They were crossing the Boulevard and then they were across it, going down an incline along the railroad tracks and past a bridge that spanned the tracks and then down into a neighborhood of ramshackle homes and cars that said poor. There were three young black guys grouped on the sidewalk ahead, in front of what looked like a country store. Two of the guys were shirtless and one of them wore a white T-shirt that had numbers written on it in Magic Marker. Alex noticed that one of the shirtless ones had a scar on his face. Pete and Billy were rolling down their windows.

"You ever been back here, for real?" said Pete. Alex could hear excitement and a catch in Pete's voice. Pete was rooting through the paper bag at his feet and coming up with one of the Hostess cherry pies in his hand. He tore the wrapper off the pie.

"Nah," said Billy, who was looking at the group of black guys, now eye-fucking them as they approached. They were thin, flat of chest and stomach, broad shouldered, and muscled out in the arms.

"You know how to get out of here, right?" said Pete.

"*Drive* outta here," said Billy, switching off the radio. "I got the wheel. You just do your thing."

"Why you goin so slow?"

"So you don't miss."

"I'm not gonna fuckin miss."

"Billy," said Alex. His voice was soft, and neither Billy nor Pete turned his head.

And now the Torino was *there*, and the young men were stepping slowly to the car as it pulled alongside them. Billy's face was stretched tight. He leaned toward the passenger window and yelled, "Eat this, you fuckin niggers!" and Pete backhand-tossed the cherry pie. It glanced off the scar-faced, shirtless young man, and Pete ducked to avoid his punch, thrown through the open window. Billy floored it, cackling with laughter, and the Ford left rubber on the street as it fishtailed and straightened and headed down the road. Alex felt the color drain from his face.

They heard the angry calls of the young men behind them.

They passed more houses and an intersection and then a very old church, and down at the end of the road they saw a striped barrier erected by the county and behind it, beside the railroad tracks, thick woods and vines in full summer green.

"It's a turnaround," said Alex, as if in wonder.

"The hell it is," said Billy. "It's a dead end."

Billy put the Ford through a three-point maneuver, slamming the automatic shifter into reverse, then into drive, and headed back up the street. The young men were standing in the road, not moving toward them, not yelling anymore. The shirtless one who had been hit by the pie looked to be smiling.

Billy tore his bandanna off his head, letting his black hair fall free. He turned left at the intersection, and the tires cried as they passed more houses in disrepair and an old black lady walking a small dog, then they came to a T in the road and all looked right and left. On the right, the road became a circle. On the left, the road ended with another striped barrier bordering woods. All of them pondered their stupidity and bad luck, and no one said a word.

Billy turned the car around and drove back to the main road. He stopped at the intersection and looked left. Two of the young men were spread out in the middle of the road, spaced so the Ford could not pass through. The other had taken a position on the sidewalk. An older black woman with eyeglasses had appeared and was standing on the porch of the country market.

Pete touched the handle of the door.

"Pete," said Billy.

"*Fuck* this," said Pete. He opened the door, leaped out, closed the door behind him, and took off. He ran toward the woods at the end of the street, the soles of his three-stripes kicking up as he slashed left and hit the railroad tracks without breaking stride.

Alex felt betrayal and envy churn inside him as he watched Pete vanish behind the tree line. Alex wanted to book, too, but he could not. It wasn't just loyalty to Billy. It was the suspicion that he would not make it to the woods. He was not as fast as Pete. They'd catch up to him, and the fact that he had run would only make it worse. Maybe Billy could talk them out of this. Billy could just apologize, and the ones in the street would see that what they'd done was nothing more than a stupid prank.

"I can't leave my dad's car," said Billy very quietly. He hit the gas and went back up the road, the way they'd come in.

She is my parents' age, thought Alex, looking at the older woman wearing eyeglasses who stood on the porch in front of the store. *She will stop this.* His heart dropped as he watched her turn and walk into the market.

Billy stopped the Torino and locked the shifter into park about fifty feet from the young men. He stepped out of the car, leaving the door open. Alex watched him walk toward the young men, who gathered around him in the street. He heard Billy's amiable voice say, "Can't we work this out?" He saw Billy's hands go up, as if in surrender. A lightning right came forward from one of the shirtless young men, and Billy's head snapped back. He stumbled and put a hand to his mouth. When he lowered his hand there was blood on it, and Billy spit blood and saliva to the ground.

"You knocked my teeth out," said Billy. "You satisfied?"

Billy turned and pointed at Alex, still seated in the backseat of the Torino.

"Take off!" shouted Billy, blood and anguish on his face.

Alex pushed the driver's seat forward and got out of the car. His feet hit the asphalt lightly, and he turned. He was grabbed from behind and thrown forward, and he tripped and went down on all fours. He heard footsteps behind him and was lifted off his knees by a fierce kick in his groin. The air left his lungs in a rush. When he caught his breath, he puked beer and bile. He panted furiously, watching his vomit steaming on the asphalt before him. He rolled onto his side and closed his eyes.

When Alex's eyes opened, he saw a foot rushing toward his face, and it hit him like a hammer.

"*Shoot that motherfucker!*"

"*Nah.*"

"*Shoot him!*"

"*Nah, man, nah . . .*"

"*Do it!*"

Another blow came down on Alex, and something was crushed. It felt as if one of his eyes had been loosened and sprung.

My face is broken. Dad . . .

A shot echoed out into the streets of Heathrow Heights.

PART TWO

FIVE

IT WAS still called Pappas and Sons Coffee Shop, as it had been for over forty years. The sign had been replaced by a new one that was exactly like the original, the words in block letters, a drawing of a cup and saucer, the letter P elegantly displayed in script on the cup's side, steam rising off its surface. "Pappas" twice the size of "and Sons." A refurbishment of the old one had been attempted, but the sign could not be saved. Its black lettering had faded, its pearl gray background irreversibly yellowed by time.

Inside, a man stood behind the counter, a pen lodged behind his ear. He was of medium height and build, with barber-cut hair, graying temples swept back, black and curly on top. His stomach was flat, and he had a good chest. Both of these things he maintained by watching his diet and through regular visits to the YMCA. For a man his age, he looked good.

Handsome, some would say, but only in profile. What ruined him was the eye. The right one, which drooped severely at its outer corner, bordered by a wormy scar, the best the doctors could do after two reconstructive surgeries. It could have been worse, considering that the socket had been crushed. The vision in that eye was blurry at best, but he had gotten used to it, refusing to wear glasses or contacts except when he was under the wheel of a car. His penance, was how he thought of it. And the physical part of it, his mark.

He doubled a clean apron over and tied it around his waist. He noted with satisfaction that the urns were full and hot. He looked up at the Coca-Cola clock on the wall. All the deliveries had arrived, and he was ready to open with a half hour to spare. The help would be dribbling in shortly, well in advance of seven, this crew being responsible and dependable, almost always on time.

Beneath the clock was a two-top that had replaced the cigarette machine. No ashtrays on the counter, no cigarettes for sale, no *Daily News* or *Washington Star*s stacked atop the D.C. Vending machine. Other than that, the coffee shop looked pretty much the same as it had when his father had opened it in the '60s. The original equipment had been repaired rather than replaced. The Motorola radio, now inoperable, still sat on the shelf. The cylindrical lamps, which John Pappas had installed with his older son one Saturday afternoon long ago, still hung over the counter.

Not that the store looked old. New tiles were installed in the drop ceiling whenever they became stained. Alex insisted that the floors and countertops be spick-and-span come closing time, and he applied a fresh coat of paint to the walls every year. Blue and white, like the colors of the Greek flag. So it looked, basically, as it had always looked. Most important, it stayed clean, the hallmark of a good eating establishment. If his father were to walk in now, he would take note of the reflection off the stainless-steel ice machine, the shine of the freshly wiped counter, the spotless sandwich board, the clear glass of the pie case, the grill bricked free of grease. He would nod his head with contentment, his deep brown eyes readable only to his son, and say, "Bravo. *Eeneh katharaw.*"

Alex Pappas had changed the menu many times over the years, but this was something his father would have done as well. He would have adapted. The Asians and college-educated Greeks had opened pay-by-the-ounce salad bar establishments, which had worked for several years and then largely faded away, victimized by bland product, overpricing, and overexpansion. When those places had been popular, Alex retreated from his burger-and-fries, steak-and-cheese staples and added chicken filet sandwiches, lean-cut corned beef and pastrami, salads, and hearty soups. He served diner-quality breakfasts: eggs prepared to order, center-cut bacon, link sausages, scrapple, and grits and half smokes for the true locals. He held his coffee charge at fifty cents a cup, with free refills if consumed in house, and this became his signature. Served the coffee in cups with the custom *P* on the side, just like the one on the sign. Human contact, the personal touch. This was what kept him in business. Try to get that at Starbucks, or the Lunch Stop, or from any of the *Keenezee*-owned establishments. The Asians knew how to run an efficient operation, and they were workhorses, but they couldn't make meaningful eye contact with their customers to save their lives. Alex knew most of his customers' names and their tastes. With many of them, he had their orders written on the guest check pad before the words came out of their mouths.

It was the chains and their patrons that were killing him. The young people were like robots; they only walked into eating establishments whose names they recognized from the suburbs and town centers where they'd grown up. Panera. Potbelly. Chipotle. And those weren't nearly as wretched as the

McDonald's and Taco Bells of the world, which Alex could not even bring himself to discuss. They served dogshit. No wonder America was fat. Et cetera.

So the clientele of Pappas and Sons was on the middle-aged side, which was not a desirable scenario for a forward-looking business. Alex had done all right up to this point and had managed to provide a decent and comfortable living for his family, but the future was not promising. The rent, though it had kept pace with inflation, had remained reasonable until now, due to the kindness of Mr. Leonard Steinberg, who had given Alex's father his original lease and liked him, as they were both veterans of the war. But Mr. Steinberg had passed away, and the new landlord, a loud young man with dull eyes in a property management office of young men just like him, had served notice that the rent would increase significantly in the coming year. Alex wasn't going to raise the prices on his product, which would drive away customers. He would not cut the pay of his help. They had kept up their end of the bargain, and so would he. That rent increase was going to come right out of his profits.

Thank God for the death insurance money, passed through his mother, distributed equally to him and his brother, Matt. Alex had not touched a penny of it, and it had grown to a sizable amount. Also, he had some commercial property on the east side of Montgomery County. He was never going to starve.

His father had suffered a heart attack in July of 1975, a month before Alex was to enter his second year at Montgomery Junior College, known then in the county as Harvard on the Pike. Alex's plan had been to ease into school, perhaps transfer to the University of Maryland once he got his grades up, but he had floundered at MJC, doing well only in English.

His social life had deteriorated, and he found refuge in music, watching films, and reading paperback novels, things he could do on his own.

He had started with the usual stoner lit, Heinlein, Tolkien, Hermann Hesse, and the like, and moved on to mystery and pulp. He became infatuated with the Travis McGee books by John D. MacDonald, though even at the age of nineteen he recognized them as the ultimate male fantasy, writ large. No job, no family ties, life on a houseboat, the freedom to kill your enemies, the convenient death of lovers, allowing you to move on to the next *Playboy*-quality piece of ass . . . But the writing was clean and addictive. He began to think, *Maybe this is something I can do someday. See my name on the spine of a book.* A good profession, one to practice in solitude.

After "the incident" he had stayed in close proximity to his family. His parents had been good to him. They did not react with histrionics to the event or, in his presence at least, obsess about his injuries. It was something that had happened to him, not something that he had initiated. Callie, in keeping with her personality, took charge and managed the aftermath. She dealt with the press, the school, the insurance company, the police, and the prosecutors, keeping Alex's contact with them to a minimum. His father became more introspective, simply choosing to hold his emotions in check. Matthew, Alex's younger brother, did not seem affected at all.

With outsiders, it was different. Alex became increasingly uncomfortable around people who were not family. He could see their reaction, even if they were polite and tried to conceal it, when they got a look at his face. It just felt better to be alone. He found it easier, not having to explain himself or repeat the story, which he couldn't help but rewrite, slightly, in his favor. None of them meant for anyone to get hurt. He was only a passenger. Billy and Pete were just horsing around. Looking to "raise a little hell" is what the prosecuting attorney said.

If Alex had thought about it logically, he would have admitted that becoming an author, or anything of that nature, was a rather foolish and unrealistic ambition given his background. In any case, his father's condition had derailed Alex's dreams. He did not reenter college that semester. In fact, he never returned to school.

Before his heart attack, John Pappas had never missed a day of work. Blizzards couldn't stop him from getting downtown. To him, illness, no matter how severe, was only a distraction. "If I can be sick at home, I can be sick at work," he said. But it went deeper than a stubborn work ethic. He had no sick leave to collect, and neither did his help. If the store was locked and dark, no one got paid, neither John nor the help nor the vendors. Consequently, the Pappas family rarely took vacations, and they never took one with their father. He said, "If a *magazi* like mine closes its doors, even for a week, it's likely that those doors gonna be closed forever." And: "What, I'm gonna sit on some goddamn beach while my customers are eatin across the street at that other guy's place? How am I gonna relax, huh? By makin sand castles?"

The doctor called it a myocardial infarction and said that it was "significant." John Pappas would be off his feet and off work for several months. From his bed in the intensive care unit, with clouded tubes going up his nose, his father had looked up at Alex and spoken softly and with effort. "We're gonna lose everything unless you do it, boy. I'm sorry."

"Don't be sorry, Dad," said Alex, hating himself for the tears that had come to his eyes. "Just get well."

"Take care of the help," said his father. "They prop the place up. Don't ever shortchange them, hear?"

"I hear you, Pop."

That night, Alex and his mother talked, sitting at the table in their kitchen. There was a cigarette going in her hand, the pack of Silva Thins neatly placed beside the blue green ashtray with the notches in its lip, which had always made Alex think of a castle when he was a boy. His mother was not wearing makeup.

"You can do it, honey," said Calliope Pappas.

"I know I can, Ma."

"You're the *only* one who can. I don't know the business like you do. Your brother's too young."

Alex had been working at the coffee shop for eight summers now, and through osmosis he had learned. He'd get the place set up before dawn, make the *caffe*, receive the deliveries, and turn on the grill. The crew knew their jobs. They would do the rest. He could run the register, and there was a paper history with the vendors, receipts and so on, so the ordering procedures would be learned quickly. He wasn't afraid. There wasn't *time* to be afraid.

"What do I do with the money?" said Alex.

"Tear off the register tape at three," said his mother. "The last two hours are for us, not the tax man. Put about fifty dollars, bills and coins, in the metal cash box and lock it in the freezer before you leave at closing time. Bring the rest of the cash home and give it to me. And leave the register drawer open at night." Calliope tapped her cigarette off into the ashtray. "Your father says it tells burglars that the register is empty. They look through the window and see that open drawer, they figure why bother breaking in."

"Okay, Ma," said Alex.

The house was quiet without their father in it. They had one of those kitchen wall clocks with the thing coming out of it, a rod and a ball that rocked back and forth and actually made a tick-tock sound. They were listening to it now.

Calliope ground out her cigarette in the ashtray and exhaled the last of her smoke. "I'm going to give these up. They made your father sick, you know. That and his mother's cooking. All that grease."

"I better get some sleep."

"Go on. Don't forget to set your alarm."

Alex went upstairs, going by the dark bathroom where at this hour his father would normally be soaking in the tub, smoking, and passing gas. Alex entered his room and got on the bed, lying on his back with his forearm across his eyes. He could hear the music coming from Matthew's room.

Matthew had never worked in the coffee shop. He played sports year-round, got excellent grades, and had recently scored high on his SATs. Matthew was bound for an out-of-state college, his path unblocked by his father's situation. As for Alex, he sensed correctly that his world had forever changed.

The next day he woke in the dark and went to work. The faith that his mother and father had put in him had not been misplaced. Initially, he made mistakes, mostly in the psychology of leadership, but as the weeks went by he felt more self-assured and began to think of himself as the guy in charge. He felt like a man. He was where he was supposed to be. Maybe that fat-assed attorney had been right: "As a writer, your son makes a good counterman." Alex took the music lyrics off the register where they had been taped. It seemed foolish to have them on display now.

His father came home from the hospital. He grew the first beard he'd ever worn. A week before Christmas, he was in the kitchen with his wife, standing beside the eating table, waiting for her to serve lunch, a tuna fish sandwich and a cup of chicken noodle soup. She was at the electric stove, her back to him, when she heard him say, "Hey, Callie," and when she turned, John Pappas had his hand outstretched and his face was the color of putty. A shower of blood erupted from his mouth and he dropped like a puppet. The doctor called it "a massive event." John Pappas had expired, most likely, before he hit the floor.

ALEX PAPPAS, fifty-one, stood looking at the Coca-Cola clock on the wall, not really needing to see it to know the time, knowing the time exactly by the change of light outside as the dawn turned to morning. The plate glass window that fronted the store was like the screen of a movie he had been watching repeatedly for thirty-two years.

He had married. He had fathered two sons. He worked *here*.

The *magazi* was what he had. It had saved him after the incident in Heathrow Heights, enabled him to reconnect with people, and given him sanctuary and a purpose. It had been his retreat after the death of his younger son, Gus. Salvation through work. He believed in that. What else was there?

Pappas and Sons.

One boy dead, one alive. But Alex would not change the sign.

SIX

He WAS a physical therapist at Walter Reed, the army medical center up on Georgia Avenue. His name was Raymond Monroe, but because of the gray salted into his hair and because he was considered to be rather old, some of the soldiers and several of his coworkers called him Pop. He had been in this line of work for many years and had been at the hospital for two. Monroe felt that he was pretty good at his job. The pay was respectable, the work was steady, and most mornings he found himself looking forward to his day. Like his father and his older brother, James, he liked fixing things.

Monroe had worked for various clinics over the years, never having the business acumen or ambition to own one himself, and he had done fine. When his son, Kenji, the product of an early marriage, had enlisted, Monroe applied for a position at Walter Reed. Much of the medical staff at the hospital was active-duty military, GS employees and contractors, but Monroe had served in the army, stateside, for four years out of high school, which had been helpful in getting him on board. He figured that the service had been good to him, as his benefits had provided the tuition money to get him through college and all

71

those postgraduate years he'd put in at the University of Maryland's Eastern Shore campus. Now he was giving back. Plus, he felt the need to do something, if only symbolically, to support his son.

Private First Class Kenji James Monroe had been deployed to Afghanistan and was stationed at the Korengal Outpost. He was a soldier in the Tenth Mountain Division, First Battalion, 32nd Infantry Regiment, Third Brigade Combat Team, out of Fort Drum, New York. Monroe had memorized all the numbers, which gave him the secure feeling, illogically perhaps, that the military was actually organized and would be equipped to protect his son. He wasn't one of those army parents who went overboard behind the flag waving, with the reveille ring tones on the cell phone and such. He was detached from all that, and still, he was very proud of his son.

Monroe had fathered only the one child. His wife, Kenji's mom, had died of breast cancer when the boy was ten. His wife's name was Tina, and she was good to the heart. Tina had pulled him out of his funk, all those years carrying that thing, worrying on his brother, holding in his bitterness and distrust, not growing out of his young and angry mind-set until she'd come into his world and helped him become a settled man. Her death had knocked him back down. But he got up, knowing he had to for his boy. Monroe, with the help of his mother, had raised Kenji himself.

He had a thing with a woman now, a nice career gal who was a licensed clinical social worker at Walter Reed. It was the first serious relationship he'd had since the death of Tina. Kendall Robertson had a little boy named Marcus. The boy's father was not in any of the framed photographs around her place, which told Monroe that the man was not welcome back. Kendall was thirty-five, fourteen years his junior, and the boy was eight. They had met at church, and in their first conversation, at coffee hour, they discovered they worked at the same facility. Monroe now spent the night at her house, a row home in Park View, a couple times a week. Marcus seemed to accept him. It was working out all right.

Monroe was seated at a small table off Kendall's kitchen, watching her get her boy ready for school. In his hand was a cooling cup of coffee, a Georgetown Hoyas mug with a drawing of the bulldog mascot on its side.

"Where's your spelling words?" said Kendall.

"In my homeroom packet," said Marcus. "You put the paper in there your own self last night."

"That's right," said Kendall, zipping up his book bag. She was leaning over him, a wing of hair fallen about her face. "Don't you forget to turn that sheet in."

"I always do."

"You forget. *That's* what you do. You don't turn it in, how's your teacher gonna know you did the work? Homework's part of your final grade."

"Okay, Mom."

"I got to get him up to Before Care," said Kendall, now looking at Monroe. "You comin out with us?"

"I'm gonna finish up this coffee and the sports page. I can still make it up to First Formation. I'll just catch the Seventy."

"Seventy-nine's less crowded," said Kendall. The Metrobus ran every ten minutes up and down Georgia during rush hour and made far fewer stops than the 70. "Quicker, too."

"If I see one, I'll get it," said Monroe.

"Wizards win?" said Marcus. He was short for his age, wiry, with an athlete's heart, and ears too big for his skull.

Monroe nodded. "Gilbert looked into his head and torched

the Mavs for thirty-nine. Caron and Antawn did some damage, too. Now, if we could only get us a center with hands . . ."

"Tell Mr. Raymond good-bye," Kendall said to Marcus.

"Bye, Mr. Raymond."

"All right, Marcus. You have a good day at school."

Kendall came over to Monroe and kissed him on the mouth. He let it linger just a moment and then pulled back, so as not to cheapen her in the boy's eyes.

"You look nice," said Monroe, looking her over.

She wore a pantsuit she had purchased at the Hecht Company, now gone, up in Wheaton. With the coupons and the sale price, Kendall had bought it for next to nothing. She didn't need to buy expensive clothes to look good. She was a handsome woman, with puppy brown eyes and a full mouth. Curvy, and not too small anywhere, which he liked.

"Thank you," she said, blushing a little. "Call me, hear? Maybe we can meet for lunch."

"Right," said Monroe.

When he was done with his coffee and the paper, he left Kendall's house, locking the door behind him. He went down to Georgia Avenue and took it north on foot. He passed the D&B market, Murray's steak and produce, a Spanish-owned auto repair. Many of the folks he was passing were dressed cleanly, on their way to catch buses or taxicabs to their jobs. The neighborhood was changing. He expected that it wouldn't be long before most of these businesses would be replaced, too. Cafés, bars that weren't about pussy or violence, a theater that would show plays, something akin to a Starbucks. It was coming.

Still, there were the usual men outside the liquor store, waiting for it to open, to remind you of what had been. Monroe said hello to the group, and one of them called out to him by name. He saw a midget wearing chains over a Len Bias Celtics jersey and boy's-size Nike boots, going for that street-retro thing. Little man was frequently out on the same corner of the Avenue. Monroe had greeted him once but gotten only a scowl in return. Dude was just the angry type, Monroe surmised. Then he thought, *I would be angry, too.*

Monroe went on. He passed a couple of bus stops before he lighted on one. He lived in his mother's house in Heathrow Heights, and he did own a car, but when he slept in town, he sometimes liked to enjoy the experience of the city. Walking and riding the bus, having contact with folks, that was how he liked to go.

IF HE got off to work early enough, Raymond Monroe would start his day at First Formation, a kind of roundup after reveille on the Walter Reed grounds. The hall where the soldiers gathered resembled an American Legion auditorium. Here, badly wounded patients mingled with those who were being treated for less-serious injuries. Amputees wore the evidence of their wounds most obviously and permanently, as did burn victims in the late stages of recovery, and men and women with rows of stitches and patches of bald spots now bearing stitches. Others did not outwardly appear to have been wounded at all but were suffering from mental disorders. Many of those who made it to First Formation were in the final stages of their hospital stay and headed for the Temporary or Permanent Disability Retirement List, which the soldiers called the TDRL and the PDRL.

Monroe had missed reveille but got into the hall in time to get up with a couple of the guys he had treated. He approached Private Jake Gross, who stood by a folding table near one of the hall's many doors, leafing through a NASCAR magazine. The table was covered with similar fare, muscle-and-drag-car periodicals, flyers offering free nosebleed seats to Wizards games and Nationals contests, crab feasts, and trips to Six Flags and other nearby amusement parks, all reflecting the geographical backgrounds, interests, and ages of most of the soldiers.

Gross, twenty, was scheduled to leave the hospital shortly, having made the PDRL, and was headed home to Indianapolis. His build and bearing were military made, but his face was still as freckled and free of stubble as a sixteen-year-old boy's. His right leg was artificial. His plastic knee was robin's-egg blue, and his shin was a metal pole that ended in a New Balance sneaker. He had come far since Monroe had met him. He was a fit and energetic young man to begin with, but athleticism was only a small part of getting him mobile. He had the necessary will and heart. He was walking as well on the new leg as anyone Monroe had treated.

"What's goin on, short-time?" said Monroe. "You ready to go home?"

"More than ready," said Gross.

"You gonna be staying with your parents?"

"My girlfriend. Her father got me a job at the big printer they got outside Indy. They're a bookmaker, like."

"Say you're gonna be a bookie?"

Gross blushed. "Not like that. They print books up and put 'em together. They printed *The Da Vinci Code* there."

"Never heard of it," said Monroe.

"Yeah, right. Anyway, it's not like a factory job. Everything's computerized. Big as a rack of football fields, too. You should see it."

"If I'm ever out that way, I'll let you give me the tour."

"Count on it," said Gross, putting his hand out. "Thanks a million for everything, Doc."

"I'm no doctor."

"Heck, you fooled *me*."

"You just made my day, Private."

"I'll stop by before I ship out."

"Do that," said Monroe.

Outside the hall, Monroe saw Sergeant Major O'Toole, a soft-spoken Vietnam veteran who had come out of retirement to work with soldiers through the army's Wounded Warrior Program. He was talking to a young man seated in a wheelchair near a couple of his friends, who were standing on the sidewalk. One of them was on new legs. Monroe had treated the wheelchair-bound young man, Private William "Dagwood" Collins, so nicknamed for his tall, thin build. Collins, the victim of a roadside bomb, had lost the use of both legs. He had initially refused a double amputation, which would prepare him for the next step, the fitting of artificial legs. But Monroe had heard that the young man was having second thoughts. Monroe caught O'Toole's eye but did not stop to talk to him or Collins. He walked across the campus to the main hospital and took the elevator up to his floor.

Raymond Monroe worked primarily in the occupational therapy and physical therapy rooms of the hospital. A therapy dog, Lady, roamed both rooms, playing with toys, sniffing at outstretched hands both flesh and plastic, and allowing herself to be petted. The facilities included free weights and weight machines, treadmills, mats and medicine balls, and a well-used pool. Raymond Monroe did much of his work on the occupational therapy room's many padded tables, stretching his patients and increasing their range of motion and flexibility through repetition. The hips and shoulders were crucial areas.

Prosthetics, burns, and scars aside, the problems he dealt with here were not much different from those he had encountered when he had worked as a PT at sports medicine clinics. He was bringing people back to some degree of active normalcy, postinjury.

Monroe's first patient that morning was Sergeant Joseph Anderson of the First Cavalry Division, who had lost his right hand near Mosul. Anderson had a wry sense of humor and a positive attitude. He liked classic rock, redheaded women, and '66 Mustangs, and he had an admirable abundance of confidence, despite the fact that his face had been badly scarred.

"Ali Baba tossed a grenade into our Humvee," said Anderson the first time he met Monroe. "I picked it up and tried to throw it back to him, as a courtesy. But I guess I was a little late."

"Word is you might have saved a couple of your men."

"I sure would like to have my hand back, though. And my dashing good looks. Didn't work out like it does in the comic books, sir."

"No need to call me sir. I'm a civilian."

"I was raised to call my elders sir. 'Less they're ladies, and then I call 'em ma'am."

"Where was that?"

"Fort Worth, Texas. As in, don't mess with it."

"You a Cowboys fan?"

"There *ain't* no other team."

"I won't hold it against you."

"You must be for the Deadskins."

"Don't play."

Anderson had a prosthetic hand. On it, he had recently tattooed something, looked to Monroe to be a word spelled *Zoso*. On the flesh of his forearm were three symbols inked in blue.

The one on his hand was known as a continuation tattoo. Many of the soldiers had gotten them applied to their prosthetics to replicate the portions of tattoos that had been lost to injury or amputation.

"You like my new tat?" said Anderson.

"If you like it, then I do, too," said Monroe, who was kneading his fingers into Anderson's forearm, doing it roughly because the young man could take it. "What's it mean, anyway?"

"It's a symbol. It looks like a word, but it isn't. They call it a glyph. Don't ask me why. Four members of Led Zeppelin each chose a symbol, and they put them on their album. Four band members, four symbols. *Led Zeppelin Four*, get it? The greatest hard-rock record ever made."

"All right," said Monroe.

"I envy you for being around when they were playin," said Anderson. "You ever see 'em live?"

"Musta missed it."

"Tell me you were a Zep fan, Pop."

"Can't say I was." Monroe issued a barely detectable smile. "Matter of fact, I didn't even know it was a group. I used to think it was *one* dude. My older brother set me straight, like he always did."

"Mine liked to school me, too."

"That's how big brothers do," said Monroe.

Later, after Anderson had left, after he had treated a couple of other patients, Monroe broke for lunch. His intention was to meet Kendall in her office.

Beyond the swimming pool, in a hall that led to a bank of elevators, he saw a general and some lower-ranking, freshly scrubbed officers; several doctors were giving the visiting uniforms a tour of the facility. The group parted as a young man and an older woman came down the hall.

The young man was a private out of Minnesota who had recently gotten his new legs. He wore a harness and a leash. His mother followed him as he wobbled on plastic knees and shin poles fitted into sneakers, his hips gyrating wildly as he took tentative steps. His face was pink with effort and concentration. His forehead was damp with sweat, and he bit down on his lower lip. The young man's mother held the leash, steadying him, just as she had done twenty years earlier in their home in Thief River Falls, when he was eleven months old and taking his first steps.

The general, the officers, and the doctors began to grin painfully and clap their hands in unison for the enlisted man as he moved through the crowd. Monroe could not bring himself to join in. He had love for the soldiers and marines he treated and nothing but respect for the countless doctors, therapists, career military, and volunteers who were making their best efforts to help them. But he wasn't about to join these officers with their frozen smiles.

Monroe walked quietly to the elevators as the private and his mother passed.

SEVEN

ALEX PAPPAS had recently bought satellite radio service for the coffee shop, as he had become increasingly discouraged by the content of modern terrestrial radio. The choices on satellite were plentiful and could satisfy the help, who were mixed in culture and thus had varying musical preferences, and the clientele, who generally resided on the upward and downward slopes of middle age.

Darlene, as the senior member of the crew, had promptly commandeered the new radio. Of the original help from his father's era, only she remained. Inez had died of liver failure in her forties, and Miss Paulette had passed away shortly thereafter, a victim of diabetes and her weight. In the '80s, Junior Wilson had been taken by the glass pipe and for all purposes had disappeared. His father, Darryl Wilson Sr., still the engineer in the building above, no longer spoke of his son.

Darlene was now forty pounds heavier than she had been at sixteen. When he looked at her, Alex still saw her lovely eyes and smile, and also those forty pounds. He gently urged her to lose weight and give up smoking, but she brushed off his suggestions with a gentle laugh.

She had given birth to four children, one fathered by Junior Wilson, and currently was the grandmother of nine. An unemployed, single daughter and two grandchildren lived in her row house in the Trinidad section of Northeast. One son was an inspector for the health department, another was incarcerated on drug convictions in Pennsylvania. The second daughter had a government job, a successful marriage, and a house in PG County. Darlene had supported various family members over the years and had managed to do it all through her job at the shop. Alex provided her a basic pension plan and health insurance coverage. She had been completely behind him from the day he had taken over, helped him get through that time of his father's illness and death, and continued to be essential in the running of the coffee shop.

Darlene exercised her radio privilege by playing the oldies R&B station Soul Street, hosted by the legendary Washington DJ Bobby Bennett, remembered by many as the Mighty Burner. When Darlene was feeling generous, she conceded the radio choices to the Hispanic employees who made up the balance of the crew: Rafael Cabrera, an energetic young man from the Dominican Republic, who managed to perform both delivery and dishwashing duties; Blanca Lopez, colds and sandwiches; and Juana Valdez, the counter waitress.

Alex only asked that during the rush the radio be set on something without vocals. Vocals annoyed him when it was busy and only added to the confusion in the store. Alex's older son, John, had suggested to his father that he play the "chill-out" sound at rush time, which he called "up-to-date and intricate." To Alex it was just rhythmic instrumental music, mildly hypnotic and inoffensive, and intricate, he suspected, only if one was high. But John was right. It was perfect background music for the lunch rush.

"The music is very important in a store like ours," Alex had said, trying to justify the expense of the satellite radio box to his wife, Vicki, as they stood before the unit in their local RadioShack. "Not just for the customers, but for the help, too."

"If you want it, buy it," said Vicki, knowing his penchant for gadgets. "You don't have to sell me on it."

"I'm just saying," said Alex.

The customers took note of the radio immediately and ribbed Alex about entering the new century seven years after it had arrived. The employees enthused over its novelty and playfully argued about the choice of stations all day long. Plus, Alex's by-the-book accountant, Mr. Bill Gruen, had told him he could write off the expense. It had been a worthwhile purchase that had improved the business. His father would have approved.

The rush was winding down. Several customers sat at the counter, finishing their lunches. Alex knew them all, the makeup of their families, what they did for a living. One of them, an attorney named Herman Director, ate a liverwurst on white every day. Alex brought liverwurst in just for him, as it was rarely requested by anyone else. Like buttermilk, which Alex also kept on hand for a big mustachioed fellow named Ted Planzos, it was an item that was fading from America's culinary radar screen.

Alex sat on the stool behind the register. He had been looking through the glass of the refrigerated dessert case at the pies and the cheesecake that remained, planning what he would take to the hospital on the way home. He ordered extra since he'd begun his routine, more than he would ever sell, so there would always be a surplus at the end of the day. The soldiers were big on cheesecake and key lime pie. They liked the rich and the sweet; not surprising, as most of them were not much more than kids.

"What do you owe me?" said Dimitri Mallios, a longtime attorney and longtime customer, stepping up to the register, sliding the guest check across the counter.

"I owe you seven and change," said Alex, barely looking at the check. Turkey and swiss on kaiser, lettuce, tomato, and mayonnaise, fries, small Diet Coke. Mallios came in twice a week, sat on the same stool if it was empty, and ate the same sandwich and sides every time. Juana would write the order on the pad as she saw him through the plate glass window, coming around the ledge bookended by twin shrubs. Blanca would start building the sandwich before he parked himself on the stool.

"Everything all right?" said Mallios, as Alex rang him, slid the bills into their respective beds, and made change.

"Business is steady," said Alex with a shrug. "But the new people, they're gonna raise my rent."

"You had a good ride with Lenny Steinberg," said Mallios, who had represented Alex and his father on the lease negotiations since the inception of the business. "We'll deal with the increase when the time comes."

"Okay, Dimitri."

"You're good, right?" Mallios was giving him the serious eye now, the question not about the store but about his mental health.

"*Entahxee*," said Alex, with a small wave of his hand. "Everything's okay."

Mallios nodded, left two on seven for Juana, and headed back to work.

Darlene walked the rubber mats down to the register, spatula in hand, humming softly. She wore a pale pink shift and sneakers whose backs she had cut off.

"How'd it go?" said Alex.

"The chicken breast sandwich went like a mug. People liked the horseradish sauce. That was John's idea."

"He's full of ideas."

"Where is he, anyway?"

"I told him to take the rest of the afternoon off. Who thought to add bacon?"

"Me. Bacon makes everything taste good."

"Get your order together for tomorrow, and see what Blanca needs, too."

"Blanca say, 'Eighty-si, corn bee,'" said Darlene, with her idea of a Spanish accent.

"Put a corned beef on the order."

Alex looked at Rafael, back by the dishwashing area, leaning on the counter, talking to an attractive, leggy woman in a short skirt and matching jacket. She had removed her eyeglasses, meaning he had gotten to her. Rafael was a handsome young man with soulful black eyes, fluid and athletic movements, and a wealth of charm. He took a shot at many of the female customers who came through the door, and though he was rarely successful, few of them took offense. They didn't seem to mind that he was nineteen, or that he washed dishes for a living. Rafael had that kind of male glow. He was well aware of it. He loved coming to work.

"What's Rafael doin?" said Alex, a mix of annoyance and admiration in his voice.

"You mean you don't know?"

"Kid's a horndog."

"He's a young man," said Darlene. "Remember?"

"She's gotta be ten years older than him."

"So? It never stopped *you*."

"No need to go there."

"That secretary, worked on Nineteenth Street, when you

were Rafael's age? Above the Korean place? You were just a kid, and what was she, thirty-two?"

"That was—"

"Fun. And don't even try and act like it wasn't."

"Go ahead, Darlene," said Alex, feeling a warmth in his face.

"You about ready for lunch, sugar?"

"Soon as these customers clear out," said Alex.

The afternoon light came through the window, a spear of it warming his hand. Alex didn't need to look at the Coca-Cola clock on the wall. He knew the time from the touch of the sun.

"YOU SAW him," said Sergeant Major O'Toole, looking at Raymond Monroe. "You were out there after First Formation."

"When I saw y'all, his friends were around."

"They left us after you went away. Private Collins told me he needed to talk to me alone."

"What did he say?" said Kendall Robertson.

"He's ready to do it," said O'Toole.

They were seated in Kendall's cramped office in building 2 of the main hospital. Kendall, an inpatient therapist for wounded soldiers and their families, had been visiting with Monroe when O'Toole knocked on her door. The three of them nearly filled the space. Around them, along with her desk, computer, and files, sat boxes of chocolates and plastic-wrapped flowers, stuffed animals holding miniature American flags, and other gifts of a similar feel-good, patriotic nature. Kendall delivered them on her rounds.

"What changed his mind?" said Kendall.

"I think just, you know, seeing the progress made by his friends," said O'Toole. "They're walking now. Shoot, some of them are running. He sees his buddies joking and smoking, and he's thinking, I need to get on with my life and get some prosthetics."

"Is he certain?" said Kendall.

"He's as close as you can get to it," said O'Toole.

"Voluntary amputation is a complex decision. It's one thing to have it done out of necessity, postinjury. But to say, I want you to remove my legs . . ."

"It's not that simple on the logistical side, either. He's got to make his request formally to a group of doctors and officers. It's almost like a hearing. I mean, it takes a while for the procedure to be approved. I'd hate to see Private Collins change his mind again while all the red tape is being sorted out."

"I'll get the ball rolling," said Kendall, "if that's what he wants. I'm due to see him today on my rounds."

"Thank you, Miss Robertson."

Kendall nodded. "Sergeant Major."

O'Toole left the office. When the door closed, Monroe raised his eyebrows at Kendall, who smiled.

"Yeah, I know," said Kendall. "When is it going to be an easy day around here?"

Monroe got out of his chair. Kendall stood and walked into his arms.

"You're doin good, baby."

"That's what they tell me."

"I guess I'm having lunch by myself today."

"Looks like it. I want to get started on this Collins thing."

He kissed her softly. They enjoyed a long embrace in the quiet of the room.

ALEX PAPPAS had secured a visitor's pass through the AW2 offices so he could get through the security gates of Walter Reed without undue hassle. Because he was making quick deliveries, he usually parked his Jeep on the grass near the Fisher Houses, estate-sized brick homes that functioned as hotels where parents, siblings, girl- and boyfriends, and spouses stayed near wounded soldiers during their treatment and recovery.

Alex retrieved his desserts, neatly arranged in a large fold-up box, and carried them around the back of Fisher House II, where wrought iron tables were set up on a patio, a quiet outdoor spot where soldiers and family could find some peace, smoke cigarettes, or talk on their cells. A rear door led to an extralarge state-of-the-art kitchen shared by the residents. Food was made available here at all hours, often in elaborate spreads.

"Hello, Peggy," said Alex to a woman who had just cleared a granite countertop and was now wiping it down. Peggy Stawinski, a middle-aged blonde, had a son who was currently serving in Afghanistan. She volunteered her time in both Fisher Houses, as well as the Mologne House, an older, more elegant structure that also served as a hotel.

"Hey, Alex. You can put that stuff down right here."

Alex set the box on the counter and pulled its contents. "Got a few things today. It all came in this morning, so it's fresh."

"What's that?" said Peggy, pointing to half a cake swirled pink and red.

"They call it Marionberry cheesecake."

"You're kidding."

"They were going for cute."

"You want some coffee? I just brewed it."

"I'm parked on the grass," said Alex. "I better get home."

"Thank you. This all looks great."

"My pleasure. How's the library doing?"

"We could always use more books."

"I'm gonna bring some paperbacks. Detective stuff. I got too many lying around. My wife is on my back to get rid of them."

"Okay, Alex. Bye."

He stopped by weeknights on his way home from work, but he never stayed to mingle with the soldiers or their families. He said he didn't have the time to hang around. He didn't want their thanks. He was parked on the grass. He had to go.

RAYMOND MONROE walked the grounds of the facility, staying after his shift to catch a ride with Kendall, who was late getting off work. Especially going west, away from the hospital, the grounds were green and landscaped with old-growth oak, maple trees, and flowering cherry and magnolia. It had been announced that the Walter Reed complex would move out of D.C. in the next ten years. Officials had been wavering on the decision as of late, but the stay of execution would only be temporary. One hundred and thirteen valuable acres in the middle of the city—it was inevitable that the facility would go.

Turning the corner of one of the Fisher homes, he nearly walked into a white man about his age, just coming out the back door. Monroe was used to deformity, what with all the wounded, amputees, and burn victims he treated. But there was something else about this man, aside from the horrible droop of his right eye, that unsettled Monroe immediately.

" 'Scuse me, buddy," said Monroe, putting his hand on the man's arm as he moved to step around him.

"Excuse *me*," said the man, who went on his way.

Monroe stopped at the back door of the Fisher House and looked at the man walking to his vehicle, a Jeep Cherokee parked on the grass. He studied the man for a moment longer, flashing on those days *after*, that painful time in court. He pushed on the door and entered the house.

Peggy Stawinski stood in the kitchen, setting out some cakes and pies on the long counter. "Raymond. Funny how you just happened to stop by as soon I put these out."

"You know I like sweet things, Peggy. Like you."

"Stop."

Monroe often came in to say hello to Peggy. Both of them had sons under fire.

"I'm waitin on my girlfriend. Killing time." Monroe reached for something on the counter, and Peggy gently slapped his hand. "That does look good, though."

"Marionberry cheesecake."

"Clever."

"Want a cup of coffee?"

"Nah, I'm good." Monroe ran a finger along his thin black mustache. "Listen, who was that man who just left out of here? Had on a white shirt and work pants."

"He owns a lunch place downtown, at Connecticut and N. Brings us desserts every night on his way home."

"Just to, what, show his support?"

"He lost a son in Iraq."

Monroe nodded.

"His name is Alex Pappas," said Peggy.

"Pappas."

Alex Pappas had been the boy's name. He knew Pappas was the Greek version of Smith or Jones. Still, there was the eye, and this erased any doubt. The boy would have carried that mark his whole life. Charles Baker had seen to that.

"You know him?" said Peggy.

Monroe didn't answer. He was thinking.

EIGHT

CHARLES BAKER sat in Leo's, a neighborhood watering hole on Georgia Avenue, near a flower-and-tree cross street in Shepherd Park. On the wood before him was a glass of draft beer that he had been nursing for some time. He was reading a newspaper and waiting on his ride.

Baker went through the *Washington Post* front to back. He did this daily. Though he had opened neither books nor newspapers in his youth, he had picked up the reading bug while in prison. The habit had stuck.

One section he skipped was employment. With his history, there wasn't any good reason to apply for a job that came with a pension, health insurance, or a future. He'd been down that funny road. Going out on interviews, employers sensing immediately that he wasn't "right" for the job, the box cutter scar on his face not helping him, the stink of his life on him permanent. When it was time to talk about his experience, he mentioned his felony convictions and incarcerations, as he was required to. Also, he liked to make straights squirm.

"It's only fair to tell you that there are a lot of people applying for this position" *(people without rap sheets)*. "Many of them are highly qualified" *(they have been to school past the tenth grade, unlike you).* "You seem like a good person" *(I'm afraid of you).* "We'll give you a call" *(never).*

Sometimes Baker just wanted to laugh out loud in their offices, but he did not. He was a good boy. On the outside.

Anyway, he had a job, a part-time thing his PO had hooked him up with. It involved bedpans, soiled diapers, trash bags, and mops, but he was on paper, so he had to get himself employed. He was part of a cleaning crew in a nursing home down in Penn-Branch, off Branch Avenue, in Southeast. He had an arrangement with the dude he worked with, some variety of African, who would cover for him when he didn't come in, assure the lady parole officer that Baker was regularly showing up for work. The African preferred to have his brother, whom he'd just brought over from the motherland, take the hours instead.

It was at the nursing home that Baker had met La Trice Brown. And through La Trice he'd gotten together with her son, Deon, and his friend Cody. Indirectly, working in that shithole had been good for him.

"What's the name of the song and who did it? And don't say Lou Rawls."

"Gimme a second. I'm thinking."

At the other end of the bar were two middle-aged white men four rounds deep in vodka. They had been talking loudly about women they claimed to have done, sports they'd never played, and cars they would someday like to own. Now they had begun to argue over the song coming from the juke. It was a pop-soul number, heavy with strings. The vocalist had a smooth voice that started calm and grew in drama. At the peak of it, the man sounded like he was about to bust a nut all over the microphone. Baker knew the song but not to name it.

"'Hang On in There, Baby.' Johnny Bristol."

"What year?"

"Seventy-four?"

"It was seventy-five."

"I was off by a C hair."

"What about the label?"

"It was MGM."

"How'd you know that?"

"I bought the forty-five up at Variety Records when I was a teenager. I can still see the lion and shit."

"You know what this song means, don't ya?"

"It means, like, don't let the world get you down."

"No, dumbass. It means, hang your sausage hard inside me and don't let it go limp."

"Inside *you?*"

"You know what I mean."

"But it's a dude singing it."

"Okay, so he's telling a broad to hold on. He's telling her, hang in there. Try not to come too fast."

"Who cares if she comes?"

"You got a point."

Baker did not look over at the fools or pay them any mind. He was into the business section now, reading one of those sidebars they had, "Spotlight On," where they profiled a successful person in the Washington area. Age, college attended, married to, kids, last book read, bullshit like that. It was in this very sidebar that Baker had first been mentally reacquainted with his man, who had made the big time. Not just an attorney, but a partner in a law firm. Bragging about how he was "involved" with kids in the inner city, had started a charitable foundation in the name of his family, through which he made "substantial contributions" to scholarship funds for "African

American" students who were bound for college but needed "a helping hand." Baker wondered if the man was running for office, or if he was just trying to show his friends that he was right in his heart. Everyone was gaming in some way.

The bartender, a heavyset guy with a big nose, asked him if he was ready for another. Baker put his hand over the top of the glass and said that he was good. The bartender went down the stick and asked the jokers if they wanted another round. They said they did and went back to their conversation.

"Hey, you ever been to Wardman Park?"

"When it was the Sheraton Park, I did."

"I'm going to an affair down there on Saturday night. A wedding reception, in that Cotillion Room they got."

"Yeah?"

"I haven't been there in years. But I got, like, a history in that place."

"What kinda history?"

"It's of a sexual nature."

"This again."

"I'm sayin, I scored my first make-out there when I was fifteen years old."

"Where, in the men's room?"

The bartender prepared their drinks.

Baker thought of the photograph of the man he had seen in the newspaper. He remembered the boy at the trial. Blond, soft-spoken, so filled with remorse. The lucky one who ran away. He didn't look anything like that boy anymore. Gray hair, nicely dressed, distinguished. Wouldn't he be surprised to meet his old friend Charles?

"Hey, pal, can we buy you a beer?"

Baker turned his head. It was one of the white dudes, short guy with a Jew boy–looking Afro. Baker had been in and out of the world for many years, but he felt certain that whites had given up on that tired look a long time ago.

"I'm about to get up on outta here," said Baker in a friendly way. "Thank you, though."

In his previous life, he might have pulled back on his jacket to show the little dude the grip of a pistol coming out the waistband of his slacks. A visual reply to his kind offer with a glimpse at something that said "I ain't thirsty." That was the old Charles Baker. Not that he didn't like to fuck with people now and again. But he wasn't about to take an automatic fall for carrying a firearm.

Time was, he carried a gun regular and cared less than nothing about the consequences. Used to be, back when he was staying with a woman he knew, over there in the high forties, off Nannie Helen Burroughs in Northeast, he'd get up in the morning, drop a pistol into his pocket, head out the door, and go to work. Walk the streets until he came up on people who looked to be weak, older females and men he could punk, then take them off for what they had. He fancied himself a beautiful, strong animal, like one of those cheetahs walking out on the plain. Going to work natural, doing what hunters did.

That was before his most recent stay in prison. In the federal facility in Pennsylvania, toward the end of that last long stretch, he had crossed over into old. Sure, he had lifted weights and done the usual push-ups in his cell. He continued to look men in the eye and he walked tall. But no doubt, age had come up on him and it had slowed him some. Upon his release, his plan was no plan, as it had been many times before, but now the lack of a road map scared him. He realized that the physicality and fearlessness of his youth would no longer carry him in the world. He had no desire to live straight, but he could read a mirror and see that his strategy had to change. He would become a manager. Use his wiles and charm to make others do what he had grown too old to do himself.

He'd need to find some young ones and put them to work. Wasn't hard to rope in the pups. Though his rep had died with those who were gone or incarcerated, anyone could look into his hazel eyes, drained of light, and see that he was real. Not in the sentimental way that graying uncles and tired rappers were afforded the OG tag. Real.

Baker's cell, a disposable, sounded.

"Yeah, where you at?" said Baker.

"Comin up on you," said the white boy, Cody.

Baker closed the phone.

A black Mercury Marauder pulled up out front of Leo's. Charles Baker dropped beer money and a meager tip on the bar and walked out into the last of the day's light. He crossed the sidewalk, stepping around one of those do-good types leading a dog out the Humane Society offices, and got into the spacious backseat of the car.

Deon Brown sat under the wheel of the Mercury. Cody Kruger was beside him. Deon looked in the rearview, and Baker studied his eyes. He had taken his pill, which was good.

"Go, boy," said Baker.

Deon pulled off the curb, swung the Marauder around in the middle of Georgia, and headed south.

LA TRICE Brown owned a duplex row house in Manor Park, a middle-class neighborhood east of Georgia near the Fourth District police station. She stood in her second-floor bedroom, beside the window that gave onto a view of Peabody Street, looking down at the curb where her son, Deon, his friend Cody, and Charles Baker were stepping out of Deon's car. Looking at Charles, she heard that voice in her head, which was her begging, saying, *Please, let him be kind*.

She worked for the Department of Labor as an administrative assistant. She had come from a strong family with roots in Southeast. She had held her government job for nearly twenty years, attended church regularly, did not smoke cigarettes or reefer, drank moderately, and had been a good mother to Deon and his older sister, La Juanda, now married and gone. Everything was right about her but one thing: she had always hooked up with bad men. Many women were attracted to reckless men in their youth. Most outgrew this attraction and learned, but La Trice Brown never had.

Deon's father was dead, shot in the face for who knew what many years back at a house party in Baltimore. La Juanda's father was a two-month error, a hustler she'd dropped off at the bus station in the way that soiled clothing got dumped at a homeless shelter. Charles Baker was La Trice's latest mistake.

To be fair, he had seemed like a good man, a knight even, when they met. La Trice's grandmother L'Annette had checked in permanently to the nursing home in Penn-Branch, suffering from advanced Alzheimer's and plain old age. When La Trice visited, she would sometimes speak with Mr. Baker, one of the cleaning men. Though there was something about him that suggested a kind of hard edge, he was always polite and asked after her grandmother, telling her that he would make sure "the old girl" was comfortable when he was on shift.

He was older than her by ten years, but attractive, with a shaved head and greenish eyes that reminded her of that movie star who played the pimp with the golden heart. To her, the scar on his face did not ruin him, but instead gave him character. He had told her straight-up that he had made some bad decisions in his life and was currently on paper. Her reply was that she believed in redemption and second chances. That was her again, being blind.

La Trice had bought her grandmother a small bottle of good perfume as a birthday gift, and one day, while sitting in the room with her, noticed it was not on the dresser where Miss L'Annette kept her precious things. She mentioned this to Mr. Baker, who said he'd look into the matter. The next time La Trice visited, the perfume bottle was back on the dresser. She found Mr. Baker pushing a mop and bucket down the hall.

"Was it you?" said La Trice.

"I took care of it," said Mr. Baker. "One of the nurses, Haitian gal, thought she was slick. She ain't gonna take nothing from grandmoms again."

"How did you get it back?"

"I just, you know, politely showed this girl the error of her ways."

Mr. Baker moved into her personal space, looming over her, powerful. La Trice was a short thing, and he was so tall.

"Thank you, Charles."

"That's the first time you called me by my Christian name."

"Would you like to have some coffee with me sometime?"

"Oh, I'd like that very much, La Trice."

He had seemed like such a good man then. La Trice heard the slam of the front door as he entered her house, and felt herself flinch.

THE YOUNG men went off to play Xbox back in the TV room. Cody rented an apartment nearby where he and Deon stored, scaled, and bagged the marijuana they moved. It was also where Cody kept his gun. Deon still stayed in his mother's house, partly to keep an eye on his mom and partly because he felt it was the wise thing to do, given Cody's reckless nature.

Baker told them he'd be back shortly. He wanted to have a word with Deon's mom.

Baker went up the stairs. La Trice had been acting funny lately. Talking back, getting annoyed when he spoke on his plans for the future, like she had heard his bullshit stories one too many times. The worst thing was, she sometimes recoiled at his touch. Once you lost that sexual hold on a woman, the relationship was done. You could only get it back temporary, but never all the way. Not that he cared about her. But he needed her son and his friend. He would have to get the girl in control of her emotions until he used the boys up.

La Trice was standing back in the corner of her bedroom when he entered. She was very short, with big breasts that were too big, if there was such a thing, when the brassiere hit the floor. She was all-right looking when she smiled, but she didn't do much of that anymore, and when she was brooding she had that cartoon character thing going on, thyroid eyes, lips out, like some animated canine. He was sick of looking at her.

"What's goin on, girlfriend?" said Baker pleasantly.

"I just got home from work. You?"

"Been *lookin* for work."

"Weren't you on the schedule today?"

"Called in sick."

"A condition of your parole is that you have gainful employment. You need that job."

"Need got nothing to do with it. I'm done with that place. I'm telling you, I can't stand the smell of it anymore."

He didn't like working with all those foreigners, either.

Like that Haitian nurse. He knew it was her who stole that perfume from La Trice's grandmother. Wasn't the first resident that girl hit. Always took from the ones who were mixed up in the head. When he confronted the Haitian about the theft, she denied it, so he went ahead and pushed her into a vacant room and pinned her to the wall with a forearm across her neck. Squeezed one of her nipples hard between his thumb and forefinger, right through the fabric of her uniform, until a tear ran down her cheek. She brought that bottle of perfume to him the very next day. His gallant act had made him a hero to La Trice.

"I got what I wanted out of that nursing home, anyway," said Baker. "I made the acquaintance of a sweet old lady named Miss L'Annette. And I met you."

Baker remembered when words like that would dampen La Trice's panties. But now she just looked away.

"We gonna be all right, girl," said Baker. He stepped to her and lifted her chin with his hand. He bent forward and kissed her still lips.

She wanted him to go away. She didn't love him. She didn't care for the influence he had on her son. They were doing some kind of dirt together, Charles and Deon and Cody. Whatever it was, it had to be wrong.

"I'm out," said Baker.

"Where you off to now?"

"Over to the apartment with the fellas. 'Less you want me to stay here with you."

"No," said La Trice. "You go ahead."

Charles went downstairs, found the boys, and told them it was time to go.

NINE

DEON BROWN had attended Coolidge High in the District, and Cody Kruger had gone to Wheaton High, out in Maryland. Deon had graduated with low grades, and Cody had not graduated at all. They met as coworkers at one of the many athletic-shoe stores in the Westfield Mall, which some of a certain age still called Wheaton Plaza. It was not the store that required its employees to wear referee jerseys. Neither of them would have done it.

The first time Deon saw him, Cody had an open gash over his right eyebrow and scrapes on the side of his forehead. Cody explained that he had been sucker punched by "a boy who was trying to see me" but that he had gone on to "punish" his attacker and that the marks on his face "wasn't no thing." Deon never actually saw Cody fight. Still, Cody talked about violence incessantly, the way other young men talked about sex. Females didn't seem to be into him, anyway. He had wide-set eyes, a pasty complexion, spaces between his teeth, and acne, chunky as vomit, on his cheeks.

They became friends. Deon had always been a bit of a loner, and for all his bluster, so had Cody. They were into weed, video games, and the same kind of music. They both liked TCB, 3D, Reaction, CCB, Backyard, and other local go-go bands, and rap, if it got combined with go-go, like with that dude Wale. They knew who Tony Montana was but not Nelson Mandela. They bought clothes with labels and disdained the brands that were common and out. They wore Helly Hansen rather than North Face, Nike Dunks over Timbs. They were both sneakerheads. The employee discount at the store was why they worked there.

Cody called all Hispanics "Mexicans" and considered them his adversaries and the thieves of American jobs. Cody wore his hair very short and only got it cut at black barbershops. Cody said "forf" for "fourth" and "bruva" for "brother," but to Deon it didn't seem like he was trying too hard, like other white boys. It was who he was.

After a chance meeting with an old acquaintance who'd become a supplier, Deon and Cody had started dealing a little weed to the other employees in the mall. There was a natural market for it, and they could do it discreetly, through the network, all the young heads who worked the kiosks, the urban-clothing stores, the hat-and-athletic-jersey places, and the shoe shops. They'd buy a pound at a time and get their own smoke free. They'd never exchange marijuana or money on the Westfield grounds. That could be done after a short drive to one of the many nearby parking areas serving the CVS, the surplus store, or the county lot behind the Wheaton Triangle. When they began to see a profit, Deon put a down payment on a used Marauder, a car he had long coveted, and Cody rented an apartment near the Fourth District police station. They stepped up their order from their supplier and turned the extra inventory without effort. They spent the profit as quickly as it came in.

Plasma television, multiple iPods, furniture bought on time from Marlo, a gun. To Cody, it was the life he had imagined for himself. Deon was not so sure. He had bouts with depression, and often, even while chilled on Paxil, he could not see the positives. If you had all this, what was there to look forward to? Mr. Charles, who had been in their lives since the start of their business, said, "More."

STEPPING OUT of La Trice's house, Baker, Cody, and Deon got into the Mercury. Deon's Marauder was tricked with Kooks headers, Flowmaster pipes with big chrome tips, twenties with Motto rims. The windows were tinted to the legal limit, and this and the other extras drew the eyes of police. Baker also knew that a black boy and a white boy seen riding together in a car were considered to be suspicious and were more likely to be stopped than same-race occupants. For this reason he insisted that the Marauder be free of contraband. For their work, they used Cody's Honda, a reliable and relatively invisible car.

They went to Cody's apartment, located on Longfellow Street. The place was always messy and smelled of unwashed clothing and food left on dishes in the sink. The carpet was littered with gum wrappers and slips of paper holding Xbox codes. The boys sat on the couch and played the latest version of NBA Live while Baker sat at a countertop-on-file-cabinet desk and fired up Cody's computer. The boys used the desktop to look at porno, rate girls on MySpace, check out the latest sports scores, and surf eBay for sneaker purchases both classic and new. Baker used it for business.

His idea had been set in motion the day he'd seen the sidebar in the business section of the newspaper. And then, after watching one of those television shows set half in the street, half in a courtroom, an episode that detailed a blackmail involving a decades-old crime, Baker had begun to see how he could profit from a similar but more reasoned scheme. By typing "Heathrow Heights" and "murder" into the search engine, Baker had eventually been directed to a site that offered a database service containing documents related to criminal trials on both the federal and state levels, going back many years. Using La Trice's credit card, he had retrieved the partial transcripts of the trial for a charge of less than five dollars. Unlike the old newspaper articles he had printed off microfilm at the local library, which had not identified some of those involved due to their status as minors, the document he obtained listed all the players by name. It wasn't too hard to proceed from there.

"I ain't want no Woods, young," said Cody, as Deon pulled the wrapper off a cigar and dumped out its tobacco. "Let's do a vanilla Dutch."

Deon kept on task. He took weed from a pile on the table and dropped a healthy amount into the Backwoods wrapper. He rerolled the blunt and sealed it.

"This some bullshit," muttered Cody. But when Deon fired the marijuana up and passed it to him, he hit it deep.

Baker worked on. For a small fee, there were all kinds of people-find searches available, which narrowed the field by age and geography. Soon he had the address and contact information for Peter Whitten. The other one, Alexander Pappas, was a bit harder to identify. There were a few with that name in the D.C. area, but the one he ultimately chose was about the right age. He still lived near the neighborhood in which he'd come up. Had to be the same boy he'd stomped.

On the word processor, Baker typed an unsigned letter that he transcribed from one that had been handwritten, showing editing marks and words in the margins. He then typed in a name and printed it on an envelope he fed through the bubble-jet machine.

Marijuana smoke hung heavy in the room. Cody and Deon laughed easily as Cody boasted about his prowess on the video basketball court. Baker didn't mind that their heads were up. They were easier to manage when they were high.

"Repeat what I told y'all about the code," said Baker.

"The Xbox codes?" Cody didn't turn his head away from the screen, his fingers working the controller.

"The code to get back into the apartment," said Baker patiently. "How I told you boys to knock a certain way."

"We got keys," said Cody. "Why we need to knock on the door, too?"

"What if someone takes your keys? Or the police come back *with* you? This way, I'm gonna know it's y'all."

"Knock knock pause knock," said Deon.

"Right," said Baker. "You two ready to tip out?"

"Hold up," said Cody Kruger, using body language to make his players do his bidding onscreen. "I'm about to slam this sucker."

"You had a dream that you did," said Deon.

"Your game is fluke, son."

"You can play later," said Baker. "We got work to do."

ALEX PAPPAS had a photograph framed and hung in the kitchen, showing his father, John Pappas, standing over the grill at the coffee shop, his apron on, a spatula in his hand, a joyous smile on his face. The grill was covered with rows of thawing hamburger patties, which he was precooking. He did this daily in preparation for the lunch rush.

"Why is he smiling?" Johnny Pappas, Alex's older son,

would ask when he was a kid. "He's just cooking burgers! It's not like he won a million bucks or something."

"You don't get it," Alex would reply.

The photo was a way of keeping his father alive to the grandsons who never knew him. Alex had mounted it beside the refrigerator so they'd see it often.

"Hey, Pop," said Johnny Pappas, entering the kitchen. "Hold that for me, will ya?"

Alex had just put a block of *kasseri* cheese inside the side-by-side, and he had yet to close the door. He kept it open while his son reached across him and removed a plastic bottle of cran-raspberry juice. Johnny swigged directly from the bottle.

"You're drinkin it like an animal," said Alex.

"I don't want to have to wash a glass."

"When's the last time you washed anything around here?"

"True that," said Johnny.

Johnny replaced the bottle, his shaggy hair brushing Alex's face, and wiped his mouth on his sleeve. Alex closed the refrigerator door and joined Vicki, who was seated at the kitchen table, several take-out menus spread before her. They were going to order food, but Alex had put out some cheese, kalamata olives, and crackers for a predinner snack. Johnny joined them at the table.

A prime-time game show was playing on a small television set on the counter. The Pappases had a nice rec room with a big-screen TV, but mostly Alex and Vicki sat in the kitchen at night, watching the thirteen-inch. The kitchen had been the central room of the house since the boys were babies.

"How'd we do today?" said Johnny.

"I took in two, three million," said Alex.

"That all?"

"We did fine."

"Dad, I been thinking . . ."

"What I tell you about thinking?"

"I was thinking we'd add some specials to the menu. Change the offering a little bit."

"Ah, here we go."

"You can't compete with the Paneras of the world. I mean, if you're trying to go head-to-head with them in sandwiches, you're going to lose."

"It's not that kinda place. I got a grill and a colds station. I don't have a big kitchen."

"You don't need any more room or equipment. I can make gourmet soups on one gas burner. Maybe sauté some soft-shells when they're in season. For breakfast we can offer huevos rancheros, and sides like apple sausages. Slice up some fresh avocados as a garnish."

"I get it. You might know how to prepare all the fancy stuff, but you're not there all the time. Who's gonna do it? And what if it doesn't move?"

"Darlene would love to learn new sandwiches and recipes. Don't you think she gets bored with the same-old, too?"

"She's there to work, not to get excited."

"If we try it and it doesn't fly, then we go back to what we were doing. I'm not telling you to throw the old menu away. I'm saying, let's do something different. Bring in a whole new kind of customer."

Alex grunted and folded his arms.

Johnny had earned a bachelor's degree in marketing and had recently graduated from a local culinary institute. For a while he had been an apprentice chef in a new-cuisine restaurant near George Washington University. Now he worked with his father at the coffee shop during the breakfast and lunch rushes, which was frequently an oil-and-water situation for both of them. Vicki, who thought her son needed the day-to-day experience of running a business, had suggested the trial arrangement.

"I saw a nice chalkboard with a hand-painted frame at a store today," said Johnny. "I think we should buy it. I can put it up over the wall phone, write the day's specials on it."

"For God's sake."

"Let me try, Dad. One new soup, one new sandwich. Let's just see if it goes."

"*Avrio?*"

"Tomorrow, yeah."

"Okay. But how about *this* for a change? You come to work on time."

Johnny smiled.

"You dining with us tonight, honey?" said Vicki, her drugstore-bought reading glasses perched on her nose.

"Depends on what you guys are having," said Johnny.

"*Ee-neh ah-paw-soy,*" said Alex, making a head movement toward Johnny. It meant that his son was to the manor born.

"I just don't want any of that chain crap."

"You think I do?" said Alex.

"How about El Rancho?" said Vicki.

"El Roacho," said Johnny.

"I don't want Mex," said Alex. "My stomach . . ."

"Mie Wah?" said Vicki.

"Me Wallet," said Alex.

"Don't be so cheap, Dad."

"It's not that. I just don't want Chinese."

"Cancún Especial?"

"Can't Cook Especial," said Alex.

"He said he didn't want Mexican," offered Johnny.

"Well, we have to eat something," said Vicki.

"Let's just get a Ledo's pizza," said Alex, the decision they had been moving toward all along.

"I'll cut a salad," said Vicki. "Call it in, Alex, okay?"

"If Johnny picks it up."

"I'm gone."

They watched him go, a tall, thin, good-looking young man of twenty-five in tight jeans and a leather jacket that looked a size too small.

"What is that look he's got?" said Alex. "Like, metrosexual, somethin?"

"Stop it."

"I'm asking."

"He's a hip young guy, is all," said Vicki, who subscribed to many magazines that could be purchased in the supermarket checkout aisles. "He looks like one of those guys in that band, the Strokes."

Alex caught her eye. "I got somethin you can stroke."

"Oh, please, Alex."

"I'm sayin, it's been a while."

"Must you?"

"A guy can dream."

"Call the pizza in, honey."

"Yeah, okay."

He went to the phone and ordered a large pie with anchovies and mushrooms. Vicki, aligning her lettuce, cucumbers, onions, and carrots near the cutting board, spoke to him as he hung up the phone.

"Honey?"

"What."

"We've got to do something about the building."

"Okay."

Alex and Vicki owned a 1,700-square-foot brick structure, formerly a Pepco utility substation, off Piney Branch Road in Takoma Park. It had been zoned for commercial use and for the past five years had been leased by an Iranian who used it as a carpeting and flooring showroom. When the man's operation had gone the way of the corded phone, he had vacated the premises. Vicki was worried about the cash flow, but Alex was not. She maintained their books, did their taxes, and managed their investments. Alex had a talent for running a business but was uninterested in the mechanics of money.

"I'm gonna find a tenant," said Alex.

"You've been saying that since the Iranian moved out. Six months now."

"The building's paid for."

"We still pay property taxes on it."

"*Okay.*"

"I'm just pointing it out, Alex."

"Just don't go stomping your little foot over there. You hear me, Thumper?"

Vicki smirked, her eyes on the cutting board as she halved a head of iceberg lettuce.

She was on the short side, with a nice figure on her still, a little belly, but that was all right. Her hair, dyed black, was cut in the *Friends* style that the Aniston girl had made famous but was now way out of date. Even Alex knew that. But on his wife it looked good. He still got excited when he watched her walking toward the bed at night. The way she turned her back shyly when she removed her bra.

Vicki had aged several years in the one since Gus had been killed, but the new lines on her face were not an issue with Alex. Grief had moved the clock forward on him, too. He knew that he and Vicki were going to be together until the end. With everything they had been through, having survived it, there wasn't any question of that.

He met her when she was just out of high school, a trainee in the accounting department in the machinists' union building, at 1300 Connecticut. The most fun-loving girls in the south Dupont area, and the nicest, worked in the machinist offices. Alex was in his early twenties, a young businessman, the owner of the lunch counter, a good catch. She was a daily morning customer, small coffee, milk and sugar, with a Danish. Her last name was Mimaros. She was Greek American, Orthodox, a *koukla*, and nice to Darlene and the rest of the help. She didn't seem to mind his eye. He took her out to dinner, and she was respectful of the waitress. Had she not been, it would have been a deal breaker for Alex. He married her within a year.

"What do you think?" said Vicki.

"About?"

"About Johnny, *boo-faw*."

"Johnny's got big ideas."

"He's excited. He's just trying to help."

"I said he could try out a thing or two, didn't I?"

"In your own way. Yes, you did."

"He bugs me, that kid."

Alex waited for Vicki's quiet reminder that was also an admonishment: *He's not Gus.* But Vicki went on shredding her lettuce and commented no further.

Alex went back to the phone and lifted it off its base. "I'm gonna call my mom."

He moved to the living room and had a seat in his favorite chair. He dialed his mother, who now lived out in Leisure World. He tried to phone her every night and visited her twice a week, though she often reminded him that she was not lonely. Calliope Pappas had not been involved with a man since the death of her husband, but she had many friends. Alex's brother, Matthew, an attorney in northern California, called infrequently and visited occasionally on holidays, so Alex's mother, now coming up on eighty, was the last connecting thread to his childhood. He often said that he had stayed in the Washington area for her. Secretly he felt that he needed his mother more than she needed him.

"Hi, Mom. It's Alex."

"I know it, honey. Don't you think I recognize your voice by now?"

After they said good-bye, Alex returned to the kitchen, replaced the phone, and went to the refrigerator for another slice of cheese. He looked at the photo on the wall, his old man in his apron at the *magazi*, flipping burgers, a look of true joy on his face. Alex had his good days at the store. He'd had some laughs with the customers and the help. But he'd never felt the way his father looked in that photograph. It occurred to him that in thirty-some years on the job, he had never experienced that kind of unbridled happiness himself.

TEN

"HOW'D THAT dude get that job?" said Raymond Monroe.

"He was a comedian before this," said Kendall Robertson.

"He's never made me laugh," said Monroe. "Not once."

"Me, neither," said Marcus Robertson.

They were in Kendall's row house on Quebec Place, eating carryout, watching that popular nighttime game show with the bald-headed host, had the trumpet-player hipster patch beneath his lower lip.

"I'd like to know where you apply for that job," said Monroe. "'Cause I *know* I could do it better than him."

"You ever see a black game show host?"

"Didn't Arsenio host one?"

"He's not funny, either."

"I could be the first. Break that game show host color line. I'm sayin, if Mr. Clean can do it, I can, too. Because this man is, like, *talentless*. Is that a word?"

"I think so."

"You wanna know how he got that job? Luck. Like,

four-leaf-clover, bust-the-casino kinda luck. I mean, this dude must have a golden horseshoe lodged up in his—"

"Raymond!"

Marcus laughed. "He's lucky."

"That's what I'm sayin, Peanut."

Monroe had given the boy the nickname because of his stature and the funny shape of his shaved head. Marcus didn't mind when he called him that. He liked Mr. Raymond, and when he gave Marcus the name, it was a sign that Mr. Raymond liked him, too.

"What are we watching this for?" said Kendall.

"You're right," said Monroe. "I don't know why they call it a game if there's no skill to it. It's all about greed."

Monroe got up from the kitchen table and turned off the television set.

"That was easy," said Kendall.

"Ought to do it more often," said Monroe. "C'mon, little man, let's have a look at your bike."

"He needs to do his math," said Kendall.

"I will, Mom."

"You promise your mother you're gonna do your homework later?" said Monroe.

"Yes."

"Let's go, then."

Kendall gave Monroe an approving glance as he crossed the room with the boy. They went out the back door, down wood stairs to a cracked sidewalk bordered by two small patches of dirt, weeds, and a little grass, and entered a small detached garage next to the alley.

Kendall had bought the house for fifty thousand and change ten years back, and now it was worth several hundred thousand dollars. She had endured the drug dealing, break-ins, and violent crime in the neighborhood, and though the problems had not been completely eradicated, her vision of a Park View transformed was beginning to take hold.

Many of the homes on her street had been turned over to new-generation ownership and were being reconditioned. Though she had made no major improvements, Kendall kept her place in clean good shape. Monroe handled the basic maintenance, which was often no more than throwing a fresh coat of paint on a wall, drilling new screw holes for those that had been stripped, caulking the bathtub and shower stall, and replacing broken windows, a skill his father had taught him and James when they were boys.

Monroe had also organized the garage. His parents had not had one in Heathrow, and it was a luxury for him. He had screws, nuts, bolts, washers, and nails in clear film canisters, labeled by Sharpies on tape, aligned on a wooden shelf. Motor oil, transmission fluid, brake fluid, rags, cleaning supplies, windshield washer fluid, and antifreeze were lined up in a row against one cinder-block wall. He had brought his toolbox down here and took it back to his mother's as needed. He supposed he was slowly moving in.

"I don't know how the tire got flat," said Marcus, as Monroe upended his bike, a Dyno 2000 with rear pegs, and set it on its saddle and bars.

"You ran over something, I expect. Go get me those tire levers off the shelf." When Marcus did not move, Monroe said, "Those blue things, thick plastic, a few inches long. Got hooks on the end."

Raymond showed the boy how to insert the thick end of the tire lever between the tire and the rim, and how to hook it onto the spoke. He instructed him to use the second lever the same way, hooking it two spokes down. By working it around in this fashion, the tire could be removed from the rim.

"Now run your hand real careful inside that tire. You're gonna find a bit of glass or a sharp twig, something like that in there. Whatever it was punctured that tube."

"It was this," said Marcus, holding a small triangle of forest green glass carefully between his fingers.

Monroe gave the new inner tube a couple of pumps of air and fitted it into the empty tire. He pulled the valve through the hole in the rim and seated one side of the tire into the rim's edge. He turned the bike around and used his thumbs and muscle to fit the other side. He completed the replacement by inflating the tire to its suggested pressure. All the while he talked to the boy, describing the process with simple language.

Marcus watched him as he worked. He noticed the veins jump on the back of Mr. Raymond's hands and how they stood out like wire on his forearms. The tight way he wore his knit watch cap cocked a little sideways on his head. His thin, neat mustache. Marcus was going to grow one just like it someday.

"You should be good now," said Monroe.

"Can I ride it down to the Avenue and back?"

"It's too dark. I'm worried about the cars seein you. But you can walk with me to the market if you want. I noticed your mother needed some milk."

On the way to Georgia, Monroe talked to Marcus about body language. "Chin up, and keep your shoulders square, like you're balancing a broom handle on there. Make eye contact, but not too long, hear? You don't want to be challenging anyone for no good reason. On the other hand, you don't want to look like a potential victim, either."

"How's a victim look?" said Marcus.

"Like someone you could rob or steal in the face," said Monroe. He had said these things to Kenji when he was a little boy. Raymond's father, Ernest Monroe, had said them to him.

Down on the Avenue, as the foot traffic increased, Marcus reached out and held Monroe's hand.

CHARLES BAKER sat in the passenger seat of Cody Kruger's Honda, looking through the windshield at a gray four-square colonial at the corner of 39th and Livingston. Deon Brown was in the backseat, shifting his considerable weight. They were parked down the block, near Legation Street. Two blacks and a white, sitting in a beat-up car in one of the city's wealthier neighborhoods. Anyone who came up on them would know they were wrong.

"These houses are nice," said Cody.

"Big trees, too," said Baker. "This here's a burglar's paradise during the day."

They were in Friendship Heights. Baker had done some break-ins in neighborhoods just like this one. Two men in, one lookout in the car. Go directly to the master bedroom and toss it. People liked to keep their jewelry, furs, and cash close to where they slept. But he and his crew had been retired from that game by the law. He wasn't about to go back to prison for a fur coat. If he was going to fall, it would be for something worthwhile.

"All this money," said Cody. "Why they not drivin nicer whips?"

"Look careful," said Baker. "They're showing that they got it in a quiet way, but they're sayin something else, too."

This was not the new-money, look-what's-in-my-driveway lifestyle of a Potomac or a McLean. The residents here had it, but they did not care to advertise it. Their cars weren't flashy, even when they were fast, but they were fairly new and environmentally correct. All-wheel-drive Volvos, Saab sedans, SUV hybrids, Infiniti Gs, and Acuras lined the streets.

"They sayin, 'Look at me,'" said Baker. "'I can afford a Mercedes, but I *choose not* to own one.' They gonna spend fifty thousand dollars on a Lexus hybrid so they can save a few miles per gallon on gas and boast about it at their next dinner party. But ask one of these motherfuckers to give a thousand dollars to a school on the other side of town, so a poor black kid can have a computer and a chance? You gonna see the door slam right in your face."

How do you *know?* thought Deon, tiring of the cynical drawl in Baker's voice. *When have you ever done anything for* any *kind of kid, poor or otherwise?*

"Ain't that right, Deon?"

Deon adjusted his body. He had big legs and was uncomfortable in the small backseat. "Right, Mr. Charles."

"I can't stand these people," said Baker, and Cody nodded his head.

"Can we go?" said Deon.

"In a minute," said Baker.

Deon wasn't comfortable in this part of the city. Even when he dressed right, even when he was straight, he got looks. It wasn't just his color, though that was a large part of the reaction. The locals could sense he didn't belong here. Once he bought a shirt from one of those stores over on Wisconsin Avenue, on what they called the Rodeo Drive of Chevy Chase, and when he took it to the register, they asked for his ID, even though he was paying cash. His mother told him he should have asked why, but he had been too humiliated to question the clerk. He never went shopping on that fancy strip of stores again.

The side door to the four-square colonial opened. A tall, thin man in a sport jacket and slacks stepped out of the house. His hair was thick, gray, and on the long side, falling a little over his ears. He held a leash, and on the end of it was a fat dachshund. The man stopped to light a cigar, then walked north.

"Every night," said Baker.

Cody touched the handle of the door.

"Not yet," said Baker. "Let him go some."

"How you know he's not gonna be right back?"

"He's off to that nice little rec center and ball field they got, just a block or so away. Takes a little while for him to get there 'cause his poor excuse for a dog got them short little legs."

"Dark ball field be a good place to rob his ass," said Cody.

"What I want can't fit in a wallet," said Baker. "His debt is bigger than that."

The man cut left on Livingston and disappeared.

"Here you go," said Baker, handing Cody a security-tinted envelope. The name Peter Whitten was printed on its face.

Cody got out of the car, jogged down the block, and placed the envelope in the mailbox beside the door of the colonial. He returned to the Honda, excited, pink of face, and short of breath.

"Go, boy," said Baker.

Cody turned the ignition and pulled out of the space. They drove east, headed back to their side of town.

VICKI HAD gone to bed early, as she tended to do since Gus was killed. She could not bear to watch the serial-killer and autopsy shows that dominated the television schedule late in the evening, and she had never been a reader. Alex spent most nights in his chair in the living room, alone, with a trade paperback and a glass of red wine. He still read novels but alternated them with biographies, battlefield memoirs written by soldiers, and nonfiction books about the politics of war.

The house ticked and settled. Johnny was out with his friends, and Vicki by now was asleep. Alex dog-eared the page and poured out the rest of his wine in the kitchen sink. He left a light on for Johnny and went upstairs.

He entered Gus's bedroom. They had kept it as it was. Neither he nor Vicki had been able to box up his football trophies, give away his clothing, or take down the posters Gus had tacked to his walls. Alex had talked about relocating, selling the house and moving on, but both of them decided that leaving the house would mean leaving Gus behind.

Alex wasn't mentally unsound. A year ago, he had been close enough to madness to know how it felt to be scrambled. After that day, after the men in uniform came to the front door, after they'd buried what was left of Gus, Alex went half crazy with bitterness and rage. He took to hard liquor for the first time in his life. He thought of burning his house down. He had violent thoughts about the president. He talked to God aloud and asked him why he had not taken him first. One black night he asked God why he had not taken Johnny instead of Gus, and cried out for forgiveness until Vicki came to him and took him in her arms.

The woman the army sent explained the stages of grief. He said, "Fuck your stages of grief," and repeated it to her back as she walked quickly from his house.

It got better. Time passed and it hurt less. He stopped drinking scotch. He grew tired of being angry. He wrote a letter to the army shrink and apologized. He had a business to run, a wife to take care of. He wanted to see Johnny settled. He wanted a grandson.

Alex looked at Gus's bookshelf, which held few books but many trophies, mostly from his days in Pop Warner, the good years for Gus that were Alex's best years, too. Driving the boys to the games, hearing their conversations, boasts, and predictions as their favorite hip-hop tunes played in the car. After the game, Gus on one knee, sometimes happy, sometimes tearful, listening intently to his coach, steam rising off his head, sweat beaded and streaked on his face, sod clumped in the cage of the helmet he cradled against his chest. Gus slept with a football then. His goal was to play for the Hurricanes. He wanted his father to move them to Florida so he could train year-round.

He was not much of a student. He was goal oriented only in athletics and at work, where he spent summers with his father down at the coffee shop, delivering food. His high school football career was a disappointment due to the limited talent and lackluster efforts of his teammates, and his grades were substandard. By his senior year, it was clear that he was not headed for college. A recruitment officer who hung around the strip mall near his high school began to talk to him. Gus was the perfect candidate: fit and strong, not particularly book smart, eager to test himself and tie his manhood to training and the battlefield. He watched commercials that made soldiering seem like a cross between a knight's quest, an Outward Bound adventure, and a video game, and they filled him with emotion. Gus wanted to scale the mountain, pull the sword from the stone, and face the dragon. He enlisted at the age of eighteen.

"Don't worry, Dad. When I come back, we'll grow the business together."

"That's what the sign says," said Alex, bringing his son roughly into his arms and hugging him tightly. "I'm keeping it for you, boy."

Shortly after his nineteenth birthday, Gus was killed by a makeshift bomb detonated beneath his Humvee, west of Baghdad.

Alex held a trophy in his hand and read its plate: Gus Pappas, MVP, 1998. At the Boys Club banquet, Gus had swaggered to the podium to receive the award, stopping to replicate the Heisman pose to the laughter of his teammates.

"Son," said Alex softly, replacing the trophy on the dusty shelf. And, as he often did on nights like this one, he thought, *Why?*

ELEVEN

DOMINIQUE DIXON had called Deon Brown on his disposable, given him the meet and time. It would be on Madison Place, near Kansas Avenue, along Fort Slocum Park.

Typically, Dixon would drive by the location first, and if he felt that it was hot he would warn Deon off and change the plan. There was rarely a problem and there had been no surprises.

Dixon had been in the marijuana business for a couple of years. He now supplied about a half-dozen dealers in the northern portion of the 20011 zip of Manor Park. Though he was not hard or a fighter, he did have a talent for reading people. Once he decided to enter into a business arrangement with someone, he treated them fairly. He reasoned that if he did them right, there would be no cause for them to betray him. Up until now, his reasoning had been sound.

Dixon grew up in a stable home in Takoma, D.C. His father and mother were good providers, attentive, and had mostly made the correct parenting moves. Nevertheless, Dominique had become a supplier. The blame fell not on the parents, but on his older brother, Calvin.

Calvin was handsome, reckless, a risk taker, thoughtless, charming, and short-tempered. He had a friend named Markos, the son of an Ethiopian father and an Italian mother, a successful Adams Morgan couple who had done well in Shaw and Mount Pleasant real estate. Calvin and Markos had met in the VIP room in a club off New York Avenue and discovered a mutual interest in high-potency marijuana, expensive champagne, mixed-race women, and Ducati bikes. Through a club acquaintance, Markos obtained a meeting with a Newark connect, who liked his sense of style. Neither Markos nor Calvin cared to work for a living, so they tapped Calvin's smart younger brother to run the business. Dominique idolized his older brother and saw a chance to grow his stature in Calvin's eyes. Markos's seed money paid for the initial order. It had been a successful venture from the start.

Dominique had run into Deon Brown, with whom he had gone to high school, up at a shoe store in the Westfield Mall. He remembered Deon as a quiet, intelligent kid, an underachiever, maybe, but straight, someone he could trust. He recalled, too, that Deon liked to cocktail his antidepressants with heavy amounts of marijuana. Deon fitted Dominique into a pair of Vans and offered them to him at his employee discount. Out in the parking lot, Deon handed him the shoes, and Dominique pressed a very small baggie of marijuana into Deon's palm.

"Trust *this*," said Dominique.

"What is it?"

"Some nice hydro. If you like it, ring me up."

"You still stayin with your parents in Takoma?"

"I got my own spot now. But you need to reach me, just hit me on my cell." Dominique gave him the number. "Don't be givin that out to nobody else, hear?"

That night, Deon and his friend Cody smoked the hydroponic weed and got stupid behind it.

Deon phoned Dominique the next day. "Hook me up with some more of this, dawg. Me and my boy want an OZ."

"I don't deal with that kinda weight."

"I'll take a quarter, then."

Dominique laughed. "You're not hearin me right."

"Oh," said Deon.

"Look, man. You want, I can tell you how you can get an ounce for free."

"When?"

"Let's do a face meet. Bring your boy, too."

They got together at a breakfast-and-lunch place high up on Georgia, just north of Alaska Avenue, past the Morris Miller's liquor store with the partially lit neon sign. The lunch place was in the last days of its operation, having been mortally wounded by the fast-food businesses flourishing around it. The area within earshot of their four-top was full of empty tables.

As Deon and Cody entered, Dominique, already seated, was initially surprised and a bit put off by Cody's appearance. That he was white did not bother him particularly, though he did prefer to deal with people his own color, if only for reasons of comfort. Cody, with his black-on-black D.C. dog-tag hat, plain black T, Nautica jeans, and black Air Force highs, looked like any rough-edged city kid his age, until you got a good look at his face. There was a slackness to the acne-dotted jaw and a vacancy in the wide-set eyes that suggested a lack of intelligence beyond the dulling effects of pot. If he was a docile idiot, then fine. If he compensated for his stupidity by being overbearing or violent, then it would present a problem. Dominique decided to sit with them, make his proposal, and see where it went.

"So," said Dominique after Deon had introduced him to Cody. "You liked the sample, right?"

"Shit was tight," said Cody.

"That's *average* quality for me."

"You told Deon we could get some free," said Cody.

"I'm gonna get to that," said Dominique.

"We listenin," said Deon.

Though they were alone, Dominique leaned forward and lowered his voice. "If I was to give you more, do you think you could get rid of it?"

"How much more?" said Deon.

"A pound, to start."

Deon felt Cody looking at him, but he kept his eyes on Dominique. "Why us?"

"You and me go back. I need to know the people I deal with."

"I ain't the only person you know from high school."

"True. But when I ran into you at the shoe store, I remembered how you and me was always straight. And I started to think, that shopping mall you work in is an untapped market. You and your boy must know a rack of heads out there, don't you?"

"Sure," said Cody with a careless shrug.

"I got no one out in that area," said Dominique. "This here is an opportunity for me but also for you. I mean, what's the next step you take after salesman at that shop? Assistant manager? I'm not tryin to be funny about it, either. I'm *askin* you."

"That's right," said Deon.

"There it is," said Dominique.

"What's a pound gonna cost us?" said Cody.

"This shit I got now is fifteen hundred wholesale," said

Dominique. "But I'm gonna front it to you. This time only, because I want to help you get started. The first fifteen comes in, you pay me back. The rest you sell for profit or keep for your personal use. It makes no difference to me."

"Sell it for what amount?" said Deon.

"What the market bears. You get two hundred an ounce for it, you gonna double your money. Time to time, I'm gonna bring in some high-intensity hydro that's more expensive. Two thousand, twenty-five hundred a pound. When that happens, you got to get three, four hundred an ounce to make your usual thing. 'N other words, you adjust."

"What do *you* pay for it?" said Cody.

"What's that?"

"I'm just interested."

"That ain't none of your business," said Dominique, smiling in a friendly way.

Cody looked at the young man in the Ben Sherman shirt with the little roses on it, his slender fingers and thin wrists, his shiny, manicured nails. Cody didn't like what he saw, but he nodded his head.

"Look, dawg," said Dominique. "The way this works, the way this got to be is, keep it simple. I'm gonna deliver what you need whenever you need it, and then it's on you to move it. But I'm just a middleman. I don't get involved in what you do, and you don't need to know the details of what I do. Understand?"

"Yeah, okay," said Cody.

"My advice? Don't get sloppy. That's what you got to keep in mind. Far as who you sell to, I'm sayin take care. Some kid who got no loyalty to you gets put in the box for possession, he might offer up your name. And then you gonna be under the hot lights yourselves, and you might say mine."

"I wouldn't do that," said Cody.

"No doubt," said Dominique. "We just talking here. But you should know, anyone gives me up, the people I deal with gonna be nervous."

"I get you," said Cody.

"You remember my brother, don't you, Deon?"

"Sure," said Deon. He didn't know Calvin Dixon but knew of his rep. "Where he at now?"

"Oh, he's out there. Still out there, you know."

Deon drummed his fingers on the tabletop. He glanced around the lunch place. He looked at Cody, then back at Dominique.

"So," said Dominique, relaxing in his chair. "Y'all ready to make some money?"

Dominique had contacted Deon and Cody at the right time. They were bored, unsatisfied with their income levels, and saw no way up or out. It would be fun, a game played outside the law, something that would blow up their self-esteem. Neither of them felt that what they were about to do was wrong. Marijuana was a part of their everyday lives, as it was for their peers. Smoking weed didn't hurt anyone. It wasn't heroin or cocaine, and they weren't corner boys. Of them, only Cody aspired to the life he had heard about in rap songs and seen on television, sung and acted by people who for the most part had never experienced that life themselves. Deon, prone to depression and treading water since high school, saw it as a positive move. He liked the idea of extra money in his pocket and free weed to smoke. Beyond that, he looked no further than the day he walked through.

"We'll do that one pound," said Deon. "See how it goes."

It went well at first. It was easy finding customers, and the ones they dealt with were friends they'd made at the mall or people those friends could vouch for. If a kid got pulled over in his car and got busted for a bag of weed in his glove box, the event ended there. The no-snitch culture had bled out from the city to the inner suburbs. The police were not respected as worthy adversaries. Uniforms were the enemy. It was unspoken and understood that no one would roll on Cody and Deon.

In the course of a year, change came rapidly. The lunch place up past Georgia and Alaska closed its doors. Another neon letter on the Morris Miller sign went dark. Cody rented an apartment and furnished it. Charles Baker came into Deon's mother's life and inched his way into theirs. Cody quit the job at the shoe store. He bought a gun, the second transaction started by a straw purchase from a firearms store on Richmond Highway in Virginia. They doubled their orders from Dominique.

Deon didn't care for the changes. At times, when he was off his Paxil, too high on weed, paranoid and confused, he thought of running away, perhaps moving to another city. But he knew no one outside D.C., and he didn't want to leave his mother. The bus he had caught was an express.

"HERE COME that boy now," said Charles Baker.

They were parked on Madison, facing west, the dark grounds of the park on their right, residences on their left. A stock Chrysler 300 drove slowly down the block, then executed a three-point turn and backed up so that its trunk was close to their hood. Dominique Dixon got out of the car and lifted the trunk lid as Cody opened the trunk to the Honda using his keypad remote. Dominique quickly retrieved two large black plastic trash bags, each holding a pound of marijuana. He closed the lid with his elbow, went around back of the Honda, and dropped the bags into its trunk and shut it.

"Kid dresses nice," said Baker, as Dominique, sporting a leather jacket over a striped designer shirt worn out over expensive jeans, came to the driver's window, now rolled down.

"Fellas," said Dominique, his eyes losing their light as he got a look at Baker, sitting in the passenger seat.

Cody handed him an envelope containing three thousand dollars cash. Dominique slipped it into the inner pocket of his jacket.

"Why don't you come on in and sit, boy," said Baker.

"I gotta roll," said Dominique.

"Don't wanna be social, huh?"

"I ain't trying to get jailed," said Dominique, attempting to keep a jovial tone to his voice. He looked into the backseat. "We good, Deon?"

Deon made a very small shake of his head. The movement told Dominique to leave them. Deon's eyes were saying "Just go away." Baker caught the signal and it made his blood tick.

"Yeah," said Deon. "I'll get up with you later."

"We could go somewhere and talk," said Baker pleasantly. "I wouldn't mind gettin to know you better."

"I can't tonight," said Dominique.

"Maybe we could go over to where you stay at. Have a drink, somethin like that."

"I got plans."

"With a woman, I hope," said Baker, and Cody chuckled. "C'mon, bro, we just wanna visit."

"I don't take my clients to my crib."

"Do I stink or somethin?"

"Look, man—"

"It's Mr. Charles to you."

Dominique exhaled slowly. He didn't make the correction. He looked at Deon pointedly and said, "I'm out."

He didn't acknowledge Baker or Cody before returning to his Chrysler. The headlights of the 300 swept across them as Dominique Dixon pulled away.

"Little motherfucker just so full of disrespect," said Baker. "Wonder where he off to for real."

"Probably back to his spot," said Cody.

"You know where he live at?" said Baker.

"Sure," said Cody. "Me and Deon dropped some cash off to him once. But he ain't ask us inside."

"Let's go, Cody," said Deon. "We need to get off this street."

At the apartment, Cody and Deon weighed the weed on scales and began to ounce it out into Glad sandwich bags. Charles Baker paced the floor as a late West Coast NBA game played on the plasma TV.

"Kobe gonna take it to the Jailblazers," said Cody, his eyes pink from the bud he'd smoked. "Lakers makin a run."

Deon's cell rang. He answered it, said, "Hey," and then, "Yeah. Hold up."

Baker watched him get up out of his chair at the table and walk down the hall.

In Cody's bedroom, Deon closed the door softly behind him. "I'm good now."

"Look here, Deon," Dominique said. "This shit with your man got to stop."

"I hear you."

"I told you before, I deal with *you*. Cody's rough, but he came with the package, and I accepted that from day one. That old man, though, he's just wrong."

"He stays with my mother sometimes. He's just around, is

what it is. I didn't ask him to be there. He got a way about pushing hisself in."

"That's not my problem. This business I got, ain't no corner bullshit *to* it. No chest thumpin, no threats, and no violence. I don't bring people like him into the circle. Are we straight on that?"

"Yes."

"You my boy, Deon."

"No doubt."

"Next drop we do, I don't want to see that man again."

"I got you, Dominique."

Deon closed his phone. He left the bedroom and went back down the hall. Baker was seated at the table with Cody as the basketball game played at a high volume in the room.

"Who was that?" said Baker, looking up.

"My mom," said Deon.

"You two got secrets? Why you had to leave out of here to talk?"

"'Cause y'all got the game up so loud I can't hear myself think."

"She ask to speak to me?"

"Nah. She got one of them migraine headaches. It might be better if she's alone tonight."

"That her talkin or you?"

"Huh?"

"Nothin," said Baker.

That pussy dead to me, thought Baker. *And fuck her soft little son, too.*

RAYMOND MONROE sat at Kendall Robertson's desk and clicked the Outlook icon on her computer screen. She had set up an e-mail address for him, as he didn't have a computer at his mother's house. He went to Send and Receive and hit it. A spam solicitation came through, but nothing else. No e-mail appeared from Kenji.

He hadn't heard from his boy in a couple of weeks. It was not unusual, but that did not cause him to worry any less.

Raymond sat in the quiet of the living room and said a short silent prayer for Kenji. His words were always the same: simple thanks for the gift of life, and the gift of life given to his son. Monroe never asked God for anything. He had no right. He thought of his brother, and then the man at the Fisher House with the bad eye. The lives ruined and taken. All you could do was hope for forgiveness and try to live a decent life. Reach out to the ones who got caught up in the ugly mess.

Monroe phoned his mother, told her he loved her, and said good night. He shut off the lights, went up the stairs, checked on Marcus, and walked into Kendall's room. Kendall was on her side of the bed, her back to him. She had left a bedside lamp on for him, and in the glow of it he stripped down to his boxers and slid under the sheets. She was naked. He got close to her and ran his hand down her shoulder, arm, and hip. She turned toward his kiss.

"This is a nice surprise," he said, cupping her breast.

"Wasn't to me," said Kendall. "I've been thinking about it all evening."

"What did I do right?"

"Plenty. The way you are with Marcus, especially."

"That boy's good."

"So are you, Ray."

"I'm tryin," said Monroe.

TWELVE

Eighty-five on the soft-shells, Juana," said John Pappas.

"Got it, baby," said Juana Valdez, running a damp rag over the countertop where a customer had eaten moments before. "One mo."

Alex heard the exchange but did not turn his head. He was busy ringing out the lady attorney who had just gotten off her stool. The lunch rush was winding down, with only stragglers left at the counter. There would be little turnover now.

"How was everything today, dear?" said Alex.

"Fantastic," said the dark-haired woman.

She looked over Alex's shoulder as he made change. The dessert case was there behind him. His father had chosen its location, thinking that customers would want a little something to take back to the office on their way out the door.

"Tempted?"

"How's that peach pie?"

"Nice. I can wrap you up a slice if you want."

"Better not. Shame to let it go to waste, though."

"It won't go to waste," said Alex.

The peach pie didn't move well at the store, but Alex brought it in because the soldiers, many of whom were Southerners, seemed to like it. He had half a cherry cheesecake in the refrigerated case as well. He planned to box them both and run them by the hospital on his way home.

"Dad." John Pappas had come down to the register and stood behind his father as the woman left the store.

"Yes?"

"Eighty-five on the soft-shells."

"I heard you," said Alex, swiveling on his stool to face his son. Johnny wore black slacks and a sky blue shirt. He looked like a guy about to order a martini, not a counterman. "That's good."

"Don't be so enthusiastic."

"No, I mean it. It's *good*. We made a profit and some new friends. I heard positive comments from the customers. Not so much about the soup, though . . ."

"I shouldn't have gone with asparagus, I guess."

"It makes your pee smell funny. People don't like it when their urine stinks, especially at work. They gotta share the bathrooms, remember."

"I didn't think of that."

Alex tapped the side of his head. "Use your *myah-law*."

"You want that last order of soft-shells for lunch?"

"Don't eighty-six them yet," said Alex. "A paying customer might want them."

"Right."

"But if they're still around in a half hour, have Darlene set me up a plate with sides. She knows what I like."

"Okay."

"And Johnny?"

"What?"

"Are we done with your music for today? Because it all sounds like the same song."

"This is Thievery Corporation, Dad."

"I don't care if it's General Motors and IBM combined. We sell food here, not tabs of X."

"*Tabs of* X?" John chuckled.

"That's not the right term?"

"Maybe you ought to stick to your own era. Love beads and bell-bottoms, like that."

"Son, that was before *my* time."

"I'm going to talk to Darlene."

"Go ahead."

"She's stoked about tomorrow's special: shrimp Creole."

"Sounds expensive."

"The shrimp's on sale this week."

"Just don't get too extravagant. This ain't the Prime Rib."

Alex watched John walk down the rubber mats. He stopped to talk to an NAB executive on the way back to the prep area. He asked him about his meal, and what he'd like to see on the menu in the future. The executive seemed pleased that his opinion was being solicited. He had been eating here for years, and he and Alex had not exchanged more than a few pleasant but weightless words.

By the grill, Darlene stood with her spatula pointed up at the drop ceiling, making a chin motion toward Johnny, then smiling at Alex. Beside her, Blanca was whistling as she began to wrap and store her colds. Rafael was doing some Latin Joe two-step back by the dishwasher. Okay, so they all seemed happier when Johnny was in the house. Not that Alex was a slave driver or a grouch. But the boy did brighten the place like a coat of fresh paint. Still, Johnny had plenty to learn.

"Love beads," said Alex as a customer stepped up to the register, guest check in hand.

"What's that?" said the man.

"My son thinks I'm a dinosaur."

"Join the club. The difference is, mine has no ambition and he can't cook."

"Come by tomorrow," said Alex, experiencing an unfamiliar twinge of pride as the man pushed bills across the counter. "He's doin something with shrimp."

CHARLES BAKER had gone into the nursing home for a few hours, on account of his PO, a nice-looking Latina gal, had scheduled a meet. It went all right. He told her he liked his job and had a real good attitude about the future, all the bullshit she wanted to hear. She said that the urine sample he'd given to the clinic had tested fine. It was no surprise to him that he'd dropped a negative. He drank just a little, which was legal for an offender, but did not smoke reefer. Even in his youth, he had not cared for it. It was just as well. The plans he had made were complicated, and for them to work out, his head needed to be right.

His African supervisor covered for him, told the parole lady that Baker had fulfilled his duties and in general was one of his Johnny-on-the-spot employees. The PO went on her way, and as soon as her car was gone, so was Baker.

He caught a crosstown bus where Branch Avenue met Pennsylvania. He was on it, headed west, when his cell rang, showing a blocked number. Baker answered his phone.

"Yeah."

"Charles Baker?"

"That's right."

"This is Peter Whitten."

Baker grinned. He cleared his throat. He sat up straight on the bench seat he was sharing with a dude who was wearing a coat that smelled like unwashed ass.

"Mr. Whitten. Thank you for calling me."

"Just to be clear, this is the Charles Baker who left a note in my mailbox, isn't it?"

"It is me."

"I think we should meet face-to-face. How does that sound to you?"

"My thoughts, too," said Baker, going for refined.

"What about tomorrow? Are you free for lunch?"

"Why, *yes*."

"There's a place I like. . . . Do you have a pen?"

"I'll remember it."

Peter Whitten gave him the name of the restaurant, its location, and the time of the reservation. "You should wear a jacket. I think they require it."

"Will do," said Baker. "See you then."

He closed his cell. He stared out the window and felt himself smile. He had expected Whitten to be angry at first, if he responded at all. But the man sounded downright reasonable. People with money just did business differently. They acted civilized. Baker wasn't accustomed to manners and reason, but he could get with it. Wasn't always violence that got shit done.

This was going to be easy.

ALEX PAPPAS stood by the register, counting out the change drawers, his left hand cupped below the edge of the counter as he slid coins into it with the forefinger of his right. His lips moved as he calculated the amounts and entered them on a calculator the size of a paperback novel. The sun had passed, leaving him in the pale yellow glow of the overhead conical lamps.

Alex cut the register tape at three to hide some profit from the tax man. He left enough money in a metal cash box to get started in the morning, locked the box in the stand-up freezer, and took the remaining cash home to Vicki, who managed their finances, just as he had delivered the *chrimahta* to his mother when he had first taken over the business. The system worked, and he felt there was no reason to change it.

Juana and Blanca were gone, always the first to leave. Rafael had finished mopping and rolled the industrial-sized bucket and wringer out to the back hall. Johnny and Darlene were by the grill area, working out a recipe in a notebook, Darlene having changed into her street clothes, an outfit complete with matching handbag. It was her routine to come back into the shop from the hallway bathroom, dressed nicely, before going home. Alex knew she wanted him to have a look at her, the way she'd done when they were teenagers. Telling him that she was a grill girl in a uniform but also a woman with a life outside the store.

Rafael ambled down the other side of the counter and had a seat on the stool nearest the register. He too had changed into clean clothing and had doused himself with strong cologne.

"Hey, boss."

Alex finished counting quarters and made an entry on the calculator.

"Rafael. You got a little behind today on the deliveries. Was there a problem?"

"Blanca send me too far away, all the way to Si'teenth Street. Then when I get there, the lady don't have the money collected for the order."

"Sixteenth's out of our delivery area."

"I know it!"

"All right, I'll speak to Blanca."

Rafael did not move to leave. Alex waited, knowing Rafael wanted one of two things. Advice, because he had no father in this country, or money, because he was always short on cash.

"One more thing, boss."

"Yes?"

"I'm takin a girl out to dinner tonight."

"One of our customers or a round-the-way girl?"

"I don't mess with the customers."

"You try."

Rafael smiled shyly. "This a girl I meet in my neighborhood. We're goin to Haydee's. You know it?"

It was a place that served Mexican and El Salvadoran food. The owner had come to America from El Salvador, worked as a waitress, and opened her first restaurant on Mount Pleasant Street and then a second on Georgia Avenue. Alex had taken the family to the Mount Pleasant location for dinner one night and bored them, no doubt, with his enthusiastic retelling of another immigrant success story.

"It's nice," said Alex. "Reasonable, too. So don't ask me for too much."

"Can I get forty dollars?" said Rafael.

Alex reached into his pocket, produced a roll of bills, peeled off two twenties. "You want it all taken out the next payday?"

"Half nex week, half the nex. Okay?"

Alex handed him the money. "Wear a rubber, Rafael."

"*Que?*"

"You heard me. You're too young to be a father."

"I don't like the raincoat."

"Do what I tell you, boy."

Rafael winked. "Thanks, boss."

Alex made a small wave of his hand. "Have fun."

Rafael headed for the back door with a cocky, athletic dip. Alex was reminded of Gus. He had had that kind of physicality and confidence. Alex had constantly reminded him to use condoms, too. "Your mother and I don't want any grandchildren yet. You don't want to mess up some girl's life." Gus, like Rafael, didn't look past the pleasure at the consequences. It was not that they were insensitive, but rather, they were insensible. Alex never had to tell Johnny to use a condom. He knew little about his personal life, but he felt that Johnny would be cautious. Gus, on the other hand, made decisions based on desire and emotion. Gus was certain he would play football at a higher level, despite his average size, and wanted to move to Florida. Gus had joined the army behind his romantic vision of the warrior. Gus had dreams and fantasies. Johnny had plans.

Alex heard a knocking sound and turned his head to see a tall black man rapping his knuckles on the glass of the front door.

"I'll get it, Dad," said Johnny.

"No, *I* will," said Alex.

He slipped the cash box under the counter, shut the register drawer, passed through the break in the counter, and stepped up to the door. Through the glass, he mouthed the word "Closed" to the man, but the man did not move. Alex flipped the dead bolt and opened the door just enough to speak to him.

"We're closed, sir."

"I'm not here for food or drink."

"What can I do for you?"

"My name is Raymond Monroe."

The name was a common one. It was also vaguely familiar.

Alex had the growing feeling that he had seen this man before.

"Can I come in for a minute?"

"Why?"

"Look, I'm not here to rob you."

"I know that," said Alex, a bit embarrassed and also annoyed.

"I saw you outside the Fisher House yesterday, at Walter Reed. You and I almost bumped into each other."

"Right," said Alex. So that was where he recognized him from. He didn't quite remember the encounter, but he had no reason to think this man would lie.

"It was Peggy. You know Peggy, don't you? She told me who you were. See, there was something about you. Well, it was your eye, you want the truth. And then, when she said your name . . . You *are* the boy that got hurt out at Heathrow Heights, aren't you?"

Alex hesitated. "I was."

"I'm one of the young men who was involved in the incident. The younger brother."

Monroe drew his wallet and held out his driver's license so Alex could match the photo to the name. Alex glanced at it, keeping his foot against the door.

"Look, I don't want anything," said Monroe.

"You've, uh, caught me off guard here."

"Just a word." Monroe placed his palm on the glass of the door. "Please."

"Certainly." Alex stepped aside. "Come in."

Monroe entered the shop, and Alex locked the door. They walked toward the counter.

"Can I get you a soda, something?"

"I'm okay," said Monroe.

"Dad?" said Johnny, standing with Darlene by the rear door.

"Go home, both of you," said Alex. "I'm just gonna have a word with this gentleman. I'll be right behind you."

After Alex waited for Johnny and Darlene to go, he gestured to the stool nearest the register. As Monroe got situated, Alex took a seat himself, leaving one empty stool between them. Alex rarely sat on this side of the counter. He didn't know what to do with his arms.

"That was your boy?"

"My oldest, yes."

"Nice-looking kid."

"Thanks."

"I have a boy, too, a soldier. Kenji's in the Tenth Mountain Division, First Battalion. Third Brigade Combat Team."

"God protect him," said Alex.

"Yes."

"Is that why you were at Walter Reed?"

"No, I work there. I'm a physical therapist."

"That's admirable."

"Well, I'm getting paid for it. So it's not like I'm donating my time. But I'm tryin to help out, you know. I felt a little useless, what with Kenji over there, doing his part."

Alex nodded. On the Coca-Cola clock, the second hand swept past twelve, dropping the minute hand with a soft click. Alex placed his forearm on the counter and ran a finger along the artificial grain of the linoleum.

"I'm sorry," said Alex. "I don't mean to be rude. It's just that I'm not exactly clear on why you came to see me."

"I'm just reaching out," said Monroe. "You move along in life, you feel the need to make the beds you left undone."

Alex nodded. He could think of nothing to say.

"We don't have to do this all at once," said Monroe, sensing the man's resistance and confusion, deciding that the rest of it would have to be left for another, more appropriate time. "When you feel more comfortable, when you're ready to talk again, give me a call."

Monroe reached for the guest check pad and the pen that was lying beside it. He wrote his name and cell number on the top sheet, tore it off, and pushed it along the counter to Alex. Alex was polite and did the same.

"I'm sorry for the loss of your son," said Monroe.

"Thank you."

Monroe and Alex got off their stools and headed for the door.

"Mr. Monroe."

"Make it Ray."

"Your brother . . . What was his name again?"

"James."

"Is he around?"

"He's alive, yes."

"How's he doing?"

"He's out. Stumbled some, but he's out now. Back in D.C., working. Yeah, James is doing good."

Monroe offered his hand, and Alex shook it.

After Raymond Monroe had left, Alex sat in the quiet of the shop, thinking about the door that had just been opened. Picturing himself walking through it, and wondering what he might find if he did.

THIRTEEN

RAYMOND MONROE drove his aging, well-maintained Pontiac out into the County and north on the Boulevard, coming into the retail district, passing the big hardware store and the Safeway, the Greek-owned pizza parlor, and the old gas station where his brother, James, had worked, now self-service, a minimart having replaced the mechanics' bays. He hooked a left at the end of the strip, before the split in the road, and rolled down the incline, along the B&O railroad tracks and into Heathrow Heights.

Adults were getting home from work, and kids were playing in their yards and riding their bikes down the sidewalks as the shadows stretched out in the dying light. Nunzio's, the local market and country store, had closed long ago and been replaced by two split-level houses, one with turquoise siding. At the bottom of the street, bordering the woods, was the government barrier, painted yellow, telling anyone unfamiliar with the layout that the road had come to an end.

Raymond waved to an old man he knew and, farther along, a girl he'd once kissed down by the basketball court, now a grandmother. He still knew most of the people who lived here.

He'd known their parents and now recognized their children. A few Hispanic families had moved into the neighborhood in the past five years, workingmen and -women with many kids, but Heathrow was still a black enclave, its people proud of their struggle and history.

Many houses had been improved, and others were in the process of being renovated. There were a couple of homes being built from the foundation up, but the new structures looked to be as modest as the teardowns they were replacing. If folks wanted to flash, they went elsewhere. Many, even those who had markedly improved their standard of living, had chosen to stay in Heathrow Heights.

Rodney Draper, the Monroe brothers' old friend, was one of those who had never left. Rodney still lived in his late mother's house, though no longer in its basement. He had a wife and three daughters, one of whom was attending college. Rodney had gone into stereo sales, then major appliances, and had worked his way up in a small operation that became a ten-store chain in the 1990s. He was now the merchandising manager for the company, worked the sixty-hour weeks common to retail, and made a solid if unspectacular living. Raymond passed his house, expanded, well tended, and bright with a fresh coat of white paint. Rodney's car was not out front. He always seemed to be at work.

Monroe parked in front of his mother's house, not far from Rodney's on the street parallel to Heathrow's main road. This street, too, concluded in a dead end. Dogs, even those who knew his smell, barked at Monroe from the yards of the surrounding houses as he crossed his lawn.

His mother, Almeda, sat in the den of their two-bedroom home. Monroe took her cool arthritic hands in his, bent forward, and kissed her cheek.

"Mama."

"Ray." Almeda's eyes went to the overnight bag he clutched in his hand. "You staying the night?"

"Yes, ma'am."

She was seated in her husband's old recliner, which Raymond had re-covered himself. Her hair was white, the moles on her scalp visible through the cottony wisps, her thin wrists and forearms prominently veined. She wore a clean floral-pattern blouse from Macy's and black pants with an elastic waistband. She was well into her eighties. The hump in her back was most pronounced when she stood.

Almeda would need professional care soon if she were to live much longer. Raymond was determined to keep her out of a nursing facility. She wasn't sick, just weak. Money was not an issue. The house was paid for, and Raymond took care of the property taxes and utilities, and performed most of the maintenance. Almeda received modest Social Security benefits, along with a check from the VA, reflecting Ernest's service in the war. They got along fine. Most of the time, Raymond enjoyed his mother's company. He liked living here.

Monroe went to the television set and turned down the volume. Almeda was watching *Jeopardy*, and like most elderly folks, she kept the sound up loud. He sat on the sofa beside her and leaned forward so she could hear him clearly.

"Something troubling you, son?"

"Not at all."

"It's nothing to do with Kenji, is it? Have you heard from him?"

"I haven't. He's busy, is all it is. Out on those patrols he goes on. I'm sure he's fine."

"Problems with your girlfriend, then?"

"Nah, Kendall's good. The both of us, we're good."

"Running back and forth between two homes is going to take a toll on your relationship."

"Trying to kick me out?"

"I'm saying, you might as well move in with her. Get a minister, have a ceremony. Do right by her and her son."

"I might. If they'll have me."

"Who wouldn't?" said Almeda. "Fine man like you."

"Listen, Mama . . ."

"What is it?"

"I visited a man today. One of the white boys in the incident, back in seventy-two."

The incident. All involved had always called it that. Almeda's shoulders slumped as she sat back in her chair.

"Which boy?" she said.

"The one Charles Baker hurt."

Almeda folded her hands in her lap. "How did you find him?"

"I ran into him at Walter Reed. Alex Pappas. I recognized his name and put it together with his face."

Almeda nodded. "And how has life turned out for him?"

"He was at the hospital delivering food. He lost a son in Iraq."

"Awful," she said.

"He owns a diner downtown. He carries the scar Charles gave him, but other than that, I don't know much about him. I didn't stay with him long enough to find out. He was uncomfortable, like anyone would be. I came up on him quick."

"What did you see in his eyes?"

"I saw good."

"Why, Raymond? Why would you seek him out?"

"I had to," said Monroe.

Almeda offered her hand. He took it, a tiny tangle of bones.

"I suppose I understand," she said.

"Couldn't be an accident that I crossed paths with him. I pray at night for my son, knowing that I'm still unclean inside. I can't *be* like that anymore."

"Will you talk to this man again?"

"I left the door open. It's on him now."

"You should include your brother if the man wants to take it further."

"I plan to."

"It was him who suffered most."

"Yes, ma'am."

"Is that all?" said Almeda.

He hadn't told her everything. He didn't want to worry her over James.

"There's nothing else," said Raymond Monroe, cutting his eyes away.

DEON BROWN was in the living room of his mother's house, alternately sitting in a chair and pacing the floor. Since the night before, he and Cody had managed to off most of the weed they had bought from Dominique. Their day was spent talking on their disposable cells, setting up meets, making deliveries in parking lots, garages, houses, and apartments, and collecting money. The balance of the ounces they had not physically unloaded had been committed. The transactions had been quick and successful, and they had each pocketed over a thousand in cash in less than twenty-four hours. Deon should have been happy, but he was not. He was tired of hanging with Cody, whose mouth did not stop, even when he was high. Cody had just about gotten on Deon's last nerve.

He had come to his mother's to find some peace, maybe have dinner with her, watch television together, talk. But to

Deon's annoyance, Charles Baker had been in the house when he'd arrived. Deon had heard Baker upstairs, raising his voice at his mother, and her sharp objections and replies. And then Baker's voice, louder still and frightening, ending the argument with intimidation and aural force. Silence after that for a couple of minutes, followed by a rhythmic squeaking sound, which was the mattress springs being worked on his mother's bed. Deon wanted to leave out the house, but he could not. He wasn't about to abandon his mother to low trash like Charles Baker. Baker was on top of his mother, thrusting, the mattress squeaking and the legs of the bed lifting and hitting the hardwood floor. Deon rubbed at his temples and paced, but he did not leave.

The house grew quiet. Deon heard his mother's door close up on the second floor, and soon Baker came downstairs. He stood at the foot of the stairs, tucking his shirt into his slacks, and nodded at Deon, now seated again in a cushioned armchair.

"How long you been here?" said Baker.

"A while."

"You heard us arguin, then."

"Sounded like you were doing most of it."

"Your mother's emotional. Women be like that."

"Is she coming down for supper?"

"She needs to rest now," said Baker with a vile grin.

"You're not stayin the night, then," said Deon. It wasn't a question.

Baker held his smile and kept his eyes fixed on the boy. He didn't like to be talked to this way, but he would allow it to pass. *I'm done with that dry hole, anyway,* he thought. *Why would I want to stay?*

"I'll be sleepin at my group home tonight," said Baker. "But

I need to get over to Thirteenth and Fairmont, to see a friend. Can you drop me?"

"I was just leaving myself," said Deon, happy to get this man out of his mother's house.

Deon drove the Marauder east, Charles Baker beside him. Night had fallen, and the glow of the instrument lights colored their faces. Baker looked at Deon, filling up his space under the wheel though the seat had been pushed far back.

"You got some size on you," said Baker. "What you go, two fifty?"

"Round that."

"You ever play football?"

"Never."

"You runnin to fat now. All them Macs and that slope food you be consumin. You need to watch yourself, 'cause, lookit, you starting to get some titties on you like a woman."

Deon kept his eyes ahead, braking and coming to a full stop at one of the many four-ways now on 13th.

"The way you built," said Baker, "wouldn't take long in a weight room to get you swole. When I was liftin, I was a beast."

When you were in prison, thought Deon.

"Anyway," said Baker. "You and your boy just don't do enough physical shit. That's all I'm sayin. Young boys be like that today, though. Your Tubes and Your Space, the chitchat rooms and all that bullshit—y'all just don't use your muscles anymore. Me, I *use* my muscles. The ones in my head *and* in my back."

Deon accelerated as he hit a gradual incline, the Flowmasters growling beneath the Mercury.

"Course, with all that money you got, I guess you don't feel the need to be getting physical. I'm talkin about real work, going out there, scrumpin and humpin. 'Cause you and Cody, y'all are flush. Am I right?"

"We're doing fine," said Deon.

"What, you two made a couple thousand, more than that, in the last day alone?"

"Something like it."

"And me emptyin bedpans and scrubbing the shit stains off of porcelain, for what? Couple hundred dollars a week? How you think that makes me feel?"

"What's your point?"

"What's my *point*. You funny, you know it? My point is, I been in your mother's world for a little while now, and I been good to her. You'd think that her son would want to return the favor and do something for the man who done right by his moms. Give Mr. Charles a little taste of that good thing you and your boy got."

"We're set," said Deon.

"But I'm not."

"What I'm trying to say is, we had our thing going before you came along, and we're not lookin to grow it. I'm happy where we at."

"You don't look too happy. I mean, I ain't seen you smiling all that much. You on them mood pills and shit, but you don't seem all that joyful to me."

"I'm straight."

"What about the white boy? He happy, too?"

"You'd have to ask him."

"Yeah, I'm gonna do that. 'Cause Cody, he seem like the ambitious type. More than you."

"Where you wanna be dropped?"

"I said Fairmont. We got a few more blocks yet." Baker drummed his fingers on the shelf of the dash. "I guess you just can't see it. You don't have that vision thing."

Deon did not ask Baker about what he could not see.

"I don't even want to be around no marijuana," said Baker. "I'm not lookin to get violated on some drug charge. And if I did try to get involved in the, uh, mechanical part of the business, I would just fuck it up. 'Cause I am no good at that detail work. Truth is, I don't know a thing about movin weed. But I do know human nature."

"What you gettin at?"

"First time I got a look at your friend Dominique, I saw a straight bitch. I got some experience in identifying those motherfuckers real quick."

No doubt, thought Deon.

"I'm sayin, you put me in a room with little Dominique? I'm gonna negotiate a better deal for y'all real quick. Get those profit margins up. That's the role I'd play for y'all. I'm not boastin about it, either. I can do it."

"Dominique got people," said Deon.

"What kinda people?"

"He got a brother who's fierce."

"Shit. They got the same blood runnin through their veins, don't they? I ain't sweatin."

"We're good the way we are," said Deon.

"You're gonna be stubborn, huh," said Baker jovially. "Okay. Fuck it, young man, I don't need nothin from you, anyway. My ship's about to come in real soon. You gonna be askin *me* for loans."

"We're here," said Deon.

"Pull over."

Just before Fairmont, Deon cut the Mercury to the curb and let it idle. Two blocks up ahead, at Clifton Street, young white people in business clothes were walking over the crest of the big hill running along Cardozo High School, coming up from the Metro station toward their condos and houses.

"Look at that," said Baker. "They think they can just move in here. . . . They don't even know where they at or what can happen to 'em. Walkin all confident and shit. They think they gonna take over our city."

"Thought you grew up in Maryland," said Deon.

"Don't correct me, boy," said Baker, his face old and grim in the dashboard light. "I don't like it when you do."

"I didn't mean nothin."

"I know you didn't, big man." Charles Baker forced a smile. "Thanks for the ride. I'll catch up with you soon, hear?"

Deon Brown watched Baker walk west on Fairmont Street, his collar casually turned up, his hands swinging free. Deon drove east, then swung a left on 11th Street and headed uptown.

Charles Baker went to the middle of the block, a strip of row houses with turrets, and cut up a walkway to the front of a building that held multiple apartments. He stepped into the foyer and pushed one of several brown buttons set beside pieces of paper fitted behind small rectangles of glass.

A voice came tinny from a slotted box. "Yeah."

"It's your boy Charles."

There was a long silence. "So?"

"I was on your street. I just thought, you know, I'd say hello."

Baker imagined that he heard a sigh. Perhaps it was the hiss of static coming from the speaker. He couldn't tell.

A buzzer sounded, and Baker opened the unlocked door of glass and wood. He passed through a short, clean hall and up a flight of stairs to a second-floor landing, where he knocked on a door marked with stick-on numbers.

The door opened. A big man with a barrel chest, dressed in blue Dickies work pants and a matching unbuttoned shirt, stood tall in the frame. His white T-shirt hung sloppily over his belly. He held an open can of Pabst Blue Ribbon beer in one meaty, calloused hand. His eyes were large and a bit blood-shot. His hair was unkempt and unstylish, a medium-length natural.

"What is it?" said the man.

"That how you talk to your old partner?"

"You want somethin. Otherwise you wouldn't be here."

"I just wanna visit. But I can't do it out here."

"I gotta be up for work tomorrow."

"Shoot, I got a big day, too," said Baker. "Can I come in?"

The big man with the barrel chest turned his back and walked into the dark apartment, the sound of a television loud in the room. Charles Baker entered and closed the door behind him.

The man sat in his favorite chair, a recliner, and took a swig of beer. It spilled some and rolled down his chin and onto his shirt. The man wiped at the wet spot, near a white oval patch with his name stitched across it in script.

"Ain't you gonna offer a man a beer?" said Baker.

"Get one," said the man.

"I *knew* you were my boy." Baker stepped toward the refrigerator in the apartment's tiny kitchen. He had no trouble finding it. He'd been here before.

James Monroe sat in the recliner and stared ahead, the light of the television flickering in his black eyes.

FOURTEEN

ALEX AND Vicki Pappas sat in their living room, nursing glasses of wine, red for Alex, white for Vicki. He had told her about their son's day at work, and of Johnny's gift for interaction with the customers and help. She said that Johnny's presence in the store was going to be good for their relationship, that it would help bring them closer together. He had been prepared to argue the point, but in all honesty, he had to agree. He did like having Johnny there. And having him in the shop was going to be good for business, too.

Alex then told her about the man who'd visited him at closing time. She listened carefully and asked some questions but did not seem particularly interested in prolonging the conversation or invested in the subject. The incident had happened years before she'd met Alex. To her, it was an abstract event that had happened to a boy she did not know and had little to do with the man she loved and had been married to for twenty-six years.

"You don't think this is some sort of scam, do you?"

"It's him," said Alex.

"I'm asking you, is this an extortion thing?"

"No. He had a nice way about him. I don't think it's anything like that."

"Will you call him?"

"*Should* I?"

"Honey, that's up to you." Vicki shrugged and got up out of her chair. "I'm bushed. I'm going to bed."

She leaned in and kissed him on the mouth. He gripped her hand and held the kiss.

"Good night, Vicki."

"*Kah-lee neech-tah.*"

After he had poured out the rest of his wine, Alex went to the family's computer station off the kitchen and got on the Web. He first searched the archives of the *Washington Post* and found several articles related to the incident, from the initial reporting of the crime in metro to the conviction announcement, eighteen months later, in the spring of 1974. He had read most of these articles at the time, had even kept a few of them, suspecting that he would someday want to revisit them, but he had thrown them out a year into his marriage, hoping that with the birth of his first son, that chapter of his life had been closed.

His recollection of that period was as hazy as the incident itself. He had not gone to the funeral of Billy Cachoris. At the time of Billy's burial, Alex had been hospitalized at Holy Cross, and then there were the two reconstructive surgeries in the fall. His stay at the hospital was one druggy, painful day after another, his only entertainment a high-mounted television set, which strained his good eye, and his clock radio, which his parents brought from home. He listened to Top 40 because he could not get the progressive stations he favored in his room, and the playlist mocked him. "Rocket Man," "Black and White," "Precious and Few." Songs that had been playing *that day*. Songs that they had joked about only hours, minutes before Billy had been killed. Introducing each song, the disc jockey on PGC would announce, "Nineteen seventy-two, this is the soundtrack to your life!" And Alex would think, *What a laugh*.

Like many teenage boys who have found serious trouble, he felt that the sun would never shine on his side of the street again. Back at home, he listened to his Blue Öyster Cult album incessantly, returning to the song "Then Came the Last Days of May" over and over again. *Three good buddies were laughin and smokin / In the back of a rented Ford. / They couldn't know they weren't going far*. It seemed to have been written for him and his friends.

Except in the presence of legal authorities, Alex had little further contact with Pete Whitten. Pete's father had forbidden him to socialize with Alex, and their few phone conversations were awkward and filled with blocks of silence. Pete would be off to an out-of-state university the following summer, unaltered by the event, as neither he nor Alex had been charged with crimes. Alex understood that their friendship was done.

For Alex, the strangest aspect of the aftermath was returning to school. He felt that his face was ugly and frightening, though of course his perception of it was far worse than the reality. His eye drooped severely at the corner, and the scar tissue around it was waxy. It would never go unnoticed, but it was far from horrific; in a way, he just looked permanently sad. He broke up with Karen, assuming she would no longer be attracted to him. One day, in the E wing hall, a kid named Bobby Cohen innocently said, "Hey, man, I heard you got jumped by some black dudes," and Alex grabbed him by the shirt and threw him up against the lockers. The boy had said nothing wrong, but Alex had been looking for an excuse to explode.

He grew more sullen every day. He was not a tough kid, but he acquired a reputation as a badass simply because he had been involved in a racial incident in which one of his friends was shot and killed. The black kids at his high school, numbering about thirty in a population of five hundred, stopped speaking to him. He had been friendly with a few of them before the incident, mostly through interaction on the outdoor basketball court near the teachers' parking lot, but that would be no more. A group of greasers, the last of their breed, reached out to him, thinking he shared their racial biases. They called themselves, unimaginatively, the White Masters, and he rejected them. His aim was to get through his senior year with his head down. He was racked with guilt over Billy's death and desired no new friends. He wanted to be alone.

Working for his father, in its way, kept him human. The customers, readers of the *Washington Post* and the *Evening Star*, certainly knew of his involvement in the event. Some shunned him, but the majority of them were polite. Inez, typically, made no mention of the incident and sometimes chuckled, as if she knew something about him that he did not, as he passed by her colds station. Whatever they were feeling, Junior and Paulette kept it to themselves. The hardest part for Alex was facing Darlene for the first time. But thankfully, Darlene was kind.

"Does it hurt?" she said, putting out her hand and touching her fingers to the scar, the only person outside his doctors and mother to do so.

"Not anymore," said Alex. "Listen . . ."

"You don't have to talk about it. It hurt me when I read about you in the newspaper, I can't lie. But part of that was knowing that you were hurtin, too. Look, anyone can get into the wrong car. Because that's all it was. That's all it *had* to be. Alex, I *know* you. So you don't have to say one more word."

Sometimes after work they'd sit in the darkened store past closing time. His father had gone, having handed Alex the key. The two of them would quietly talk and listen to music from the portable eight-track deck Darlene carried with her to and from the job. Marvin Gaye, the Isley Brothers, and Curtis Mayfield, most memorably the tape called *Curtis*, with the cover photo of the man sitting casually in his lemon yellow suit. Timeless songs like "The Other Side of Town," "The Makings of You," "We the People Who Are Darker Than Blue," Curtis's beautiful falsetto and his dreamy arrangements playing softly in the shop as two teenagers spoke to each other about teenage things, sometimes holding hands but never going past that, the two of them friends.

As for the trial, Alex's part in it was minimal. He had been coached by the state's attorney, a prosecutor named Ira Sanborn, but on the stand there was little for him to relate. He hadn't seen the actual shooting. He hadn't *seen* the young man who'd ruined his face. He could only describe the sounds, sensations, and words he had heard. On the cross-examination, the defense attorney assigned to the case, a young man named Arthur Furioso, attempted to paint Alex and Pete as young racists who were ultimately responsible for the murder by putting the event into play, but Sanborn provided enough character witnesses to refute his claim. To the jury, there was the fact of a murdered teenager and the sight of Alex's face. Also, there had never been any question as to who had pulled the trigger. The older of the two brothers, James Monroe, had confessed to the shooting hours after the incident occurred. He, his younger brother, Raymond, and their friend Charles Baker, who had admitted to the beating of Alex, were charged with murder, assault with intent, and multiple gun offenses. The only question, Sanborn told the Pappas family in private, would be the final degree of the murder charge and whether Raymond Monroe and Charles Baker would also be convicted and serve time.

Alex, sitting in front of the computer screen, got out of the *Post* site without reading the last article in the archives. He typed "Heathrow Heights" and the word "murder" into a search engine and eventually found a site that sold partial transcripts of trials going back fifty years. Using his credit card to pay the access fee of four dollars and ninety-five cents, he printed a document that read *"State of Maryland v. James Ernest Monroe,"* along with the case number and date, a Judge Conners presiding.

Alex Pappas moved the crane neck of a desk lamp toward him. He sat back and read the document.

On a hot summer day, three boys drove into the Heathrow Heights area of Montgomery County and, "on a lark," threw a cherry pie and yelled a racial epithet at three young black men standing on the street outside Nunzio's market. The court document described their action as a "perverted form of entertainment." One of the occupants of the vehicle, Peter Whitten, testified that the plan was initiated by the driver, William Cachoris (the third occupant, Alexander Pappas, testified that he could not recall who had decided to drive into Heathrow Heights). After the pie was thrown and the epithet delivered, Cachoris attempted to drive the vehicle away but came to a dead end and was forced to turn the car around. At this time Peter Whitten left the vehicle on foot and escaped into the woods and down the railroad tracks. Cachoris and the remaining passenger, Pappas, drove back up the road, which was now blocked by the three young men. Cachoris got out of the car and tried to reason with the young men, asking, "Can't we work this out?" One of the young men punched him in the face, knocking out a tooth and loosening several others. Alexander Pappas attempted to escape on foot but was captured and assaulted, resulting in serious injuries to his body and face. One of the young men then produced a pistol and shot William Cachoris in the back, the bullet puncturing his lung and heart. He was pronounced dead at the scene.

Police arrived and locked down the neighborhood. A woman, her name deleted from the document, had been watching from the window inside Nunzio's market at the time of the shooting, and told the store manager to call the police. Upon questioning, she described the young men who had been involved in the crime but claimed she could not identify them. Upon further, more intense questioning, she recalled the names of the young men.

Police raided the home of Ernest and Almeda Monroe, who were both at work, and arrested their sons, James and Raymond Monroe, without resistance. They found a cheap .38 pistol in the dresser drawer of the older brother. The woman in Nunzio's had described the shooter as a tall young man wearing a T-shirt with numbers hand-printed upon it. James Monroe, when the police found him, was wearing the shirt. It appeared to be stained with blood. At this time, James Monroe admitted to firing the gun that killed William Cachoris. Ballistics tests would later match the bullet to the gun.

Police next arrested Charles Baker at the residence of his mother, Carlotta Baker, an unemployed, unmarried hairdresser. Later, at the police station, Charles Baker confessed to the assault on Alexander Pappas.

Alex felt blood move slowly to his face as he read on.

At the trial, Baker testified against James Monroe in exchange for a dropping of the murder charge and a reduced sentence, provided he pleaded guilty to the assault charge. In accordance with the terms of the prearranged deal, the state would then recommend a sentence for Baker of less than one year. In court, on the stand, Baker said, "James shot the boy," and pointed James Monroe out for the jury. Furioso, the defense attorney, asked Baker about his deal, which he readily described, and then asked him if the police had coerced his confession in any way. He said, "The police bought me a bottle of Sneaky Pete. I drank it, but that ain't what made me talk. My conscience was bothering me." Furioso moved for a mistrial on the grounds of bribery, but Judge Conners found his reasoning weak and unjustified, and his motion was denied.

James Monroe was found guilty of manslaughter in the first degree, assault, and multiple gun charges. Baker drew a conviction for assault with intent to maim. The younger brother, Raymond Monroe, was acquitted of all charges.

Alex dropped the trial document and returned to the *Washington Post* archives, where he brought up the last recorded story on the event. It described the sentencing of James Monroe.

At a hearing before the sentencing, Furioso handed the judge a petition that had been signed by more than one hundred residents of Heathrow Heights, pleading leniency and declaring that William Cachoris, Peter Whitten, and Alexander Pappas had enacted a "racially motivated aggression" against their "peaceful community and its citizens" that had directly caused the shooting. Judge Conners stated that he would take the petition under consideration. But at the sentencing, he rejected the notion that the circumstances of the "prank" should be given any weight. "William Cachoris and his friends made a bad decision that day, a very stupid and hurtful decision . . .

but in no way does their foolishness excuse the taking of a human life." Conners went on to say, "This kind of thing goes on in the county all the time. We all put up with racial nonsense. I see it in my own neighborhood, and there is never any retribution of this kind." The *Post* reported a rising murmur in the courtroom, perhaps a reaction of incredulity, as it was known that Conners lived in Bethesda, one of the whitest and most affluent areas of Montgomery County.

Judge Conners sentenced James Monroe to ten years in prison on the manslaughter charges. He would be eligible for parole in two and one half years. In addition, Conners sentenced Monroe to two years in prison for the assault charges and three years on the gun charges. These sentences would run concurrently with the sentence for manslaughter. Baker received the agreed sentence of less than one year. Defense attorney Furioso vowed to appeal. There were no further stories related to the case listed in the archives of the *Washington Post.*

Alex Pappas sat for a while longer, moving a finger in the dust that had settled on the computer table, making a line and another line through it that formed a cross. He switched off the lamp, went to the front door of the house, checked the lock, and left a light on for Johnny, who was at a movie with a friend. Upstairs, he passed Gus's room but did not go inside.

Alex had convinced himself that Gus's death had been random. On the last day of Gus's life, the driver of the Humvee he was riding in had taken one road rather than another, and on the road he'd taken was a makeshift bomb hidden underneath debris. Did God send the driver of the Humvee down that road? Alex could not believe this. God gave us life; after that, he neither protected nor harmed us. We were on our own. But what about sin? There had to be punishment for sin.

Alex could have gotten out of the Torino that day. Alex could have demanded that Billy stop the car. He knew that what they were about to do was wrong. He'd let it happen. Because of his inaction, many lives had been broken. Two young men had gone to prison. Billy was dead. Gus was dead, too.

Alex undressed and got into bed. Vicki stirred beside him. Alex touched his hand to her shoulder and squeezed it.

"Vicki?"

"What?" she said, her eyes still closed.

"I'm going to call that man," said Alex.

"Go to sleep."

Alex extinguished the bedside light. But he didn't go to sleep.

FIFTEEN

JAMES MONROE'S apartment was very small. Its single main room held a double bed, a cheap dresser, a couple of chairs, a television set on a stand, and a compact stereo on a wire cart. Monroe could barely turn around in the kitchen. When he sat on the toilet in the bathroom, he had to keep his arms in tight or they would touch the walls.

James Monroe and Charles Baker sat close to each other in the room's two chairs. Both of them were drinking beer. Monroe was watching television, and Baker was talking.

Monroe did not particularly care for the show they were watching. It was the autopsy series set in Miami, and he didn't believe one thing about it. But it was easier to watch the show than give his full attention to Baker.

"Now Red gonna shoot someone," said Baker. "In his designer suit and sunglasses. You know that's some bullshit, too."

"What is?"

"I'm talkin about crime scene investigators drawing their guns out and shootin people. You know that shit don't never happen. Even real police don't pull their guns out, most times.

166

But Red here, he kills a motherfucker with his gun every week. With that pretty head of hair he got, blowin in the breeze."

From one of the many books Monroe had read in prison, he remembered a passage about American television shows that dealt with crime. The author said that it was a "fascistic genre" because in these shows the criminals were always apprehended, and the police and prosecutors always won. The shows were warning the citizens, in effect, to stay in line. That if they dared to break the law, they would be caught and put in jail. Monroe had chuckled a little when he'd read it. People *wanted* to be reassured that their lives were safe. These television writers were just making money by feeding citizens the lies they craved.

"Hmph," said Monroe.

"That all you got to say?"

"I'm tryin to watch this."

"What about the other thing?"

"What thing is that?"

"What I been tellin you about. My date."

Baker had come to tell Monroe about the lunch appointment he had made with Peter Whitten the next day. Monroe had just shaken his head a little and kept his eyes unexpressive and focused on the TV.

"Well?"

Monroe swigged from his can of beer.

"I *need* you, man," said Baker. "Need you to come *with* me. You don't have to say nothin; just sit there beside me and be big. Send a message to this man so that I don't have to threaten him direct. He'll see it. He *got* to."

Monroe wiped something from the corner of his eye.

"Man's got money," said Baker. "We could get some of it.

It's *due* us, understand? I'm gonna be generous and give you a piece of it for coming along. Not half or nothing like that, but somethin. After that, I'm gonna put my finger on the other one. Just go ahead and do him the same way. You *know* they got to be carrying guilt. In the newspaper, Mr. Whitten was braggin on how he's a great friend to the Negro. Well, I'm gonna give him an opportunity to show it. If he doesn't, he got to know, I'm gonna burn his reputation down."

"No," said Monroe.

"What?"

"I don't want any part of it."

"You in it already."

"No, I'm not."

"Your handwriting's on the original letter. How you gonna say you *not* in?"

It was true. James had marked up the first draft of the letter, composed with pen on paper, after being prodded by Charles. Because James had been drinking too much beer that night, was exercising alcohol judgment, and hadn't thought the ramifications through. Because Charles was too stupid to write the letter, legibly, grammatically, and without spelling mistakes, himself. Because James had just wanted Charles out of his apartment and it seemed the only way to get him to leave. He never thought Baker would deliver it. He thought Baker had been talking his usual brand of shit.

He'd had a problem with saying no to Charles since the incident. It had brought him all kinds of trouble. Once, it had led him back to prison.

"I don't want any part of it," repeated Monroe.

"I guess you don't want money, either."

"I work for my money."

"In a cold garage."

"Wherever. I work."

Baker got up out of his chair. He paced the room in a small arc. He grew tired of it and pointed a finger at the face of Monroe. "You owe me."

Monroe rose and stood to his full height. His eyes narrowed, and Baker dropped his hand to his side.

"Look, man. I'm only sayin—"

"*That's past,*" said Monroe. He paused to slow his breathing some. When he spoke again, his voice was low and controlled. "Listen. You and me, we are over fifty years old."

"That's what I'm talkin about. Time's getting short."

"It's time we *learned*. Be thankful for this opportunity we got to start new."

"What I got to be thankful for? My stinkin-ass job?"

"Damn right. I go to work every day and I'm glad to have it. Happy to rent this apartment that I can walk out of any time I please. Gaming people, doing dirt . . . that train left the station a long time ago, for me."

"Not for me," said Baker. "I can't make it any other way."

Monroe looked into Baker's hard hazel eyes and saw that it was so.

"Those white boys fucked up our lives," said Baker.

"I said no."

"Don't make a mistake. I still got the letter written with your hand."

"I didn't write a letter. I made a few marks and corrections because what you wrote was all messed up and damn near unreadable. I was just trying to teach you somethin. I *did*n't think you were dumb enough to send it off. I was just doing you a favor."

"I appreciate it. But still, the corrections you made are in your hand."

"That a threat?"

"I wouldn't."

"You wanna say something, say it plain."

"Ain't no hidden meaning to it." Baker twitched a smile. "You and me, we joined at the hip. That's all."

"I been a gentleman and let you visit. Now it's time for you to go."

"I'll get up with you later."

"Go on. I got to get some sleep."

After Baker closed the door behind him, James Monroe threw the dead bolt, went to the Frigidaire, and found another Pabst. He sat down in his chair and stared at the television but did not pay attention to the images on the screen.

He reached for the phone and made a call. The conversation he had was short and emotional.

Later, Monroe switched the channel on the television to a late Wizards game, broadcast from Seattle. He pulled up the tab atop the can of beer, tilted his head back, and drank deeply.

SUNSHINE HOUSE was one of the many food pits found on Georgia Avenue, both in the District and in downtown Silver Spring. The neon sign in the window advertised "Steak and Cheese, Seafood, Fried Chicken, and Chinese," a shotgun approach that produced mediocrity and, ultimately, heartburn and diarrhea. The proprietor's name was Mr. Sun, hence the store's name. Sun owned three operations in D.C., Montgomery, and Prince George's County; lived in a house off Falls Road in Potomac; drove an E-Class Mercedes; and had kids at MIT and Yale. Cody Kruger called the place Sun's Shithouse. He and Deon ate there often.

Deon had just finished a plate of orange chicken, a side of

fries, and a large Coke. His stomach hurt already. He had been driving north, seen the sign in the window of Sunshine House, and pulled into the lot. When he was stressed he tended to seek out food. The antidepressants he took were supposed to lessen his appetite, but they did not.

Deon wiped grease from his face and threw his napkin in the trash. He pushed on a glass door and walked out of the store toward his Marauder, parked in a spot facing the Armed Services Recruitment Center, a plain brick structure beside Sun's. He got under the wheel and fitted the ignition key but did not turn it. He didn't want to go to the apartment and listen to Cody. He didn't want to go to the house on Peabody and see his mother's swollen eyes.

He did not know, exactly, how he had gotten here. In elementary school, he had been an average student with limited social skills. In middle school, he had two close friends, Anthony Dunwell and Angelo Ross, but they were athletes and he was not, and in high school, they began to run with a different crowd. It was in his early high school years that he first experienced shortness of breath and nausea when he was asked to stand before the class and present his work. Meeting new people, he often stammered when he spoke. His mother took him to a shrink, who called his problem social anxiety and diagnosed him with panic disorder. Deon was prescribed Paxil, and that seemed to help. So did good weed. He became less socially retarded and, for a while, had a nice girlfriend, Jerhoma Simon, and then another with a brilliant smile who went by the name of Ugochi. For reasons he couldn't recall or didn't want to, those relationships did not last. After graduation there was a dry spell without girlfriends or new male friends, until he met Cody up at the shoe store. After that, there was one bad decision after another, and the entrance of

GEORGE PELECANOS

Charles Baker, and here he was, nineteen, with money in his pocket and nothing ahead but more money or jail time, sitting in a parking lot.

Deon touched the key in the ignition slot but dropped his hand away.

The boxed sign over the recruitment center was brightly lit. He recalled that down in Park View, in a similar recruitment office near the old Black Hole, the sign had always been lit and the windows kept smudge free. A clean storefront in a strip of run-down businesses, a beacon for the young men in the neighborhood who were looking for a job or a way out, many of them high school dropouts, many of them running from temptation and trouble, some of their own making, some not.

The times he'd been to places like Chevy Chase and Bethesda, Deon had never seen recruitment offices of any kind. But it made sense. Why would the army, navy, or Marine Corps waste their time, money, and effort on kids who were never going to sign up and serve? Those kids were going to college. *Those kids* had parents who would pay for their tuition and room and board, and later help usher them into the job market via their network of successful friends.

Looking through the plate glass of the center, he saw two life-size cardboard cutouts of soldiers, one black, one Hispanic, in full dress. In between the cutouts, large wire racks held dozens of pamphlets. He could guess that some of the pamphlets were printed in Spanish. Behind the racks were dividers, the kind that formed cubicles in offices. Deon wondered what these folks didn't want citizens on the street to see.

On the window itself were numerous posters touting service. A picture of an aircraft carrier loaded with planes, troops, and equipment, ready for action, below the words "Life, Lib-

172

erty, and the Pursuit of All Who Threaten It." A photograph of a black woman, beautiful and proud eyed, a beret cocked jauntily on her head, the caption reading "There's Strong. And Then There's *Army* Strong." Other posters mentioned enlistment bonuses of up to $20,000, thirty days' vacation pay per year, 100 percent tuition assistance, and full health and dental benefits. Guaranteed training in a chosen career. The chance to travel.

Yellowish light bled out from beneath the padded dividers. Someone, some officer, was in there, burning the oil, alone and ready to talk.

Deon had nowhere special to go. He had the need to talk to someone, too.

He got out of the Mercury, passed under the bright, inviting light of the big sign hung over the recruitment office, and tried the handle of the front door. The door was unlocked. But Deon did not step inside.

SIXTEEN

RAYMOND MONROE stepped out of the therapy room a little after noon, intending to call Kendall and have lunch with her down in the cafeteria. As he pulled his cell from his pocket, he passed a young man, blinded in one eye, shrapnel wounds forming crescent scars around the socket, his head shaved and stitched on the side.

"Pop," said the young man.

"How's it going?" said Monroe.

"Awesome," said the young man without sarcasm or irony, and he walked on in a square-shouldered stride.

At the elevator bank, Monroe waited for the down car beside a man his age who stood with his hands on the grips of a wheel-chair. A young woman of about twenty sat in the chair, her hospital gown worn over a T-shirt. She had short black hair, blue eyes, and a bit of a mustache, most likely a growth spurred by steroids she had been taking postinjury. Both of her legs had been amputated high in the femur, not far below the trunk. One stump was badly burned and scarred with "dots," small bits of shrapnel still embedded close to the skin surface. The other stump did not appear to have been burned but was twitching wildly.

"Hey," said the young woman, looking at Monroe.

"Afternoon," said Monroe. "How's everybody doing on this fine day?"

"How am I doin, Daddy?" said the young woman.

"She just got fitted for her new legs," said her father. His eyes were the same shade of brilliant blue as his daughter's. "Won't be long before Ashley's walkin again."

Both Ashley and her father had deep southern accents. Both of them smelled strongly of cigarettes.

"And after that," said Ashley, "I'm gonna swim from one shore to the other and back again."

"She wants to swim in the old lake," said the father. "We got a nice clean one down by our home."

"I will, too," she said.

"Next summer, maybe," said the father, as he reached down and touched her cheek. He smiled, his lip quivering with melancholy pride.

"Maybe you and I will get a chance to work together in the pool," said Monroe.

"I'll make *you* tired," said Ashley.

"My little girl is game," said the father.

"No doubt," said Monroe. As the elevator doors opened, Monroe's cell phone chimed in his hand, indicating that he had a message.

Outside the main building, he checked his messages. Alex Pappas's voice told him he'd like to meet. Monroe hit auto-return and got Alex on the line.

"Pappas and Sons." He sounded stressed amid the considerable noise in the background.

"It's Ray Monroe."

"Mr. Monroe, you got me in the middle of my lunch rush."

"Call me Ray. Look, I didn't know—"

"If you'd like to talk again, I'm stopping by Fisher House after work. Same time as the other night."

"Okay. I was thinking we'd take a drive, go visit my brother."

"I can't talk now. I'll see you then." Pappas abruptly cut the connection. Monroe stood looking at the phone for a moment, then dropped the cell back into his pocket.

He went into building 2 and took the elevator up to Kendall's floor. When he knocked on the open door to her office, he could already see that she was not there. Gretta Siebentritt, the outpatient therapist who shared the office with Kendall, swiveled her chair to face him.

"What's up, Ray?"

"Lookin for my girlfriend. Is she hiding from me?"

"Hardly. She's in conference with Private Collins. He's been occupying a bit of her time."

"The soldier about to do the voluntary amputation?"

"Him. Anything you'd like me to tell her?"

"I'll get up with her later."

Monroe ate lunch alone, thinking about James, Alex Pappas, Baker, and the trouble that was bound to come.

FOR HIS lunch appointment, Charles Baker had chosen to wear a deep purple sport jacket with white stitching on the lapels, triple-pleat polyester black slacks, a lavender shirt, and a pair of black tooled-leather shoes that almost looked like gators. He had put the outfit together over the past year, shopping at thrift places and the Salvation Army store on H Street in Northeast. He had never before had the occasion to wear the rig in full, and looking in the mirror on the way out of his group home, he felt that he looked clean and right.

"Where you off to?" said a man called Trombone, a recovering heroin addict with a very long nose, one of the four men on paper with whom Baker shared the house. "You look like folding money."

"I got people to meet and places to be," said Baker. "And none of 'em are here."

Baker did feel like a million dollars, walking out of the house.

But when he got downtown, coming off the Metro escalator at Farragut North, moving along into the bustle of Connecticut Avenue, he got that feeling again, the feeling he had whenever he left his insular world, that he was out of step and wrong. Around him, workingmen and -women of all colors, finely and effortlessly attired, carrying soft leather briefcases and handbags, walking with purpose, *going somewhere*. He did not understand how they had gotten here. Who taught them how to dress in that quiet, elegant way? How did they get their jobs?

Baker put his thumb and forefinger to the lapel of his purple sport coat. The fabric felt spongy. All right, so he wasn't in step with all these silver spoons down here. He'd dazzle Mr. Peter Whitten with his personality and force of logic. Flash him some Dale Carnegie smile.

The restaurant was an Italian place with an *O* on the end of its name, on L Street, west of 19th. He entered to the sound of relaxed conversation, the gentle movement and soft contact of china, silver, and crystal. Murals had been painted on the walls, looked to Baker like those fancy old paintings he'd seen at a museum he'd been to once, when he was coming in from the cold, wandering around, down on the Mall.

"Yes, sir," said a young man in a black suit, stepping up to meet Baker as he walked through the door.

"I'm havin lunch with somebody. I got an appointment with Mr. Peter Whitten."

"Right this way, sir." The man made an elaborate movement with his hands and swiveled his narrow hips. The word *prey* flashed in Baker's mind, but here was not the place to be scheming, and he followed the young man through the maze of tables, along the granite-top bar, where a solid-built dude in a leather blazer sat, eye-fucking him as he passed. Even the brothers down here took him for ghetto, thought Baker. Well, fuck them, too.

Peter Whitten was waiting at a two-top covered with a white tablecloth, close to the bar. Everything about him, from the natural drape of his suit to the carefully cut, just-over-the-ear hairstyle, said money. His face was neither friendly nor confrontational, and all of his features were straight. His hair was silver and blond, his eyes a light blue. Like an actor cast as the wealthy father on a soap opera, he was handsome in a predictable way. He didn't get up but stretched out his hand as Baker arrived.

"Mr. Baker?"

"It is me," said Baker, taking his hand and giving a smile. "Mr. Whitten, right?"

"Have a seat."

The young man had pulled his chair out, and Baker dropped into it and maneuvered his legs under the table. Baker touched the silverware before him, moved it a little, and almost at once another man in a tux was beside the table, setting down a menu and asking Baker if he would like something to drink.

"Would you care for a beer or a cocktail?" said Whitten helpfully.

Baker looked at Whitten's glass.

"I'll just have water," said Baker.

"Flat or sparkling?" said the waiter.

"Regular water," said Baker.

The waiter drifted. Baker opened the menu, looking to do something with his hands, not knowing how to start the conversation. He was aware of Whitten staring at him as his eyes scanned the menu. *Prima piatti*, *insalata*, *pasta e risotto*, *secondi piatti*. How'd they expect an American to know what to order in this piece? *Fagottini* . . . Baker knew there was something he didn't like about this restaurant.

"Do you need some help with the menu?" said Whitten. He wasn't smiling, but there was something like a smile in his eyes.

Baker had made an error. He shouldn't have met Whitten here. It was wrong, arrogant even, for him to presume he could play on the man's home court.

"I'm all right," said Baker. "It all looks so good. I just need some time."

"Maybe we better talk first," said Whitten, folding his hands on the table, at peace in his world.

Baker closed the menu and laid it down. "Okay. You read the letter, so there's no mystery as to what this is about."

"Yes."

"I'm lookin for a little help, Mr. Whitten."

Whitten stared at him.

"I feel like I got some, uh, reparations comin to me, if you know what I mean. Since that day you and your friends drove into our neighborhood, my life has been hard. It's not like I haven't tried to make it, either. I'm not a bad person. I have a job."

"What do you want?"

"Some compensation for what you and your friends did. I think that's fair. I'm not tryin to break the bank or nothing like that. I mean, look at you; obviously you've done good in life. You sure can spare it."

"Spare what?"

"Huh?"

"How much do you want?"

"I was thinking, you know, fifty thousand dollars would be about right. That would do it. A good *foundation* for me to build somethin on. Get me back on the track that I would have been on from the beginning, if you and your friends hadn't come into our world."

"And what would you do if I said no?"

Baker's face felt flushed. The waiter poured him water from a pitcher, and Baker drank a long swig at once.

"Are we ready to order?" said the waiter.

"We ain't ready just yet," snapped Baker.

The waiter looked at Whitten, who shook his head slightly, telling him that everything was all right and that he should leave.

When the waiter was gone, Baker allowed his emotions to subside.

"Don't take me wrong," said Baker.

"No?"

"We're just having a conversation here. I'm asking you, gentleman to gentleman, for some help."

"Your letter said something about damage to my reputation."

"That wasn't a threat. That was just, you know, an incentive for you to contribute. I was just referring to . . . Look, you wouldn't want those people at your law firm knowing about your past, would you? You don't want those kids you reach out to, those black kids you help, to know what you did. Do you?"

"They already know," said Whitten. "All of them. They know because I've told them about it, many times. It's an element in my journey. I want the kids to know that there *are* second acts in American lives. That they can make mistakes, but it's not the end. They can do dumb things and still have success, make a positive contribution to society. I think it's important that they know."

"Oh, you *do*."

Baker felt his mouth turn up in a smile. The kind he used to punk anyone who had a dream about stepping to him. The kind that usually gave men pause. But Whitten's expression did not change.

"Yes, I do," said Whitten. "I believe in second chances. Which is why I agreed to meet with you today. Because I do know that you've had a hard life."

"You looked into my life, huh."

"My associate Mr. Coates did. Mr. Coates is a private detective my firm uses in various capacities. He's sitting right behind you. He's the fellow wearing the black leather jacket, at the bar."

Baker did not turn his head. He knew who the man was.

"You're on parole right now, Mr. Baker. Do you know how severely you'd be violated for attempting to commit extortion and blackmail? I have all the ammunition to put you on the road back to prison, immediately. I recorded our conversation yesterday, in which you stated that it was you who sent me the letter. It may or may not be admissible as evidence in court, but nevertheless the tape is in my possession. I have the letter and the envelope, which most likely hold your fingerprints. The printer you used can probably be traced to your residence."

"So?"

"I'm giving you a break. Walk out of here right now, quietly, and do not pursue this further. Don't ever contact me in any way again. Don't come near my house or my place of business. If you do, I'll take swift and decisive action."

"Fancy man with your words." Baker's voice was soft and controlled. "Tryin to act like you doing me a favor."

"Mr. Baker, consider very carefully what you say and do here. For your own sake."

"Motherfucker."

"We're done."

"Coward-ass bitch. Throwin pie out a car window and running your bitch ass away. Leavin your friends behind."

Whitten's face grew pale. His fingers were now tightly laced together. "Do something right. Be smart and go."

Baker got up carefully from the table, so as not to spill his water or rattle the silverware. He walked past the man in the black leather jacket and did not look his way. He did not want to see the hint of a smile or victory because he would then be tempted to steal the man in the face. He wasn't about to get violated for something cheap like that. Because he wasn't ready to go back to the joint. He wasn't done.

He stepped around some folks who were grouped by the host stand, mindful not to make physical contact, and he pushed on the front door and went outside.

His mistake had been to try and reason with Whitten. If this life had taught him something, it was to take from the weak. That the things he wanted could only be got through intimidation and force.

A man in a trench coat was coming toward him on the sidewalk, talking on his cell. Baker bumped the man's shoulder roughly as he passed and got the desired reaction. There was fear and confusion in the man's eyes.

This is what I know. This *is what makes me feel right.*

Baker laughed.

SEVENTEEN

RAYMOND MONROE leaned against his Pontiac, watching Alex Pappas, wearing a blue cotton oxford and Levi's jeans, emerge from the Fisher House. Monroe wondered how Alex would take the information he was about to give him. The man did seem reasonable.

"Ray," said Alex, shaking Monroe's hand.

"Alex. You look clean for a man been working all day."

"I went home and changed. I wanted to talk to my wife. Explain what I was doing with you and all that. I don't get out much."

"It's not like we're gonna be clubbin. I just think it would be good for you to meet my brother. He's working this evening."

Alex shrugged. "Let's go."

Pappas drove his Jeep off the hospital grounds and parked it on Aspen, the street that ran alongside Walter Reed. He got into the passenger side of Monroe's Pontiac and settled into the seat.

Monroe drove down Georgia, past a small Civil War graveyard, and hooked a right onto Piney Branch Road. It soon became 13th Street, and Monroe took it south.

"I've been seeing a lot of contractors and construction guys on the grounds of the hospital," said Alex.

"They're making upgrades and repairs. Now we're hearing that they're not going to close Walter Reed down. For the time being, anyway."

"Because of those articles in the newspaper?"

A series in the *Washington Post* had detailed the subpar physical conditions of the facility, the misplacement of paperwork and attendant benefits delayed to soldiers, the denial of compensation to those suffering from PTSD due to questionable claims of preexisting conditions, and a general climate of incompetence. The revelations had made world headlines and had precipitated the firing of many high-ranking officers and managers.

"Those articles caused a whole lot of things to happen," said Monroe. "Improvements that *should* have happened a long time ago. 'Cause people knew what was going on. Took some newspaper articles to shame them into taking action."

"But I see good being done there."

"Well, that's the thing. The reporters, it wouldn't have hurt if they had done one more article, talking about the good. You got committed people, army and civilian alike, working hard to make the lives of those wounded kids better. And those young men and women, considering what they're facing, they've got positive attitudes for the most part. What I'm sayin is, people at Walter Reed are trying. They got caught shorthanded, is what it was. No one knew the war was gonna last like it did. No one knew the number of wounded that were going to be flooding in.

"But you wanna know the real story? The one they should be talking about? Ten, twelve years ago, before my father died, I took him down to the veterans hospital off North Capitol

Street. His leg had swelled up, and my mother was worried he had a clot. So we go in there, and after the security guard shakes us down and makes us jump through all kinds of hoops, we go to the waiting room. My father was the oldest one in there, probably the only veteran of the Big One. The rest were Vietnam vets and guys who'd served in the Gulf War. And, I'm not lyin, they sat there for hours without getting any kind of help. Dudes hooked up to machines, in wheelchairs, Agent Orange cases, and no one would give them a straight answer or the time of day. I mean, these veterans got treated like genuine dogshit. And that's what these Iraq war vets are gonna be looking at twenty-five years from now. They're going to be the Vietnam veterans of their day. By then I suppose we'll be on to the next war, and those folks will be forgotten."

"That's not new."

"But it's not right."

"Just pray that your son comes back whole."

"I do. When your boy's over there it's all you can think of." Monroe looked at Pappas. "I'm sorry, man."

"It's okay," said Alex. "Your boy's in Afghanistan, right?"

"He's at the Korengal Outpost. They call it the KOP. You heard of it?"

"I haven't."

"Basically, it's a fortified camp surrounded by rough terrain and the enemy. The Taliban, namely. About as dangerous an environment as you can be in. Kenji's light infantry. Which means he's mostly out on foot patrol, carrying an M4 and looking for hostiles."

"Do you hear from him much?"

"When he's in the camp. They got a couple of laptops, and he sends me e-mails when he can. If the bad weather rolls in, the signal, or whatever you call it, goes on the fritz. He's pretty good about staying in contact. But I haven't had mail from him in a while. I'm guessing he's out on patrol."

Alex nodded. He remembered those long periods when he hadn't been in contact with Gus. During that time, Alex had lost sleep, weight, and hair. He and Vicki had stopped making love. He'd been constantly aggravated with Johnny and often short of temper with customers and the help.

"I'm talking your ear off about my son," said Monroe. "Where was *your* boy serving?"

"Gus was in the Anbar Province, west of Baghdad. He was nineteen years old."

They drove through the Arkansas Avenue intersection and went up a long grade.

"What happened to your brother?" said Alex.

"What *happened* to him?" Monroe shook his head. "Not much good."

"How long was he in prison?"

"James did the full ten years for the shooting and then some. He didn't handle it well on the inside. He got challenged and he took the challenge, if you know what I mean. He got in fights. Finally, he stabbed a dude with a triangle made out of plastic. I don't know how or why it went down. I imagine he got pushed to the wall, 'cause he wouldn't have initiated it on his own. James is not the violent kind. I know what you're thinking, but he's not. Anyway, he did it, and he paid. It was twenty years before he came out."

"And then?"

"Then he hooked up with Charles Baker, and things kept getting worse. You remember Charles."

"Yeah."

"Charles is trouble. Always was. He had been in and out himself, in Jessup mostly, and prison just made him worse. He and James got to gaming, kiting checks and the like. Then Charles got James involved in a burglary thing, breaking into houses in Potomac and Rockville during the daytime while folks were at work. Fella name of Lamar Mays was with 'em. James was the lookout and driver, since he was always good with cars. Charles thought their action was foolproof. They timed themselves in the houses, in and out quick, hit the bedrooms only, picked the Jewish names out of the phone book, Charles thinking that the Jews like to keep their money and jewelry close at hand. But Charles was wrong, like he always been wrong. They got caught. And Lamar, stupid as he was, had a gun on him when the police arrested them. What with the charges heaped on top of charges, and his record, James drew another big sentence."

"He's been out how long?"

"Couple, three years now."

"And Baker?"

"He's out, too."

"I don't get it. What you've been telling me is, your brother is basically good. So why would he keep going down the road with a guy like Baker?"

"It's way too complicated to explain tonight," said Monroe. "What about you?"

"What do you mean?"

"What's it *been* like for you? Your life."

"Normal, I guess," said Alex. "My dad died when I was nineteen. I took over the business and I'm still there."

"That's it?"

"Work and family."

"No dreams?"

"I thought I wanted to write a book, once. And I tried it, quietly." Alex bit on his lip. "I've never told anyone this. Never even told my wife. I got a few pages down on paper and I knew, reading it over, that I didn't have the talent for it. You gotta admit who you are, right? You've got to be realistic."

"So you're sayin that you're happy in your work."

"Not exactly. I wouldn't say happy. Resigned to it. I mean, what else am I gonna do? I didn't graduate from college. I know how to run a small operation, but other than that I have no skills." Alex shifted his weight in the seat. "Anyway. I guess I'm gonna find out what else is out there for me. I plan on handing over the reins of the coffee shop to my older son sometime soon."

"The nice-looking young man I saw in the store?"

"Yeah, him."

Alex hadn't told Vicki yet. He hadn't told Johnny. This was the first time he'd said it aloud, and it surprised him. He had no close male friends. He didn't know why he was telling Raymond Monroe these things, except for the fact that he was comfortable with him. The man was easy to talk to.

"We're near James's job," said Monroe. "He's got a little apartment around here, too."

Monroe cut the wheel. They were in Park View, between 13th and Georgia, going east on a side street. Monroe pulled the Pontiac to the curb, near a break in an alley, and let the car idle.

"Why are we stopping here?"

"I want to talk to you before we see James. The garage where he works is just down that alley."

"But this is all residential."

"The man who owns the garage got it zoned commercial through a grandfather clause. It's not much of a shop. Unheated and un-air-conditioned. James only works on old cars 'cause that's the only kinda car he knows how to fix. He never did get updated on the new technology, computer diagnostics and the like. His boss knows he can't get a job anywhere else and he treats him like it. James doesn't make much more than minimum wage. But he's working; that's the important thing. The man needs to work."

"What are you trying to tell me?"

"He still makes all kinds of bad decisions. He drinks too much beer, like our father did, and it alters his judgment. He stayed in contact with Charles Baker. And Charles . . . well, Charles got an influence on him."

"Where is this going?"

"Charles had James help him write a note to your old friend Peter Whitten. Well, James kinda *edited* the note, see?"

"What kind of a *note?*" said Alex, hearing the impatience in his own voice.

"The kind asks for money. Charles wanted Whitten to know that if he didn't pay, he was going to let that law firm he works at know all about his past. I'm talking about the incident in Heathrow Heights. Matter of fact, Charles had an appointment to meet with Whitten today. I don't know how that went."

"This is *bull*shit. How stupid is Baker? Pete's not going to give him money to hush up something that happened thirty-five years go. I doubt Pete Whitten even cares if anyone knows about it."

"I agree. But if Charles gets turned away, he might just come to you next."

Alex nodded his head rapidly, coming to an understanding of something he did not care for. "You told me you reached out to me for some kind of closure."

"I did. But now there's this problem here I've got to deal with, too. I'm just being straight with you, man."

"What do you *want?*"

"I want you to meet my brother. I want you to see what he's about. Once you do this, you're gonna know that he's not wrong. That he deserves a chance out here to find some peace."

"Speak plainly, Mr. Monroe."

"If Charles was to come to you and ask the same thing he's asking of Whitten, I would hope that you wouldn't go and get the law involved. Because of that note, that would land James right back in prison. And he cannot go back. He's doing his best to stay right, Alex. He *is.*"

"You're forgetting something," said Alex. "Your brother killed my friend."

"That's right. Your friend is dead. Don't think I'm brushing that aside or that I ever will. What I'm asking is for you to try and forgive."

Alex looked away. He touched the wedding band on his finger and made a careless hand motion toward the head of the alley.

"We're here," said Alex. "Let's go see your brother."

"There's no room in that alley for us to park," said Monroe. "We'll walk in."

After locking the car, Monroe and Alex went down the alley on foot, along row house backyards, some paved, some grass and dirt, passing freestanding garages, shepherd mixes and pits behind chain-link fences, trash cans, and No Trespassing signs. They made a turn at the alley's T and came to what looked like another residential garage showing an open bay door with a hand-lettered sign nailed above it. Written in red paint that had dripped, it read "Gavin's Garage." It looked like one of those Little Rascals signs, a clubhouse thing made by kids.

Inside the garage, crowded with tools and just large enough to hold one car, was a first-series, unrestored, gold-colored Monte Carlo, its hood up, its engine illuminated by a drop lamp whose cord was knotted on the bay door rails running overhead. Beside the Chevy stood a big man with a belly to match his size, in a blue work shirt, matching pants, and thick Vibram-soled shoes. On the shirt, the man's first name, James, was stitched inside a white oval patch.

Raymond and Alex entered the garage. James Monroe stepped up to meet them. Alex noticed a bit of a limp in James's slow gait. He had seen it in others who had bum hips.

"James," said Raymond, "this is Alex Pappas."

Alex put his hand out. James shook it weakly, looking Alex over with large bloodshot eyes. Alex did not speak, knowing that anything he said would sound trite.

"What are we supposed to do now?" said James to Raymond. "Sit around the campfire and sing a song?"

"Talk a little, is all," said Raymond.

"I got to get to work on this MC," said James. "Gavin gonna be in here any minute, asking why it's not done."

"Can't you talk and work?"

"Better than you."

"Go ahead, then. We won't bother you."

"There's beer in that cooler," said James, pointing to an ancient green metal Coleman set on the concrete floor. "Get me one, too."

Raymond went to the Coleman to get his older brother a can of beer. James turned his attention to the car.

EIGHTEEN

"WHERE YOUR boy at?" said Charles Baker.

"I don't know," said Cody Kruger. "I called the shoe store and they said he left out early. Told them he had a stomach-ache or sumshit like that. I drove by his mom's house earlier, but his car wasn't out front."

"I phoned his mother myself. She say she don't know where he at."

"He'll turn up."

"We don't need his ass anyway."

"For what?"

"For what we gonna do," said Baker. "Put that joystick down and let's talk."

Kruger was seated on the couch in the apartment, playing The Warriors on Xbox. He liked the video game more than the movie because in the game there was more blood and the heroes could fuck up police. Kruger almost smiled when he heard Mr. Charles call the controller a joystick. But he didn't smile, and he dropped the controller to the floor.

Baker had been pacing the room. Kruger could see from the tightness in his jaw that he was amped. He'd met a man earlier in the day, and the meet hadn't gone well. That was all Mr. Charles had said. Cody knew not to push to find out why.

"Let me ask you somethin," said Baker.

"All right."

"You satisfied with all this here? All these things you got?"

"I'm doin okay."

"But you could be doing better."

"Sure. I plan to."

"How you gonna get it?"

"Step it up, I guess."

"How?"

Kruger's mouth hung open stupidly.

"I'm here to tell you how," said Baker. "That boy Dominique, the one who sell you your shit. Do you respect him? Is that the kind of man you gonna take orders from and look up to?"

"Not rilly."

"I wouldn't, neither. For the life of me, I can't see why you let him talk to you the way he do. You smarter than him and you stronger than him. *Ain't* you, Cody?"

"Yes."

"What we gonna do is, we gonna pay that little motherfucker a visit. Tell him how things gonna be from here on out. Maybe take some of his shit on consignment, rearrange the terms of the relationship. How's that sound to you?"

"I don't know."

"You don't *know*. What are you, Cody?"

"I'm a man."

"That's right. Anyone can see that you are. Comes a time, a man got to decide who he is. Either you serve all your life or you become the other kind. My question to you is, you gonna serve bitches like Dominique or are you ready to be a king?"

Baker saw a light come to Kruger's dull eyes.

"But what about Deon?" said Kruger.

"*Fuck* Deon, man. That boy got no ambition. But you do."

Kruger stood, chest out.

"Get that thing," said Baker. "We gonna need your iron."

Kruger returned with a Glock 17, the MPD sidearm coveted by many young men in the District who fancied themselves outlaws. Guns were readily available to those who asked around. This one had been straw-purchased at a store on 28 South, between Manassas and Culpeper, in Virginia. It had then been sold to Kruger.

"Let me see that," said Baker, taking the nine in hand. He checked the serial numbers to be sure that Kruger had not filed them down. It meant extra years if he were to be connected to a gun with shaved numbers. Baker gave the Glock back to Kruger, who slipped it into his dip.

"You ever have need of my gun," said Kruger, "I keep it in my dresser drawer, underneath my boxers."

Baker looked at Kruger, wearing his sweatshirt with the hood over his head, as he'd seen it done in videos. He reached out and pulled the hood down.

"You don't want to draw attention to yourself, now, do you?"

"No, Mr. Charles."

"You said you knew where Dominique stay at."

"I do."

Baker jerked his chin toward the front door. They left the apartment.

JAMES MONROE leaned on a shop rag draped over the lip of the Monte Carlo's front quarter panel and unscrewed the wing nut atop its air filter. He dropped the nut onto the hat of the filter so he'd know where to find it later on, then pulled the filter up and free and set it aside without disconnecting it from its hose. The old Chevy's carburetor was now in sight and serviceable.

"What you doing now, James?" said Raymond.

"Gonna adjust the air and fuel mix."

"You already did the plugs and wires?"

"What do you think? Carb adjustment's the last thing you do. I been telling you that for thirty-some-odd years."

"James keeps my Pontiac correct," said Raymond to Alex. "In exchange, I work on that hip of his."

"You don't work on it as good as I work on your vehicle."

"This garage isn't exactly the optimum place for man got a hip condition. You're on your feet too much to begin with. Gavin ought to bring some heat in here, too."

"I got that space heater," said James, referring to a small unit, currently unplugged, sitting by the tool bench in the rear of the space.

"If it was worth a damn, you'd have it on."

"Summer's comin, anyway."

"It ain't here yet."

Alex and Raymond were standing, as there was no room for chairs in the garage. Alex held a can of beer in hand, nursing it. Darkness had come, and with it the chill of a D.C. evening. It was mid-spring, but temperatures routinely dropped into the forties at night. Alex had erred in forgoing a jacket. He was cold and a bit dizzy. James had ignitioned the Chevy, and the smell of the exhaust was nauseating. Alex didn't know how James could stand working here in these cramped and unhealthy conditions.

Alex stepped closer to the car. He watched as James attached a vacuum gauge to the intake manifold. His hands were raw and callused, with a dirty Band-Aid wrapped around one index finger.

"You see that Wizards game last night?" said James.

"West Coast games come on too late for me," said Raymond. "But I read about it in the paper. Gilbert had forty-two. Sonics almost climbed back in it behind Chris Wilcox."

"Yeah, but Agent Zero put the nail in the coffin with two seconds on the clock. They get Caron Butler back from that injury, they gonna go deep in the playoffs. 'Cause when the defense double up on Gilbert, you gonna have two other weapons, Caron and Antawn, out on the perimeter, ready to score."

"They ain't going all that deep without a center," said Raymond.

"Michael Jordan didn't need an outstanding center to get the championship for the Bulls."

"Gilbert ain't Michael."

"Hand me that ten-inch flat-head, Ray. It's over there on the bench."

Raymond went to the tool bench and retrieved a long-shafted flat-head screwdriver with a vinyl handle. James took it and fitted the head into the slot of one of two screws located on the lower face of the carburetor. He turned the screw clockwise until it was tight.

"Takes five outstanding players to win a championship," said Raymond, intent on making his point.

"Not always," said James, moving to the second screw and tightening it the same way he had the first. "Course, there *was* the old Knicks team, so there's always an exception. The greatest starting five in the history of pro basketball."

"Clyde Frazier and Earl Monroe," said Raymond. "The Rolls-Royce backcourt."

"Willis Reed," said James, fitting the flat-head back into the slot of the first screw. "Dave DeBusschere."

"Bill Bradley," said Alex.

"Princeton boy," said James, not turning away from his task. "Had that pretty jumper from the corner."

"Frazier was the key, though," said Raymond. "He won the ring with Dick Barnett beside him. He didn't need Earl."

"How about the seventy-three playoffs against the Lakers?" said James. "Jesus worked some miracles in that series."

"Please," said Raymond. "Clyde ran the offense and played tremendous D. He *hawked* that ball. You *know* this."

"If you say," said James. He began to reloosen the carburetor's screws.

"Me and my brother been having this argument our whole lives," said Raymond, smiling to himself. Alex saw his smile fade as they heard footsteps.

A security light came on outside, illuminating the alley. A short balding bantamweight with large ears under patches of kinky gray hair entered the garage. He quick-stepped past Raymond and Alex without acknowledging either of them, placed his hands on his hips, and stood next to the car. He looked like a child beside James.

"Is it done?" said the man.

"I'm close, Mr. Gavin," said James. He was now slowly turning the screws counterclockwise.

"I told Mr. Court it would be ready by now."

"Court said his gas mileage was off. New points and plugs alone are not gonna fix that. I gotta adjust the mix."

"Just get it done, James. I'm not paying you to entertain company in here. Court's on his way to pick up his car. I need it to be ready. Not tomorrow. Now."

"It'll be ready, Mr. Gavin."

Gavin walked out without further comment. For several moments there was only the sound of the running car in the garage. Alex was embarrassed for James Monroe.

"Two and a half," said Raymond, breaking the tension. "Right, James?"

"That's right." He had turned the screws back two and one half times, and was now adjusting them in quarter-turn increments while listening to the engine.

"Mighty Mouse was a little short and to the point, wasn't he?" said Raymond.

"He short," said James with a chuckle. "Ain't nobody gonna dispute that."

"He got no reason to talk to you like that, either."

"That's his nature," said James. "God made him little, and now he's angry at me. Anyway, it's work. It isn't supposed to be easy or fun."

As James turned the carburetor screw, the engine sputtered.

"Too far," said Raymond.

"Right," said James. He readjusted the screw, and the engine began to run smoothly. He tinkered with it a little bit more, and it ran smoother still. "It's singin now."

"I don't hear nothin," said Raymond.

"Exactly," said James.

James took a long swig of beer. He put the can down, removed the vacuum gauge from the intake manifold, and reached for the air filter. He began to fit it back atop the carb.

"You hear Luther Ingram passed?" said James.

" 'If loving you is wrong,' " said Raymond, " 'I don't want to be right.' "

" 'If being right means being without you,' " said James, " 'I'd rather be wrong than right.' "

"Straight-up beautiful," said Raymond. "Nineteen seventy-three."

"It was seventy-two, stupid."

"Why you always got to teach me?"

"I'm just sayin."

"It was one of those cheatin-is-good songs that were popular back then. Remember?"

" 'Me and Mrs. Jones,' " said James.

"Billy Paul," said Alex. "That was seventy-two as well."

James was replacing the wing nut on the air filter. He stopped for a moment, turned his head slightly, and looked at Alex out of the corner of his eye.

"My father had a radio in the coffee shop when I was kid," said Alex. "He kept the dial on WOL. For the help."

James tightened the wing nut. "If there was an OL or WOOK on the air today, I'd have a radio in here to keep me company. But there's no stations playing the music I want to listen to."

"You need to update your tastes," said Raymond.

"I believe it's too late for that," said James. He straightened and began to wipe smudges from the car's quarter panel with the shop rag. "I better finish up before Court gets here."

"We'll get on our way," said Raymond.

Alex finished his beer and tossed the empty into a trash can topped with others. He went to James and, once again, extended his hand. James shook it.

"I'm glad we met," said Alex.

James nodded, his eyes unreadable. He and Raymond exchanged a long look. James then returned to the Monte Carlo. He lowered the hood and pushed on it until it clicked.

"Call Mama," said Raymond, heading for the open bay door.

"I always do," said James.

Alex and Raymond walked down the alley, out of the glow of the security light, into dark.

"His boss is a douche," said Alex.

"George Jefferson and Napoleon Bonaparte had a baby, and they called him Gavin."

"Why does he put up with it?"

"James feels he has to take it. He's happy to have the job."

"There's got to be a better place for him. He's good at what he does."

"He doesn't know how to work on the newer vehicles. And there's not too many employers looking to hire convicted felons. I'd help him if I could."

They walked out of the alley toward the Pontiac.

"We didn't really talk about anything," said Alex.

"That's all right."

"I'm saying, we didn't even mention the incident."

"There's time for that."

"So what was I doing there?"

"I think we're all lookin for a little peace with this thing. The first step was, I wanted you to get acquainted with my brother. He did fuck up when he helped Charles with that note. But you can see, a man like James, he does not deserve to be locked up."

Alex agreed but made no comment. He was thinking of what he would do when Baker threw his shadow on his family's front door.

NINETEEN

"I THINK he's comin," said Charles Baker, speaking into his disposable cell. "If that's his Three Hundred, it's him."

"Copy that," said Cody Kruger, holding his disposable to his ear, using the shorthand code like special agents did on TV.

Baker, seated on the passenger side of Kruger's Honda, stared through the windshield as the big Chrysler, looked like the Green Hornet car, rolled slowly across the lot of the garden apartment where Dominique Dixon lived. Kruger had parked on Blair Road, across from the lot.

The Chrysler pulled into an empty spot next to a white, windowless Econoline van that was parked beside a brown Dumpster. Dominique Dixon got out of the car. He was dressed in beige slacks and a Miles Davis–green button-down shirt. Over the shirt he wore a black leather blazer to cut the chill. It bunched up behind the shoulder blades, betraying the slightness of Dixon's frame.

"It's him," said Baker.

"Copy," said Kruger.

"You ready?"

"You *know* I am."

Dixon locked his car and headed for the open stairwell that led to his apartment. Kruger was up there, one floor above Dixon's place, his back pressed against a brick wall, jacked on nerves because this was new to him. One sweaty hand gripped the nine.

Baker watched Dixon and the confident switch in his walk. Baker knew who Dixon was, even if Dixon did not.

Baker was going to enjoy this. He always did when it was someone weaker than him, who had more than him, who thought *this* could never happen.

Baker got out of the Honda, locked it with the electric gizmo the white boy had left him. Behind him, past a park and basketball court darkened by night, a Metro train made its soft clopping sound on the rails as it headed south. As Baker walked by the Chrysler 300, he dug Kruger's key into the front quarter panel, taking off a line of enamel all the way to the trunk lid without breaking stride. It was something a kid might do, and he knew it, but still it gave him pleasure, and he smiled.

In the stairwell, he found Kruger on the steps, holding his gun on Dixon, who was standing by his door with his hands raised. Kruger's face was flushed with excitement, his acne gone pale yellow and throbbing on pink flesh. Dixon was openmouthed and visibly shaking. Baker came up onto the landing.

"Put your hands down, boy," said Baker. "Get us inside, quick."

"Why?" said Dixon.

"I ain't tell you to talk," said Baker. "Just turn the key."

They went in, Baker closing the door and seeing to its dead bolt. The apartment was as he had expected and hoped it would be. Furniture a cut above the department store kind, a big television mounted like a picture on the wall, a portable bar stocked with all types of liquor, a martini shaker, straining and fruit-cutting tools set atop glass. The garden complex was ordinary on the outside and close to run-down. But Dixon had hooked up his crib luxuriously behind the walls.

A smart, successful marijuana dealer did not flash. The Chrysler was nice but not showtime, cool enough to turn the heads of heifers but not police. Baker had seen no expensive jewelry on Dixon's wrists or fingers, none around his neck. Yeah, Dominique Dixon was smart, and this annoyed Baker rather than impressed him. Why did so many people know so much more about getting it than he did? He could have asked these smart folks questions, learned something, maybe. Instead he just had the urge to fuck them up.

"Sit your ass down on that couch," said Baker, pointing Dixon to his red linen sofa. To Kruger he said, "Hold him there. I wanna have a look around."

Baker tossed Kruger the Honda's key, then walked down a hall to a bedroom. In it was a king-size with a simple rectangular headboard behind it and wooden end tables to match, all of the pieces low to the carpet and streamlined. A dresser had the same basic design as the end tables and carried the same dark shade of wood. Baker saw a copy of *Maxim* on the floor and a straight-out stroke magazine by the bed. So the young man did like women. But why did he dress and act like a bitch? Baker had been locked up too long. He did not understand this new world.

He went through Dixon's dresser drawers, ran his hand under his jeans and undid his balled socks. He found a couple hundred dollars in twenties flat in the folds of Dixon's underpants. Baker pocketed the cash. In a padded box he found an Omega watch with a blue face, and an onyx ring, and he stuffed them both into the other pocket of his slacks. He went into the bathroom, sniffed the colognes the boy had, and splashed something he liked, smelled like trees, onto his face. The bottle was a nice green color, manly, and Baker checked the cap to see that it was tight. He dropped the bottle into the inner breast pocket of his old caramel-colored leather jacket.

He went back down the hall, thinking, *This is what it feels like to have money.* But he was not satisfied or done.

Kruger was out in the living room, dutifully training his gun on Dixon, still seated on the couch. Baker almost laughed, seeing Kruger holding the nine sideways like in those slope movies, but he held his amusement in check because the white boy was just so obedient that it kind of warmed his heart. It had been a while since anyone had listened to him the way Kruger did.

"Anything?" said Kruger.

"Nah," said Baker. "Nothin. Didn't even find a dollar."

Baker went to the bar on wheels and scanned the bottles. He wasn't much of a liquor man, preferring the control that came with the predictable effects of beer. The occasion did call for a little something, though. He passed over a bottle of vodka, had white birds flying across its side, and picked up a bottle of scotch, Glen something or other, aged for fifteen years. He sloppily poured a few fingers' worth into a tumbler and had a taste. It was smoky and it bit, and he walked it over to a chair set across from the couch. It was a matching chair, covered in red linen, and he noted the height of it and that it would be a good place to take the boy when the talking got to something else.

"So," said Baker, swirling the scotch in the tumbler. "Let's get down to why we here."

"It ain't good," said Dixon bitterly. "You forced me into my own place at the point of a gun."

"You and me gonna get along better if you don't try to act so big and bad. 'Cause we both know you're not that type." Baker looked at Kruger. "Lower that gun, Cody. We don't need it. Leastways, I don't think we do. *Do* we, Dominique?"

"What do you want?" said Dixon, the air gone out of him.

"I'm gonna get to that. Want to tell you a story first." Baker had a healthy sip of scotch and placed the tumbler on the glass of the table before him. "When I was up at Jessup, I got to know a lot of fellas out of Baltimore. That's a different breed of criminal they got up there. I'm not sayin they more fierce than the boys come out of D.C. Just different. 'Cause they do all kinds of unnatural shit to get what they want. I knew this one hitter, shot his victims with a little old twenty-two. Shot 'em in the same place every time, somewhere down at a special bone in the neck. He said it was guaranteed darkness. This other dude, Nathan Williams, went by Black Nate, used to take off drug boys by cracking a bullwhip right on the sidewalk. I'm sayin, this man carried no gun. *Only* a bullwhip. Wore it coiled up on his side, like a gunslinger wears a holster. Corner boys would give it up immediately, just drop their packages right at his feet. That was Black Nate.

"But there was this one cat, he outdid them all. I'm gonna call him Junior. When Junior was a teenager, he hooked up with some stickup boys, rip-and-run artists who were robbing drug dealers. Eventually, the rest of his crew got doomed or went to prison, and he lit out on his own. Junior only went after the big boys, never the kids on the corner. What he wanted was to find out where the money was, and he'd do anything to get that information. Threatening to kill a dude doesn't work all the time, 'cause they know they dead anyway if they give up the bank or their connect. And torture, that's just loud and messy. So Junior, he got to sodomizing motherfuckers to make them talk. You know what that word means, don't you, Dominique?"

"I know," said Dixon, the corner of his lip twitching on the reply.

"Yeah. A dude just responds to the mention of it. You tell him you're gonna steal his manhood, and he gonna answer any question you ask, all the livelong day."

"What do you *want?*"

"I want your inventory, man. I want your list of clients. I want to have all these nice things you got. You don't deserve to keep havin them, 'cause I'm stronger than you. Law of the jungle, right? I know you heard of Darvon."

Dixon nodded his head. He knew the name that Baker was reaching for, but he did not correct him.

"Now, we both aware that you're movin weight. So why don't you tell me where you keep it at?"

"I don't have it here." Dixon spread his hands. "I don't have it *any*where right now. I already moved it to my dealers."

"Not all of it, man. Don't talk to me like I'm stupid, because I am not."

"It's gone."

"Gone, huh. You just sold Cody and Deon a couple pounds, what, two nights back? And you, supplying half a zip code of dealers? Nah, I don't think it's gone. You got plenty left, I reckon. So you lyin to me. And I don't like that, Dominique."

"Look, man—"

"Thought I told you to call me Mr. Charles."

"Mr. Charles. Let's call Deon. Deon knows how my operation works. He'll tell you I move it in and out real quick."

"Deon got no say in this."

"Where's he at?"

"He ain't here."

"I can see that, but—"

"What I mean is, he can't help you."

Baker finished his scotch in one long pull and placed it loudly on the glass tabletop. He stood from the chair as if sprung and moved behind it.

"Get up, boy, and come over here."

Dixon stood slowly from the couch. He walked unsteadily to where Baker stood. Baker backed up to give him room.

"Now turn around and face the back of this chair. Put your hands on the shoulders of it."

"What for?"

"Right now."

Dixon did as he was told. His hands gripped the back of the chair. He had to bend over to do it, and as he did he realized what was happening, and he said, "No."

Baker produced a knife from the right patch pocket of his jacket. There was a button on the imitation-pearl handle, and he pushed it forward. A blade sprang from the hilt. At the unmistakable sound of it, Dixon shut his eyes. Baker, close behind him, touched the blade to Dixon's neck, brushed it delicately there until he came to the bump of Dixon's carotid artery, where he applied more pressure but did not break the skin.

"Where the marijuana at?" said Baker.

Dixon could not raise spit or speak.

"Let me help you find your tongue, boy."

With his free hand, Baker reached around and undid Dixon's belt buckle, then tore the button from the eyehole on the front of his slacks. He pulled down roughly on the slacks until they dropped to the floor, gathering at Dixon's booted feet. Dixon stood in his boxer briefs, his bare legs skinny and shaking. His eyes had filled with tears.

Cody Kruger was nearby, the gun hanging at his side, the color drained from his face. He seemed to have lost his bravado. He looked very young.

Still holding the knife to Dixon's throat, Baker stepped in and pressed himself against Baker's behind.

"You feel kinda emotional now, huh," said Baker. "But see, from where I'm standing, this ain't no thing. All that time I was inside? Shoot. Your asshole is just another hole to me. I feel the same way about your mouth."

"*Please*," said Dixon. A string of mucus dripped and hung from his nose.

"Please what? You want me to?"

"I'll tell you where it is."

Baker chuckled. "For real?"

"In a white van. Parked beside my car. The keys are in my pocket, the *left pocket* of my pants."

"Get the keys, Cody," said Baker.

Kruger retrieved the keys, gingerly, from the pocket of the slacks heaped at Dixon's ankles.

"I'll take care of it, Mr. Charles," said Kruger. He seemed eager to leave the apartment.

"You go ahead," said Baker. "Take your car and put it behind the van. Load whatever he's got in there into the Honda. Mind that no one's watching, hear?"

"I will."

"Hit me on my cell when you're ready to go."

Baker stayed behind Dixon, hard and tight against him, after Kruger had gone. Baker could feel a quivering in Dixon's shoulders.

"Cry if you need to," said Baker. "It's hard to learn who you are."

"I wanna sit down."

"Go ahead," said Baker. "But we ain't finished yet."

ALEX AND Vicki made love after he had come home from his visit with the Monroe brothers. It was unexpected for both of them, happening at once as Alex slipped into their king-size. He had expected her to be sleeping, as she almost always was when he came to bed, but she was awake, and she turned toward him and fitted into him the way a wife and husband do, comfortably and naturally, after so many years. They kissed and caressed each other for a long while, because this was the best part of it for both of them, and completed it with Vicki's strong thighs squeezed against him, her lips cool, Vicki and Alex coming quietly in the darkness of the room.

Afterward, they talked about his night, Vicki's head on his chest, Alex's arm around her.

"He wasn't angry with you?"

"The older brother? No. Indifferent is more like it. He paid his debt, and I guess he's past hating. It's like he didn't care about my presence one way or the other. He's trying to get beyond everything that's happened to him. It hasn't been easy to do that."

This led to a discussion of Charles Baker, and the mistake James had made in editing the letter.

"Are you worried about this Baker character?" said Vicki.

"No," said Alex. It was a lie.

"But what if he comes around? You promised the younger brother that you wouldn't involve the police."

"I never promised anything," said Alex. "Besides, there's no sense in worrying about it now."

It felt good to be with Vicki, naked in bed, talking as they had not talked for a while. He told her about his tentative plan to turn the business over to Johnny, and she was happy and held him tightly and admitted that she was also scared, asking him what would come next, after he let their son take control of the coffee shop.

"I'm a young man," said Alex. "I am. I've got another twenty years of work in me, maybe more. This time it's not going to be about obligation. It'll be about passion."

"But what will you do?"

In the dark, Alex stared up at the ceiling, pale white from the moonlight seeping through the bedroom blinds.

After Vicki had gone to sleep, Alex got out of bed and went to the kitchen, where he poured himself a glass of red wine. He took it to the living room and had a seat in his favorite chair. His intention was to sit here, nurse his wine, and wait for Johnny to come home. Go upstairs at the sound of Johnny's car as it pulled into the driveway, so as not to embarrass his son. A young man Johnny's age didn't need to know that his father still stayed awake at night, worrying about his son.

Having lost one boy, he found it hard to let the other stand on his own. But he knew he'd have to do that so he and Vicki could move forward. The window was closing. As the years progressed, it seemed to Alex that time moved faster. He wanted to be rid of *that thing*, the pinch on his shoulder that had nagged him for thirty-five years. Now it felt possible. He was ready to be rid of it and run to what was next.

Alex was glad Ray Monroe had walked into his shop. He

was glad to have met James. In a way, it was as if the clouds had broken, if only just a little.

Alex thought of the Monroes and the conversation that had gone on in the garage hours earlier. The usual topics discussed among men, the rhythmic banter, the gentle ribbing that went on between brothers. A look that had crossed Ray Monroe's face.

And he thought: *Something is not right.*

TWENTY

P ETE WHITTEN walked into Pappas and Sons around two thirty, after the lunch rush, when most of the customers had cleared out. He took a seat on the stool closest to the register, where Alex stood counting cash. Alex stopped, put a stack of bills into the tens bed, and closed the register drawer. He reached across the counter and shook Whitten's hand.

"Pete."

"Alex. Long time."

"Too long."

It had been over twenty years. The last he'd seen Pete, not counting when he'd seen his photograph in the newspapers, was at the funeral of Billy Cachoris's father, Lou Cachoris. Mr. Cachoris had died in the eighties, a dozen years after the incident in Heathrow Heights. Some said he deliberately drank himself into his grave after the murder of his son, but that was Greeks being Greek about death; the newspaper said that the cause of his passing was cancer of the brain.

It was at the viewing of Lou Cachoris, held at the Collins Funeral Home on University Boulevard, that Alex had run into Pete, recently married and sporting a wide-shouldered, wide-lapeled suit with a red power tie. His hair was gelled and spiked with Tenax, in the de rigueur "punk" businessman look of the time. If he had been outside he would have been sporting Vuarnets.

"Meet my wife, Anne," said Pete.

Alex said hello to her, a good-looking blonde, thin waist, thin ankles, wearing something expensive, and introduced them both to Vicki, wearing something off the department store rack. They all seemed aware of their status and where their lives were or were not headed, though they were only in their twenties, and still, Alex was proud to be with Vicki and to show her off. She looked, well, *nicer* than Anne.

Alex had debated going to the service, knowing that he would be on the receiving end of the *mootrah*, the whispers, long faces, and stares from the Cachoris relatives. They all knew he had been in the car that day and had done nothing to help his friend. But he felt that it was proper, due to his relationship with Billy, to pay his respects to the father.

After talking with Pete and Anne, Alex went to the open casket. He kissed the *ikona*, did his *stavro*, and looked down at the corpse of Lou Cachoris. His face seemed to have been flattened by a mallet. Someone had slipped a photograph of a teenage Billy under the sleeve of his burial suit, and Alex impulsively bent forward and kissed Mr. Cachoris's forehead. It felt as if he were kissing one of the artificial apples his mother had always kept on their dining room table. He said a silent prayer for Billy, and for the way things had gone for the father and son. As he opened his eyes, an uncle or cousin was standing next to him, telling him quietly and firmly that the family didn't want him there and that it was time for him to go.

He looked around, not seeing Pete or his wife, who had already left the building, and got Vicki's attention. They walked out together as the priest from Saint Connie's arrived. Going down the center aisle of the viewing room, Alex felt many gazes directed at him, the boy who had not stood beside his friend against the *mavres*, who now carried the mark, the ugly eye. Out in the lobby, he heard the attendees begin to sing the "Everlasting Be Thy Memory" song, which was supposed to make everyone feel better but instead made them feel sadder than shit. That, at least, was how it felt to Alex whenever he heard that song thereafter. Sadness, and something close to shame.

And now Pete Whitten was in his shop, handsome, successful, and relatively unravaged by time. The suit would be a Canali, the tie Hermès, the sunglasses in the breast pocket Revos. His hair was perfectly disheveled, and his jacket fit him impeccably. Pete did look good.

"I've got to apologize," said Pete.

"For what?"

"I've been working a few blocks from here for most of my career, and I've never stopped in to say hello or patronize the place."

"It's okay."

"Mostly my lunches are business lunches. All of them expensed. So normally I'm in restaurants."

"This is a restaurant," said Alex.

"You know what I mean."

"Sure."

Pete took his arm off the counter and brushed something that was not there off his sleeve. He looked around and nodded his head approvingly.

"It looks good," said Pete. "You've got a nice place here."

"We keep it clean." Alex pointed to the prep area, where Johnny and Darlene were looking at a book spread out on the colds board. "That's my son John."

"Good-looking boy. Named after your dad?"

"Yes. Johnny made a good tuna fish salad today. With curry in it. It's a combination I never would have thought to try, but the customers loved it. Would you like me to have them make you a sandwich?"

"I've eaten, thanks."

"So what can I do for you, Pete?"

"Alex, we've got some catching up to do. We should try and get together. You, me, our wives. Have dinner or something."

"Okay."

"But that's not why I stopped in today. I have some rather disturbing news."

Pete told him about the letter and the meeting he'd had with Charles Baker. Pete described the Baker conversation thoroughly, recounting the details as Alex would expect an attorney to do. Alex feigned surprise. It had gone, apparently, as Alex thought it might, given Pete's professional experience and personality. Pete had, in effect, shown Baker the door and threatened him with legal action if he did not cease his attempts at extortion.

"And what was your impression?" said Alex. "Do you think this is over?"

"I have no way of being certain, which is why I'm here. I wanted to warn you that this Baker character was out there in the world. If I remember correctly, he's the one who assaulted you."

"Yes."

"Well, he might come to you next. I'm saying, it's possible. Of course, I clearly stated the ramifications of any further contact in my meeting with him. But my impression was that he's not very smart. Also, he could be violent. He has a history of it, after all."

"I see."

"And there might be others involved. I'm speaking of the boy who shot Billy. And wasn't his brother there, too?"

Alex took a moment, to give the appearance that he was thinking it over, and then nodded his head.

"The three of them could be in this together," said Pete. "You know how these people are."

"These people?"

"*Criminals*, Alex. You're not going to get sensitive on me, now, are you? Because we're talking about facts and statistics here. Criminals, in general, don't change their stripes. I live in the real world, and I would think that you do, too. I'm only trying to make you aware of what's going on here."

"Okay," said Alex. "The question is, what should I do if I'm contacted by Baker?"

"I gave him his last chance. If he contacts you, call the police immediately." Pete reached into his breast pocket and pulled out a business card, which he slid across the counter. "And certainly you're going to want to get me involved. I have, well, I have resources that you probably don't have. Private detectives, police . . . I know people down in the U.S. attorney's office. If Baker rears up his ugly head again, we can take care of this quickly."

"I appreciate it, Pete," said Alex, taking the card and placing it atop the deck of the register. "I do."

"I felt it was serious enough to contact you. He came to my house in the Heights and delivered the letter himself, apparently."

"The Heights?" Alex couldn't resist.

"*Friendship* Heights," said Pete.

"And the letter . . ."

"Was typed and printed off a computer. He thought he

was being slick, but the printer can be traced. His prints as well."

"Right."

"It won't be a problem. But you needed to know about it."

"Absolutely."

"It's funny," said Pete. "Meeting Baker brought back that day to me. I hadn't thought too much about the incident as the years passed because, well, I guess it's because I've changed so much. It doesn't even seem like I'm the same person that I was at seventeen. Does it feel that way to you?"

"Yes," said Alex, not wishing to prolong the conversation any further.

Pete slid off the stool and shook Alex's hand. "I've got to get back to the office. Let's do that dinner and catch up."

"Sounds good."

"Take care, Alex."

"So long."

Alex watched him go. There would be no dinner. Neither of them wanted it. Pete was still the person he'd been at seventeen, but he'd never know it. He had run that day and freed himself. He'd then gone on to college and law school, a solid and lucrative career, a house in the Heights. He was still running, in a way. Billy, on the other hand, had stood his ground. The last thing Billy had done before he was shot was point at Alex and tell him to go. Among the many things Billy had been, some not of his own making, he had been a friend. As for Alex, he had not acted. He was simply the kid in the backseat of the car.

"Dad?"

Alex turned. "Yes."

"What did you think about the special?" said John Pappas.

"It worked. The curry was a nice, what do you call that, *complement* to the tuna. Only . . ."

"What?"

"You gonna turn this place into an Indian joint?"

"Yeah, Dad, that's exactly what I'm going to do."

"Next thing, you're gonna throw away the silverware, and the customers will be eating with their hands."

"That would be Ethiopian."

"Oh, really?"

"I don't think you have to worry."

"I'm saying, you sold twice as many burgers and chicken cheesesteaks as you did tuna fish sandwiches today, right? Don't forget your bread and butter. That's all."

"I don't plan on it."

"Good. Here you go." Alex reached into his pocket and pulled out a set of keys that worked on the front and back doors and the freezer. He handed them to Johnny. "I made these for you."

"Thanks."

"You're doing a real good job."

"*Thank* you."

"So I'm gonna let you close today. I've got somewhere I need to be. I was thinking I'd take the rest of the afternoon off."

"For real?"

"There's nothing to closing. The help know their side work and cleanup duties. Darlene will help you with the ordering. Cut the register tape off in a half hour. As far as the money goes, tomorrow is not a day for bills, and it's not payday, either. So leave about fifty bucks in bills and change, put it in the metal cash box, lock the box in the freezer, and take the rest home to Mom."

"I can do that."

"Don't worry about making a mistake. Just make sure the

doors are locked behind you. I can deal with anything else in the morning."

"You trust me?"

"Sure, why not?"

"I don't know. After you're gone, we might all decide to, like, drop tabs of X or something."

"You," said Alex with a wave of his hand. Get out of here. You bother me. I love you.

John Pappas smiled at his father, walking down the mats. Darlene had her back to the grill board, watching Alex, twirling a spatula in her hand.

"I'm gone for the day, Darlene."

"That's a first."

"Get used to it."

He neared Rafael, using the overhead spray nozzle to power-wash a pot.

"You leave, boss?" said Rafael.

"Yeah. How was your date with that girl?"

Rafael smiled and winked.

"Good boy," said Alex. He exited through the back door.

RAYMOND MONROE sat beside Kendall Robertson in her office, the two of them holding hands, talking quietly in the late afternoon. Kendall had drawn the blinds. She had been crying a little but was finished now and held a balled-up tissue in her free hand.

"I'm sorry," she said.

"Don't apologize. Everyone around here deserves a good cry now and again. Not just the patients."

"They're stronger than I am, most times."

"What did it today?"

"Oh, I don't know. I was with Private Collins again, the one they call Dagwood?"

"The young man thinking about the voluntary amputation."

"He's not on the fence anymore. I put in his request yesterday. I was just checking in on him, to see how he was doing with it."

"And?"

"He's fine. It was me who got angry, walking out of his room. And then that anger turned into emotion." Kendall tossed the tissue into the wastebasket by her desk. "I was over on Wisconsin Avenue the other day, in Maryland, walking by a theater. It was the movie with the girl got the machine gun implanted in place of her amputated leg. And you just know young people were gonna be in that theater, watching it, clapping and laughing behind that bullshit. While young men and women are dying, losing arms and legs, and for what? So those well-off kids can put gasoline in the cars that their mommies and daddies bought them? So they can buy their two-hundred-dollar jeans?"

"They were told to do that," said Monroe. "Take your tax cut and go shopping."

"They're supposed to forget that there's a war. No coffins, no dead. I wasn't around and neither were you, but didn't this whole country contribute and sacrifice during World War Two?"

"My father used to talk about that all the time."

"Used to be 'Ask what you can do for your country.' Now it's 'Let's watch *Dancing with the Stars*. Let's go to the mall.'"

"So if you give up," said Raymond, "is that gonna make things better for these soldiers?"

"Please. I'm not going *any*where."

"You do have fire, Kendall."

"I need to burn off some of this negative energy." Her finger traced a circle in his palm. "You coming over tonight? Marcus would like to see you, too."

"You know I want to. But I got some issues with my brother that I need to keep an eye on. And I want to make sure my mother's all right."

"Man who's fifty years old—"

"I'm forty-nine."

"Still staying with his mother. I'd say it's time for that man to reevaluate."

"I get your point. But see, you of all people . . . You been talking about taking responsibility, how we all gotta pitch in. When someone sacrifices, the ones who didn't, well, they need to show support."

"I know, Ray. You got that thing that you're carrying. But look, I'm not asking you for vows or a ring. I'm just tired of looking at your overnight bag on my floor. You could have your own dresser, for starters."

"True."

"And Marcus needs a man around full-time."

"You think I fit the bill?"

"Stop playin. Marcus loves you, Ray."

"I feel the same way. Far as he goes, I was thinking about taking him to a Wizards game. They're about to make a home stand. Seats gonna be nosebleed, but hey."

"He gets *near* that Verizon Center, he's gonna smile."

"You could come, too."

"It'll take more than a ten-dollar seat and a hot dog to buy me off."

Monroe squeezed her hand. "Just give me a little time."

TWENTY-ONE

THE PRESIDENT of the historical society had an office in a civic building near antique-and-tea-shop row. The building was in a section of town filled with Victorians on lushly landscaped grounds. Within sight of the civic building sat a six-bedroom house once owned by a man named Nicholson. Thirty-five years earlier, Raymond Monroe, a kid from the all-black neighborhood nearby, had thrown a rock through one of the bedroom windows after being shortchanged by Mr. Nicholson on a lawn-cutting job. The policeman who came to the Monroe house had given him what was known as a Field Investigation and a stern warning, telling the boy's father, Ernest Monroe, that his son was a "hothead" who would only be given one more chance.

Alex Pappas knew none of this as he sat in the small office of Harry McCoy, the society's self-appointed archivist. McCoy was a large man with tattooed forearms and a gut; his wire-rimmed glasses lessened, somewhat, his stevedore appearance. He had enthusiastically welcomed Alex into his office, relishing the chance to talk local history. There were framed photographs of businesses, streets, homes, and residents, going back to the turn of the previous century, hung throughout the office. All of the people in the photographs were white. None of the photos, Alex assumed, depicted life in Heathrow Heights.

"You're talking about Nunzio's," said McCoy after Alex had described the market with the wooden porch.

"Yes, that's it."

"It's closed now, of course. Houses were built where it once stood. The man who was running it retired and sold the property, but he would have gone out of business eventually. He couldn't compete with the Safeway up the road."

"Do you have his name?"

McCoy had pulled a file and was inspecting its contents on his desk. "That's what I'm looking for. Here it is." He glanced over the tops of his glasses. "Salvatore Antonelli. His father, the man who founded the market, was named Nunzio."

"Is Salvatore alive?"

"I don't know, but it's easy enough to find out. I believe they were locals. Unless he passed or moved away, that's a name that should be in the phone book. You're welcome to have a look."

Alex scanned the white pages and wrote down some information on a pad.

"If you need more," said McCoy, "there's a man who lives in Heathrow Heights who's kind of their historical caretaker."

"I don't see any pictures in here of that neighborhood."

"Well, the residents prefer to keep those things in Heathrow. They have an old schoolhouse that turned into a rec center after *Brown versus Board of Education*. Their photographs are on display there."

"Do you have that man's name?"

"Yes. I'll give you his number, too. He doesn't mind talking to people about his community. He's proud of it, as he should be. Nice fellow, this Draper."

Alex stood as McCoy handed him Rodney Draper's contact information, retrieved from the Rolodex on his desk.

"You say this is your hobby?" said McCoy.

"I run a business that was first owned by my father. I just like to talk to people, immigrants and their ancestors, who have had similar family businesses. Those kinds of places are going away, you know."

"As are most of the things we hold fondly in our memories," said McCoy. "You must have a passion for history."

"Not really," said Alex. "Let's just say I'm interested in the past."

DEON BROWN closed the trunk of his Mercury and parked in the alley behind Peabody Street, tight alongside the fence bordering his mother's row house. He had retrieved the clothing he needed, his shaving gear and toiletries, his Paxil, a bag of weed, all of his money, the title to his car, and the few special items from his childhood that he could fit into the duffel bag he had purchased from the surplus store in Wheaton. He had quit his job at the shoe store in the Westfield Mall. He had just stowed his things in the back of the car and he was ready to go. But he needed to talk to his mother first.

Deon's cell had been ringing all day and most of last night, but he had not answered it. He had allowed the calls, from Cody and Dominique Dixon, to go to his voice mail. From listening to the messages, Deon had managed to construct a disturbing scenario. Cody Kruger and Charles Baker had robbed Dominique of his product and were clumsily attempting to take over his business. Though Cody had not said as much, he indicated that he had some good news for Deon and that Deon should call or come by the apartment as soon as possible to get the news personally. "I need you to *be* here, dawg," said Cody. Deon had the impression that Cody had summoned him to his spot because he didn't want to be alone with Baker, who had certainly set the plan in motion. There was a kind of desperation in Cody's voice that Deon had not heard before. Cody had done a bold thing and was boosted by it, but he also seemed to know that he had fucked up.

The messages from Dominique confirmed this. Dominique said that Baker and Kruger had taken him off at the point of a knife and gun. Dominique, with barely controlled rage, said that he and his brother wanted to see Deon right away. That Deon needed to answer his phone. That if he did not respond, Dominique and his brother would have to assume that Deon was in on the plan.

Toward the end of the day, Deon had turned off his cell and thrown it down a storm drain on Quackenbos Street. He'd buy another disposable on his way out of town.

A light went on in his mother's kitchen. She had just gotten in from work. She liked to make herself a snack when she got home, to tide her over until dinner.

Deon had enlisted the day before. He'd gone back to the Armed Services Recruitment Center on Georgia Avenue, talked to a Sergeant Walters for a couple of hours, and signed up. The sergeant spoke of adventure and personal growth, but Deon's decision was more practical than spiritual. The service was the only clean way out of his present life that he could see. He had some time before he was to report to basic training, at Fort Benning, Georgia, and he would spend that time heading there, driving his car around the South, burning his cash on hotels and nice meals. He heard Myrtle was a whole rack of fun. He wanted to go to Daytona and drive his car on the

beach. He'd sell the Marauder in Georgia, before entering
BCT.

His mother was going to be upset, and worried, too. He'd
tell her that he wasn't going to see combat, necessarily. That
the army would decide what he was best suited for once he got
through basic. There were all sorts of ways a young man in
uniform could serve, said the sergeant, though he did mention
that one of those ways could be as a soldier in a theater of war.
"There's a price for freedom," said the sergeant. "It isn't free."
Deon's mother would ask him about his depression and medi-
cation. She'd wonder how they could take a boy with his problems. Sergeant Walters had said that this was "not an issue."
The sergeant had assured him that everything was going to be
all right.

What Deon had to do was get her out of the house. Con-
vince her to gather up what she needed and move to La Juanda's place in Capitol Heights. His sister had a family, but she
would take their mother in. It wouldn't be permanent. Just
long enough for this bad thing with the Dixons to go away. As
for Charles Baker, she had never given him a key. If he came to
the house on Peabody, he'd find a locked door.

All of this would have to be dealt with now.

His mother, La Trice, had stepped out the kitchen door and
was standing on the back steps of her row house. He went to
the chain-link gate of the fence and stepped into the yard. She
studied him as he approached, and because he was her son, she
read his face and knew, despite the calm appearance he was
affecting, that something was wrong.

"What is it, Deon?" she said.

"Mama, we need to talk."

"Come in. I'll fix us something to eat."

He followed her into the house without objection. He

wanted them to have that meal together. There was time enough for that.

THE ADDRESS on Salvatore Antonelli that Alex Pappas had pulled from the phone book seemed to be a match for the man at first glance. Located on a street off Nimitz Drive, in a postwar GI Bill housing community in Wheaton, not far from Heathrow Heights, the home was a wood-shingled Cape Cod with a one-turn wheelchair ramp leading to the front door. Antonelli would be of that era, a veteran most likely, probably in his eighties. The ramp would have been built for him.

As Alex went to the door, he could see a painting crew through the bay window, working inside the empty living room, a drop cloth beneath them. He knocked on the door and waited for it to open. Soon a stocky young man with deep brown skin stood in the frame.

"Yes?"

"I'm looking for Mr. Antonelli," said Alex. "Salvatore, an old man."

"The old man die."

"I'm sorry to hear that."

"We paint. The family, now they're going to sell the house." The resourceful young man handed Alex a business card. "You need paint? We do good work, cheap."

The name on the card read Michael Sobalvarro. Below it were the words "We Paint."

"Thank you, Michael. I'll keep it in mind."

Back in his Cherokee, Alex phoned the number for Rodney Draper. A woman answered, and when Alex told her he had a historical question about Heathrow Heights, she gave him Draper's work number. Alex thanked her, called the number, and got the main-office receptionist for a major appliance and electronics retailer named Nutty Nathan's. Alex knew the company, a bait-and-switch house that nevertheless had character the chains lacked. He had bought a television set from a fellow named McGinnes, at the Connecticut Avenue location, many years back. Alex remembered him because the man, extremely personable and knowledgeable, was quite obviously high.

"Draper," said a voice on the other end of the line, after Alex had been put through.

"Yes, my name is Alex Pappas. I'm wondering if I can ask you a quick historical question with regard to Heathrow Heights. I was referred by Mr. McCoy from the historical society."

"Who are you with?"

"I don't represent anyone other than myself. This was about a shooting incident that occurred outside the old Nunzio's market, back in seventy-two. I'm trying to locate a woman . . . the woman who was in Nunzio's the day of the incident. She testified at the trial. It was a very high-profile case."

Alex did not hear a reply. He thought the call had been dropped.

"Hello?"

"I remember it," said Draper.

"I'd like to contact her if I can."

"Listen, Mr. . . ."

"Pappas."

"I'm going to have to get back to you. I've got an ad to mock up here, and the sales rep from the *Post* is outside my door, waiting on it."

"Can I give you my cell number?"

"I've got a pen."

Alex said his phone number. "Please call me."

The line went dead. There was nothing to do now but go home. Alex was not encouraged. He had the feeling that he might not hear from Rodney Draper again.

CODY KRUGER sat at the kitchen table, scaling and bagging ounces of weed. A hill of sticky-bud hydroponic was before him. Kruger was careful, as Deon had convinced him to be, when weighing and compartmentalizing the marijuana. He liked to think that he worked more quickly and more efficiently when he was high, but in actuality the THC slowed him down and made him more susceptible to error. A blunt in a vanilla Dutch wrapper was burning in the ashtray beside him. "Kryptonite," a TCB tune recorded live at the Club Neon, was playing loudly in the room from Kruger's iPod, which he had hooked into his system. Kruger was baked and singing off-key the chorus to the song.

Charles Baker, annoyed and impatient, went to the system and turned the volume down.

"Ain't you done yet?"

"Wanna do it right," said Kruger. "If you don't scale this shit out correct, you gonna hear about it."

"Look, man, what you figure we fixin to make on all this?"

"Three, four thousand. It was only two pounds in the van."

"Chump change," said Baker.

"You can't get it all in one day."

"True. But once we hook up with that connect, everything gonna be elevated."

"I thought you said Dominique didn't give it up."

"He claimed he didn't know who his connect was. Claimed that only his brother did. Dominique said he was gonna talk to his brother and call you on your cell to set up a meet."

Kruger nodded but did not comment. The mention of Dominique's brother had unsettled him. From what Deon said of him, Calvin Dixon was not going to take what had been done to Dominique with a smile. He sure wasn't going to hand over his connect. A dealer would take a bullet before he gave up his source, even Kruger knew that. But Mr. Charles did not seem to understand it. Mr. Charles thought he could just keep taking and not pay.

"Did you hear me, boy?"

"I heard."

"You so fucked up you can't speak."

"Nah, I'm good."

"You fearful of all these moves we be makin?"

"No."

"If you afraid, then say so."

"I'm *not*."

"Good," said Baker. "'Cause I'm lookin for you to assist me on something tonight."

"What?"

"I need a ride out to Maryland. A man there owes me some money."

"We got money on this table right here."

"This is on a whole 'nother level. Man been owin me for over thirty years. I'm sayin, the interest been compounding. Payday gonna be large, too."

"I got to see to this. You can borrow my car."

"How am I gonna drive a car with no license? The po-po pull me over, I'm going back to jail."

Kruger wetted the tail of a baggie with his tongue and sealed up an ounce. If he kept working, maybe Mr. Charles would drop the plan.

"I asked this old friend of mine to take me, but he gone soft on me. Now, I know you aren't gonna turn your back on me like he did."

"I'm busy here."

"Thought you had some rod on you, man."

"I got product promised to some customers in the morning. I need to get this done before I can think of anything else."

"Okay, then. I'm gonna walk on over to the Avenue, find me a bar stool, and have myself a beer. You should be done in a couple hours." Baker shook himself into his leather. "What's the door code when I come back?"

"I know what it is."

"Say it."

"Knock knock pause knock."

"Right. See you in a bit, young man."

Kruger scaled and bagged diligently after Baker had slipped out the door. He would have been happy to sit here all night, working, getting blazed, listening to music, thinking about the things he could get with the cash this weed would bring. The new Vans and Dunks, the T-shirts with the rock star look, the Authentic jerseys with lids that matched.

If Deon were here, they'd talk, joke, and dream on the things that they might buy. He wondered where Deon was at and why he wasn't answering his cell. Deon had been his boy, and now it seemed that Deon had up and walked away. What Kruger had left was Charles Baker.

Kruger had thrown his gun down a storm drain in the parking lot outside Dominique's after he had transferred the weed from the white van to his Honda. It had made him sick to hold a gun on a boy his age while Mr. Charles did what he did. Kruger didn't want to have a gun anymore. He didn't want to do anything like that again.

Cody Kruger began to lose his high. He knew that Mr. Charles would not forget about that ride out to Maryland. He would be back soon, knock knock pause knock. There was no way to deny Mr. Charles when he set his mind to hunting. Kruger would drive him to see the man who owed him money, because with Deon gone, Mr. Charles was his only friend. Kruger was dim-witted and fried, and there was nothing else that he could see to do.

TWENTY-TWO

RAYMOND MONROE, standing in Gavin's Garage, closed the lid of his cell and slipped the phone into the pocket of his jeans. James Monroe was under the hood of an '89 Caprice Classic, loosening a crippled water pump that he intended to replace. An open can of Pabst Blue Ribbon was balanced on the lip of the quarter panel. James stood straight, picked up the can, and took a long pull of beer.

"That was Rodney Draper just called," said Raymond.

"Rod the Rooster," said James, smiling, recalling the nickname they'd given him as kids on account of his funny nose. "Who'd 'a thought that boy would be running a company someday?"

"Rodney always did work hard. I'm not surprised."

"What he wanted?"

"Alex Pappas called him today. Said he had a history question. Rodney didn't answer it direct. He wanted to speak to me first."

James looked into his beer can, shook it, then took another swig.

"Alex is tryin to find Miss Elaine," said Raymond.

"Why?"

"To talk to her, I suppose. I'm guessing he's looking to put all this to rest."

"What did you tell Rod?"

"I told him to wait."

"Ray . . ."

"What?"

"Charles Baker contacted me today. He was looking for a ride out to Pappas's house. Wanted me with him, he said. He didn't say why."

"Did Charles say how it went with Whitten?"

"He didn't."

"That means it went wrong. And now he's gonna try and shake down Pappas. This time it's not gonna be over lunch in some fancy restaurant. This time Charles gonna do it his old way."

"Well, I told him I wouldn't do it," said James. "I told him this ain't none of my business."

"It is if Charles hurts that man or his family. It is to me if he keeps trying to pull my brother down into the dirt."

"Charles can't help what he is."

"Plenty of folks had bad childhoods. They found ways to carry it."

"He never killed anybody," said James.

"No," said Raymond, meeting his brother's stare. "He never did that."

"Let me get back to this water pump."

"Go ahead," said Raymond Monroe.

CALVIN DIXON and his friend Markos sat on plush chairs in the living room of Calvin's luxurious condominium, located on V Street, behind the Lincoln Theater, in the heart of Shaw.

They were smoking cigars and drinking single-barrel bour-
bons, neat with waters back, the bottle set between them on a
table made of iron and glass. They had everything young men
could want: women, money, good looks, vehicles that went
fast. But on this night they did not look happy.

"Did you make the call?" said Markos, a handsome young
man with his father's Ethiopian skin tone and his mother's le-
onine features.

"I was waiting to talk to you," said Calvin, a bigger, cut,
more rugged version of Dominique.

"You want some more water? I'm about to get some."

"Sure."

Markos rose and went to the open kitchen, equipped with
a Wolf cooktop and wall oven, an ASKO dishwasher, and a
Sub-Zero side-by-side. He poured filtered water into two
glasses from a dispenser built into a marble countertop and
brought the glasses back to the table. He used his hand to re-
trieve ice from a bucket and dropped cubes into the water.

Calvin poured more bourbon from a numbered bottle of
Blanton's. They tapped tumblers and drank.

"How you like that stick?" said Markos, referring to the
Padrón cigar Calvin was drawing on.

"Nice," said Calvin. "The sixty-four got the twenty-three
beat, you ask me."

A woman opened the bedroom door and stood in the frame.
She was very young, black haired, and supercharged, a mix of
Bolivia and Africa. Her breasts strained the fabric of her
button-down shirt, and her ass was the inverted heart so many
times invoked but rarely realized. Her name was Rita. Calvin
had retired her from a haircutting salon in Wheaton after she
had given him a shampoo and scalp massage.

"Did you call me?" said Rita to Calvin.

"Nah, baby. Let us have some privacy for a little while longer, okay?"

She pouted for a moment, then went back into the bedroom, closing the door behind her.

"Girl must have thought we said her name," said Calvin.

"I asked you 'bout your stick," said Markos. "I didn't say 'trick.'"

Calvin smiled a little, taking no offense. Rita was gorgeous, and a slut. They both felt the same way about women, even each other's occasional girlfriends.

"How's Dominique?" said Markos.

"Stayin at my parents' for the time being. He don't want to be at his apartment right now. He might be out for good. I don't know."

"We can get someone else to move weight for us."

"I agree."

"Question is, what are we gonna do about our problem?"

"The old man damn near ass-raped my kid brother. The white boy held a gun on him and watched."

"'Damn near' ain't rape."

"That's a hair so fine you can't split it. Tell that shit to Dominique."

"What about the other one they were in with?"

"Deon? Dominique says he wasn't involved. We been tryin to reach him to confirm that, but he's not taking his calls. That cell probably ringin at the bottom of the Anacostia River right now. If he's smart, he dumped it on the way out of town. But I'm not worried about him. It's the other two."

"Comes back to the original question: what are we gonna do?"

Markos dragged on his cigar and looked at his friend. Both of them were tough and skilled fighters who in their youth had regularly taken home trophies from the Capitol Classic, the annual martial-arts tournament held at the old D.C. Convention Center. They had never run from any type of physical challenge or confrontation. But this was different, a step they had yet to take. Neither of them saw it as a moral decision. They simply loved their lifestyle and did not want to endanger it with the possibility of prison.

"I talked to Alan," said Calvin. Alan was in security management at a club they frequented. He had a personal history that connected him to the underworld of the city to the north.

"And he said what?"

"He said these boys would take a lethal injection before they gave us up. That promise and the way they carry it is how they grow their business."

"Is this what you want to do?"

"Don't put it all on me," said Calvin. "I need you to say you good with this, too."

Markos nodded at the RAZR lying on the table. "Make the call."

Calvin flipped open his cell.

"HOW LONG we gonna sit here?" said Cody Kruger.

"Not too long, I expect," said Charles Baker.

"You know this is his house?"

"The people-find site brought me here. There were three Alexander Pappases in the area, but only one the right age. And this is near where he grew up at. Got to be him."

"Okay, but why you think he's gonna come outside?"

"Because I'm smart," said Baker. "Tomorrow is trash pickup day in Montgomery County. You see all those cans and recycling bins out by the curb?"

Kruger said, "Uh-huh."

"Mr. Alex Pappas ain't brought his out yet. But he will. All these suburbanites do it the night before, so they don't have to fuck with it in the morning."

They had been on the street for an hour or so. Because no one was walking through the clean middle-class neighborhood and many of the homes had gone dark, it seemed very late. Rain had fallen, and in its aftermath the streetlamps were haloed with rainbows and mist.

"Why don't you just go and knock on the man's door?"

"'Cause I could pull a trespassing charge," said Baker patiently. "I get to him out on the street, that's public property."

A car rolled down the road behind them, its headlights sweeping the interior of the Honda. Baker and Kruger watched it pass and slow down, then come to a stop at the curb in front of the Pappas residence. It was a light blue Acura coupe, well maintained; a woman's car, thought Baker, until a nicely dressed young man began to step out of the driver's side.

"Stay here," said Baker, seeing it all at once, moving quickly because that was how a decisive man ought to. It had to be the man's son, and that was good. Deliver a message to the boy and you'd send a message to the man real clear. Do what I'm asking because I can get to your family. I can and will.

Baker stepped down the street as the young man, looked to be in his middle twenties, locked the car with one of those gizmos he held in his hand. He was aware of Baker coming up on him, and he tried not to act frightened. He looked Baker in the eye and nodded a greeting but kept moving around the car in an effort to get up on the sidewalk and into his house.

"Hold up a minute, young man," said Baker, blocking his path, careful not to touch him or get too close.

"Yes?" said John Pappas in a friendly but guarded manner.

"Is this the Pappas residence right here?"

"Yes. I live here. What can I do for you?"

What can I do for you? Baker almost laughed. The young man taking a real firm tone now, like he was gonna defend the castle and shit. Trying to be something he was not. Baker studied him, trim and decked out in nice clothes, the black shirt worn tails out the way all these stylish young men liked to do. Baker looked at John Pappas and in his mind he saw the word, flashing like a sign outside a bar that was named *Prey*.

"Just give me a minute of your time," said Baker. "Okay?"

ALEX PAPPAS was lying in bed beside his sleeping wife, waiting for Johnny to come home, when he heard the sound of his Acura coming to a stop. Then he heard two car doors slamming shut, one after the other. And soon after that, voices. Alex got out of bed. Johnny never brought anyone home late at night, men friends or women. He was respectful that way.

Through the bedroom window that fronted the house, Alex saw Johnny in the street, standing close to an older black man. The two of them were talking. The black man was smiling and Johnny was not. Two houses down, an old Honda was parked and idling, smoke coming from its tailpipe. It looked like a young white man was under the wheel.

Alex quickly put on jeans and tied a pair of New Balance sneakers onto his feet. Because he kept no guns or weapons of any kind in the house, he grabbed the heavy, long-handled Mag-Lite he kept beside the bed, ignoring Vicki, who had woken and was asking, "What's wrong?" and "Alex, what's *wrong?*"

He passed Gus's bedroom and went down the stairs.

"YOU SAY you're his friend?"

"Oh, I'm not claiming that we're friends, exactly," said Baker. "More like acquaintances."

"Excuse me," said John. "I really have to get inside."

He tried to step around Baker, but Baker moved in front of him.

"I ain't done," said Baker. He put his index finger to the corner of his eye and pulled down. "I gave that to your daddy. That's right. Me."

John narrowed his eyes and felt warmth come to his face. "Make your point."

"Ho, look at you," said Baker with a chuckle. "You got your little fists in a ball and your cheeks is pink, just like Raggedy Andy. You ain't gonna hurt me, are you?"

"Get out of here."

"Okay." Baker laughed. "I will. But not because a fellow like you told me to. Just tell your old man I came by. Just tell him, fifty thousand dollars. That's all he needs to know. I'll contact him next and make the arrangements. He calls the law, you're the one who's gonna suffer. You hear me, pretty? *Tell* him."

Baker began to walk toward the Honda. He heard the door to the house open, a commanding voice and rapid footsteps on concrete, and he kept pace and got to the Honda's passenger side, turned and smiled at the shirtless middle-aged man who was running toward him with eyes on fire and something like a steel club in his hand. Baker opened the door and dropped into the seat.

"Go, boy," he said. Kruger gunned it off the curb.

Alex Pappas broke into a sprint. He ran alongside the Honda, and it passed him, and he continued to chase it, knowing he could never catch it.

"Stay away from my family!" shouted Alex.

The Honda turned the corner and was gone. Alex slowed down and came to a stop in the middle of the street. He bent over and put his hands on his knees and tried to catch his breath. His heart was beating rubbery in his chest.

"Dad," said John, standing behind him. "Dad, it's all right."

Alex stood and turned. John had his cell phone out and was making a call. Alex reached out and took it from his hand.

"Don't," said Alex. "No police."

"What, are you kidding?"

"I'll explain. Come on, let's go inside."

They moved toward their home. Alex put his arm around his son as they walked.

"You okay, Dad?"

"Yes. Did he say his name?"

"He said that he was the man who gave you your eye."

"He didn't hurt you, did he?"

"No." John looked at the Mag-Lite and smiled with affection at his father. "What were you going to do with that?"

"Damn if I know. I didn't have a plan. I saw him out here with you and I just grabbed it and ran."

Vicki was waiting for them at the front door.

IT WAS very late when Raymond got the call on his cell. He was at his mother's place, seated in his father's old recliner, watching television and not watching it, as someone does when his thoughts are intense. The phone rang in his pocket, and he answered it and heard Alex Pappas's voice. Gone was the gentle tone he had come to like and grow comfortable with in the past couple of days.

Alex described the visit from Charles Baker, his attempt at extortion, and his conversation with John.

"He was talking to my son, right outside my home," said Alex. "Where my wife sleeps. Do you understand, Ray? He came to my home and threatened my son."

"I do understand," said Raymond. "Did you—"

"No. I didn't call the police. But next time I will. I need to be clear with you on that."

"I got it," said Raymond. "Thank you, Alex. Thank you for thinking of my brother."

"You've gotta do something about this," said Alex, the anger gone out of him.

"I will," said Raymond.

He next phoned James, now at his apartment on Fairmont.

"Where does Charles Baker stay?" said Raymond.

"Why?"

"Tell me."

"I don't know exactly. He's in a group home on Delafield. One of those places for men on paper. Said he's in a house on the thirteen hundred block, in Northwest."

Raymond ended the call abruptly. He got up out of the recliner and went down to the cellar, quietly, so as not to wake his mother. There, on a workbench, he found his father's tools in a steel box. Ernest Monroe, the bus mechanic, had kept them orderly and clean. Since his father's death, Raymond had used them infrequently and left them in their proper sections, as his father would have wished.

Ernest had never kept a gun in the house. He said it was dangerous and unnecessary, that with boys around, it would just be a temptation that would lead to tragedy. But he had modified certain tools, and shown them to his sons, in the event that the family was in need of protection. One of them was a heavy-shafted flat-head machinist's screwdriver whose tip Ernest had bench-ground to a point.

Raymond lifted the screwdriver from the box.

TWENTY-THREE

ON HIS way to work, Alex Pappas often topped off the tank of his Cherokee at the gas station on Piney Branch Road. This served two purposes. The gas was relatively cheap at this particular outlet, and if he desired, he could check on his investment property, situated directly behind the station, while he was there.

It was not smart to have unrented property, as the absence of a tenant left the owner vulnerable to vandals and possibly even squatters. But Alex did not have much cause to worry, as his property was in a decent neighborhood and was visible from a heavily traveled road. Also, it was well fortified by design, solid brick with no windows. The electric company had built the substation with the intent of blending it in, as much as possible, with the rest of the neighborhood.

Still, as secure as the building was, he needed to find someone to lease it, if only to get Vicki off his back. She was right, of course. She was almost always right when it came to money.

Alex was pondering this, looking at his building as he set the pump's nozzle into his vehicle. He could see the wide, corrugated bay door that fronted the property, and the small parking lot, which the Iranian, the last tenant, had enlarged at his own expense to accommodate his flooring and carpet customers.

When the tank was full, Alex drove around to the front of the building and parked. From the glove box he got his Craftsman measuring tape and a set of keys holding one that operated the bay door.

Later, he drove down Piney Branch Road, tapping his fingers on the steering wheel. Piney Branch became 13th, and farther along he turned onto New Hampshire Avenue and headed toward Dupont Circle. It was the same route he had taken for over thirty years. Most days, his mind was focused on day-to-day minutiae and the mundane. But not today.

RAYMOND MONROE found his mother in the living room, watching a morning news show on the television. He held his overnight bag in his hand.

"I'm off, Mama."

"To work?"

"Yes."

"I heard you talking to those people at the hospital on your phone. Something about you had an appointment."

"Yeah, I got something I need to take care of. I was just telling them I was gonna be in late."

"And I can see that you won't be coming home tonight."

"I'm staying with Kendall and her son."

"I'll be all right."

"I know it. You're like that Energizer bunny."

"That winds down, too, eventually." Almeda Monroe looked up at her son, her beautiful eyes set deep in a face plowed by time. "Your brother doing okay?"

"He's fine. Drinks too much beer, but hey."

"So did your father. If that's the worst you can say about a man . . ."

"Right."

"I was married to a good one. And I raised two fine sons. I would say that my life has been a success. Wouldn't you?"

"Yes, ma'am," said Raymond. He bent down and kissed her. "I'll call you tonight, hear?"

"Have a blessed day, Raymond."

Going down the road in his Pontiac, he went by Rodney Draper's house. Raymond was reminded that he needed to give Rodney a call. He did so as he drove toward Northwest, heading for a street called Delafield.

"HELLO."

"Can I speak to Alex Pappas, please?"

Alex, standing at the register, looked over his shoulder. John, Darlene, Blanca, Juana, and Rafael were beginning to mobilize for the lunch rush, all of them moving about without being told to, fulfilling the duties of their respective stations.

"Speaking."

"It's Rodney Draper. I'm getting back to you."

"I'm glad you called."

"Well, I wouldn't have, quite frankly, given the circumstances. It was Ray Monroe who asked that I help you. He said that you kept up your end of the bargain, whatever that means. He told me to give you any information you need."

"I've got a pencil."

The woman's name was Elaine Patterson. The kids in Heathrow had always called her Miss Elaine. She was in her mideighties now and in poor health. The victim of a stroke, she lived in a nursing home off Layhill Road, past the Glenmont Metro station in Wheaton.

"She's one of our treasured citizens. Miss Elaine took classes in the one-room schoolhouse, before the courts sent our kids out into the public system. The stroke shut down some of her brain functions and sharpened others. She has very strong memories of the distant past but often can't remember what she did yesterday. Her speech is halting and she can no longer read or write. I've been doing oral history work with her when I find the time."

"I'll be mindful of her health. I promise you I won't stay with her long. Could you let her know I'm coming, so this won't be a shock?"

"I will. But I'm not sure what you're looking for, exactly."

"Thank you, Mr. Draper. I appreciate the call."

Alex hung up the phone and turned to find Darlene standing behind him. She was looking at him with her big brown eyes, now heavy with bags. For a moment he saw the girl with the large Afro under the newsboy cap, small decorative mirrors patterned above the visor. He smiled.

"What are you, eavesdropping?"

"Nope. I came down here to tell you we're eighty-six on the roast beef today."

"I saw one come in this morning."

"It smells funny. I wouldn't serve it to my dog."

"You need to call the meat man and tell him to get one over here before lunch starts. He's not gonna like it, but that's too bad."

"I was thinking we'd let Johnny do that. Have him experience the conflict you and I deal with every day. He's gonna have to get used to solving problems like that."

"Right."

"What with you disappearing more and more."

"Uh-huh."

"You cuttin out early again today, sugar?"

"Matter of fact, I am."

"You're not fixin to leave your old friend completely behind, now, are you?"

"Not completely. John's not ready to take over one hundred percent. But you will be seeing less of me around here, and that means a little more pressure on you. Don't worry, there's gonna be a raise in it for you."

"There you go, spoiling me again."

"You're worth it. This place doesn't function without you."

"Am I blushing? I feel kinda hot."

"Stop it," said Alex. "Go on, get ready for lunch."

He watched her walk down the rubber mats, twirling a spatula to the music in her head.

RAYMOND MONROE parked the Pontiac in the middle of Delafield Place and studied the block. The majority of the houses here were detached four-square colonials with large front porches showing lacquered white columns, shaded by huge oaks and situated on a gentle grade. It was a lovely street, and Monroe could not see that it would be a viable location for a house of offenders. But as his eyes continued along the block, he noticed the odd houses that were not so fine. Fronted by Formstone rather than wood or vinyl siding, and with weedy, overgrown yards and hoopties parked out front, there were two or three candidates that bore the run-down mark of group homes.

A knock on any door would have told him what he needed to know. Longtime residents who took pride in their homes were always eager to point out the homes of those less inclined to take care of their properties. But he didn't want anyone to remember him later on. Squinting his eyes, he noticed the mailboxes stuffed with flyers and letters. The mailman had an early route here, and that was good.

Monroe got out of the Pontiac and adjusted his loose nylon jacket. The screwdriver, now tipped with cork, lay in the inner jacket pocket, handle up, point down.

He walked to the first run-down house nearest his car and stepped up onto its porch, looking around at the streetscape as he moved along. He went directly to the mailbox and quickly checked its contents. A dog rushed to the closed door, barking. Monroe saw that all of the letters were addressed to a couple of individuals with the same last name, and he moved off the porch and back down to the sidewalk. The dog was still barking as Monroe crossed the street and headed for a house sided by pink and green Formstone. Its yard needed to be mowed, and there were old chairs set up on its porch. Monroe checked the mailbox. It held letters and advertising material addressed to several different male names. Raymond felt his heart race as he knocked on the door.

A man with a comically long nose stood before him as the door swung open.

"Yeah."

"Baker here?" said Monroe.

The man blinked hard. "He's here."

Monroe stepped into the foyer of the house. His eyes told the man to step aside and let him. Before Monroe was a long staircase. Beside him, through open French doors, was a living room that had once been nicely furnished but was now trashed. A big man sat in a shredded armchair with the sports section open in his lap.

"Where's he at?" said Monroe, looking at the man who had opened the door.

"Who are you?" said the big man.

"Where is he?" said Monroe to the man with the trombone nose.

"He sleepin, most likely."

"You ain't his PO," said the big man.

"What room is he sleeping in?"

"You ain't his PO and you got no right to be in here," said the big man.

"If I was talkin to you, you'd know it," said Monroe.

"I'll call the police."

"No, you won't." The big man looked down at his newspaper. Monroe turned his attention to the man with the long nose. "What room does he stay in?"

The man jerked his head up. "First door to the right of the bathroom."

Monroe took the stairs. The flame grew inside him as he hit the landing and went to the closed door and kicked it at the jamb. It did not crack, and he kicked it a second time. The door swung open, and he blocked it on the backswing as he stepped inside. Charles Baker, bare to his boxers, was throwing off the sheet, swinging his legs over the side of his bed. Monroe drew the sharpened screwdriver in one motion, tore off its corked tip, and leaped onto the bed. He punched Baker with a sharp left to the jawline that sent him back to the mattress. Monroe straddled Baker and pressed his left forearm to Baker's upper chest. It pinned him there, and Monroe put the sharp end of the screwdriver to the top of his neck. He pushed it until it punctured the skin and Baker moaned. Blood trickled down over his Adam's apple.

"Quiet now," said Monroe softly. "Don't speak. I'll push this pick straight up into your brain."

Baker's hazel eyes were still.

"Stay away from Pappas and his family. Stay away from my brother forever. I will kill you. Do you understand this?"

Baker did not respond. Monroe pushed the weapon farther and saw the tip of the screwdriver go deeper into Baker's skin. Blood flowed freely down his neck. Baker made a small high sound against the pain, but still his eyes were steady. It was Monroe who blinked.

He felt sick and a sudden chill. The flame died inside him. He pulled the screwdriver out of Baker's neck, got off him, and stood away from the bed.

Baker wiped at the blood. He sat upright, his back against the wall. He rubbed at his jawline where Monroe had struck him and he stared at Monroe and smiled.

"You can't," said Baker. "You could have once. But you can't today."

"That's right," said Monroe. "It's not in me and I'm not you."

"James and Raymond Monroe," said Baker with contempt. "The good boys in the neighborhood. Sons of Ernest and Almeda. Lived in the clean house had the fresh coat of paint on it each year. Everything so clean and nice. Only thing missing was the apple pie gettin cool on the windowsill and the bluebirds flyin around it. Weren't you the lucky ones."

"You got wronged when you were young," said Monroe. "But that don't excuse you now."

"I *deserve* things."

"Leave us alone, Charles."

"I'll think on it," said Baker.

Monroe replaced the screwdriver in his jacket, exited the room, and went down the stairs. The men in the living room did not look at him as he left the house.

In his room, Baker pressed fingers to his neck and walked to the landing at the top of the stairs.

"Trombone," Baker called down to the living room. "I need you up here, man. Bring some of that medical shit you got, too."

Trombone, the house mother, slowed the blood from Baker's puncture wound as best he could, cleaned it and dressed it with Neosporin, and sprayed it with Mastisol, a liquid adhesive. Over that he taped a gauze bandage. Almost immediately the bandage became dotted with blood.

"You better have someone look at that," said Trombone.

"Yeah, all right."

Baker dressed in black slacks, a lavender shirt, and the tooled leather shoes that looked like gators. He wore his deep purple sport jacket with the white stitching on the lapels. He was not shook up. Instead, he felt almost jovial as he prepared to leave the house. The visit from Ray Monroe had only confirmed what he knew. He was like one of those strong animals, walking proud in plain sight, a hunter who had no need to hide his intent. Because who was going to stop him? No one, it seemed, had the will.

Charles Baker took Delafield east on foot. He'd catch the 70 on Georgia Avenue, go on over to Cody's apartment. The boy was out delivering his weed, but he'd be back. There Baker would compose another letter, this one to Pappas, with none of the niceties that his letter to Whitten had contained. Cody could help him with the spelling and grammar. He wasn't as smart as James Monroe, but he would have to do.

Baker hummed a tune as he walked down the block, confidence in his step, his knobby wrists protruding from the too-short sleeves of his sport jacket, his hands swinging free.

TWENTY-FOUR

ALEX PAPPAS had his head down, counting out ones below the counter, not with any real purpose but because he liked the feel of paper money moving between his fingers and thumb. As he worked, he turned the bills around so that all the heads of George Washington were facing the same way. For his father, it had been a meaningless fetish and it had become his as well.

He could tell by the dying noise in the shop that the lunch rush was done. He knew this also by the touch of the sun that had just begun to come through the plate glass window. He didn't need to look at the Coca-Cola clock on the wall to find the time.

After the ones, he counted the fives, tens, and twenties, and replaced them in their respective beds. He took note of the sole fifty-dollar bill, which he had slipped beneath the change drawer. By figuring the average percentage of cash to credit card sales, he could calculate the take of the day. He had spent his adult life working this register and had become adept at retail math.

Alex closed the register drawer and walked along the inner

counter, his feet treading the mats. He said good-bye to Juana and Blanca, who were laughing at something one of them had said in Spanish, and came up on John and Darlene, who were discussing next week's menu. All seemed to be in good spirits. It was Friday.

"Grab your jacket," said Alex to John. "Let's go outside for a few minutes." To Darlene he said, "Where's Rafael?"

"Lover Boy's out on a delivery."

"I saw the ticket. It was for Twenty-second and L, so he should have been back by now. Give him a call on his cell and tell him to quit socializing. The dishes and silver are backing up."

"Got it," said Darlene. "We'll see you on Monday, right?"

"I'm opening," said Alex. "Same as always."

Alex and John got their jackets off a tree by the dishwashing station, went through a break in the counter, and exited through the front door. Outside, John followed his father to the ledge decoratively bookended by shrubs. Alex had a seat on the ledge and looked at the shiny bits of quartz embedded in the concrete.

"I used to jump over this thing all day long when I was a kid," said Alex.

"So did we," said John. "Me and Gus. We'd be out here playing while you were working inside."

Alex could see them, John, eleven or so, and Gus, around six, John standing on the deep side of the ledge, ready to up-right his younger brother in case he caught the toe of his sneaker on the concrete and tripped.

"I remember," said Alex. He rubbed at his shoulder unconsciously as he spoke.

"Dad, are you all right?"

"I'm fine."

"All that running you did last night." John chuckled. "With your shirt off."

"I looked good, didn't I?"

"Seriously, Pop. Your father died of a heart condition. You need to take care of yourself."

"Ahh." Alex waved his hand dismissively. "My father smoked and had a poor diet. I stay in shape."

"I know it."

"But I'm not gonna be around forever. We do need to talk. About the future, I mean. I want to get things in order with you, in case I happen to kick."

"Dad, don't be so Greek."

"I'm just sayin. I want you to know my intentions."

"Okay."

"You see that front window there?"

"Yeah?"

"If you count the early days when I came to work for my father, I've been looking through that window, at this street, for forty years. It's like I've been watching the same movie over and over again. It's time for me to look at something else."

"You're selling the business?"

"*No.* But we're gonna try something new, starting next week. It's not doing either of us any good, the two of us working together. You're not gonna learn much more with me around, and the way you're catching on, I'm becoming as useless as tits on a mule."

"I don't get it."

"A mule is sterile. It can't have little mules, so its teats are there for no purpose. There's no offspring to suck on 'em."

"I'm asking you, what are you trying to say?"

"Why don't we do this? Starting Monday, I'm gonna open

the shop the way I always do. I *like* that time of day, and you're a young man who still needs a social life. I remember when I was young, working down here, and I had to get up at five in the a.m. It made an impact on my love life because I couldn't have any late nights out." Alex casually pointed to his bad eye. "Plus, I had this."

"None of that stopped you from hooking up with Mom."

"That was just one of those chemical things." Alex grinned lasciviously. "The first time she came into the *magazi*, she couldn't take her eyes off me."

"Stop bragging."

"Anyway, like I said, I'll open, and you can plan on coming in around eight, to work breakfast. I'll stick around for the first hour of lunch and shove off by one o'clock. Little by little, I'll pull back on my hours and grow yours. We'll play it by ear, but I don't think it'll be too long before you're able to run the whole thing by yourself."

"Dad, I . . ." John looked down at his feet.

"You're speechless, for once."

"I can't say I don't want this. I *do* want it. But I didn't expect you to hand it to me. I never felt like I was entitled to it."

"You'll do a fine job. I have no doubt. But you have to understand the magnitude of this commitment. We don't own the real estate. Our equity is the business itself. Every day you're starting all over again. Every day you've got to turn that key. The help gets sick, but you can't. They take vacations, but you can't. If you lock the front door and go on vacation—"

"—'the customers are gonna try someplace new.'"

"Make fun if you want."

"I'm not."

"I'm telling you, you've got challenges up ahead. The chains, you know about. You said yourself you can't go head-to-head with them. The big unknown is the new landlord and the property management company. They're tryin to raise the rent. Let Mr. Mallios negotiate with those *malakas*. Dimitri will put them on their knees."

John turned his head. Rafael was coming down N Street, walking and talking with a woman five to ten years his senior. She was a professional, dressed in a business suit, and seemed to be enjoying his company.

"Kid's girl crazy," said Alex, trying for cynical but conveying admiration.

Rafael said good-bye to the woman, broke away from her, and headed for the store.

"You're late," said Alex as he neared.

"I was just—"

"I got eyes. You have dishes to take care of. Go on, Rafael, move it. Get on your horse."

Rafael nodded and motored in through the front door.

"He's a good worker," said John.

"They all are," said Alex. "The best crew I've ever had. Look, you don't make this possible and neither do I. The help does. You gotta take care of 'em, John. There's gonna be the occasional slow week; bills are going to come due. There are times when you might not be able to pay yourself. But even if it comes out of your own pocket, you've always got to take care of the help. Make sure they're compensated in full on payday. Give them loans when they need it. On holidays, put extra in their envelopes so their kids and grandkids can have nice presents."

"Yessir."

"I'm giving Darlene a bump in pay."

"Absolutely. She deserves it."

"One more thing: I expect you to keep making the run to

Walter Reed. The contact woman is Peggy, out at the Fisher House."

"I'll leave some nice desserts with her after I get off work. I'll do it every night if you think I should."

"The soldiers like sweet stuff. Peach pie, cherry cheesecake, things like that. Don't get too fancy."

"Got it." John looked at Alex sheepishly. "Dad?"

"Yes."

"If you're turning it over to me, I'm going to want to, you know, modernize the look a little bit. Make some alterations in the decor."

"I expected that."

"You don't mind?"

"Two things I'm gonna ask you not to change," said Alex. "First one is the lights over the counter. I know you don't like them. But your grandfather and I hung those lights together, many summers ago. Those lights mean something to me."

"All right."

"And the sign. The sign stays."

"I wouldn't touch it, Dad. I'm proud of it."

"I am, too."

John Pappas's eyes were heavy with emotion. Alex slid off the ledge and stood before his son.

"What is it?" said Alex.

"I'm going to get my own place to stay," said John. "An apartment or a condo. I think it's time."

"If you'd like."

"I'm twenty-five years old. It's not cool that you're still waiting up for me at night. I see the lights going out in your room when I pull up in front of the house."

"I can't help it, Johnny. But listen, if you want to move out, I think you should."

"I've been considering it for a while. I didn't do it before because I thought it was best to stay with you and Mom. That you would want me to stick around, after Gus died."

"I know."

"You were so crushed. Because Gus was . . . well, I know that Gus was the most important person in your life."

"John, don't."

"It's all right for us to admit it. He was special. It's okay to say that he was."

"John—"

"So I thought it was important that I stay with you and Mom. The truth is, I needed you guys as well. I was pretty sick inside. I loved Gus, too, Dad. Gus was my kid brother."

"I *know*. But we're better now. We're going to be."

John took a step toward his father.

Alex pulled his son into his arms and hugged him tightly. They held each other there beneath the sign.

ALEX DROVE back out to Maryland. He stopped at the property once more to check on some questions of space and feasibility that had been nagging at him since the morning. When he was done measuring and eyeballing the interior, he was satisfied that his original instincts were sound.

Going through Wheaton, heading for the nursing home where Elaine Patterson stayed, he thought of his son John and the pain that he'd been in since Gus's death. How inward and selfish Alex's focus had been. It hurt him that Johnny knew that Gus had been his favorite. Alex had not denied it, and this was something that John would carry, perhaps for the rest of his life. There would come a time when they could talk about their relationship more freely. For now, turning the store over to him, a gesture and an affirmation, was a start.

But we're better now. We're going to be.

It was not completely a lie. Alex *was* better than he had been. He had come to terms with his sadness. He'd become resigned to the knowledge that he would never be cured of Gus's death. That he would grieve for Gus until his own passing.

But he had Vicki and he had John. The wounds he'd suffered at seventeen were beginning to heal. A new challenge lay ahead. There was room for grief, and good things, too.

TWENTY-FIVE

LADY, THE brown house dog at Walter Reed's occupational therapy room, trotted across the carpeted floor to Sergeant Joseph Anderson, who sat snapping the fingers of his right hand. The Lab came to him and smelled his hand, licked it, and allowed Anderson to rub behind her ears. The dog closed her eyes as if in pleasant sleep.

"She digs it when I rub her there," said Anderson.

"And she doesn't even have to guide you," said Raymond Monroe.

Sergeant Anderson's left forearm was flat on a padded table. Monroe sat beside him, kneading his muscles. This arm ended with a prosthetic hand that was decorated with a continuation tattoo, the word *Zoso* spanning flesh and synthetics.

"I don't like it when a woman tells me where to put my hand," said Anderson. "I like to find that spot my own self."

"You're into the challenge, huh?"

"When they get to moanin, it's like, yeah, I just did something special. Like the sign said: Mission Accomplished."

Monroe said nothing.

"Do you think I'm gonna do all right, Pop?"

"What do you mean?"

"With the women. Am I gonna be hittin it when I get out of here?"

Monroe looked into the young man's eyes. He pointedly did not look at the raised red scars crisscrossing the left side of his face.

"You're gonna do fine," said Monroe.

Lady broke off and walked across the room to a soldier who had said her name.

"I'm not exactly what you'd call handsome anymore, am I?"

"I'm no Denzel, either."

"No, but I bet you were plenty handsome when you were young. You had your strut in the sun, didn't you?"

"Yes, I did. And so will you. Women gonna be all over you, boy. With that personality of yours. What do they call that? *Infectious*. You're gonna do fine."

"We'll see," said Anderson. "Still, I been feeling like, you know, the best times are behind me. You ever get like that?"

"I do," said Monroe. "But that's part of being a middle-aged man. You're just getting started."

"It doesn't feel that way, sir."

"Maybe you ought to talk to the shrink about all this."

"It's easier talkin to you."

Monroe rubbed his thumbs deeply into the brachioradialis, the major muscle of Anderson's forearm.

"It's funny," said Anderson. "People think we were in some kind of living hell over there. Make no mistake, it was rough. But alongside the confusion of war and the general shitstorm we were in, there was also . . . well, I was at peace. Strange to say that, I know, but there it is. I woke up every morning knowing exactly what my job was. There wasn't any doubt or choice. My mission was not to liberate the Iraqi people or bring democracy to the Middle East. It was to protect my brothers. That's what I did, and I never felt so content. Don't laugh at me, but that year I spent in Iraq was the best year of my life."

"I'm not laughing," said Monroe. "They say men are goal oriented. You had your mission and it made you feel right."

"That's what's got me down, Pop. I should *be* back there, with my men. Because I didn't finish. I wake up in the morning now and I feel like there's no reason to get out of bed."

"You want to do something? Go out there and tell people your story. *Say* what you did. Folks in this country are so divided right now, they need good people like you to tell them that we're one community. That we've got to rebuild."

"Don't go putting me up on a pedestal. I'm not proud of everything I did."

"Neither am I." Monroe stopped working on Anderson's arm. "Look, Sergeant. You're gonna realize something as you get older. Hopefully it'll come to you quicker than it did to me. Life is *long*. Who you are now, the things you did, how you're feeling, like your world is never gonna be as good as it was? None of that is going to matter as you move along. It only will if you let it. I'm not the person I was when I was young. Shoot, I had an incident today . . . Let's just say I had to walk a whole lotta miles to learn how much I've changed. Whatever you did before doesn't matter. What matters now is how you make the turnaround. You're gonna be all right."

"Did you get all that off a greeting card, Pop?"

"Aw, screw you, man." Monroe blushed. "I told you to see a professional."

"I should have known a Redskins fan would be an optimist. Me, I don't see any Super Bowls in your future with Coach Gibbs at the helm. What is he, ninety?"

"You think he's old? Cowboys coach wears his pants any higher, he's gonna choke hisself."

"We'll see you this fall."

"Twice," said Monroe.

He went back to his task. He turned Anderson's arm over and worked the flexor ulnaris and radialis.

"You know, sounds to me like you got some real depression," said Monroe. "You really ought to talk to the house shrink."

"She's not as entertaining as you." Anderson grunted. "That feels good, Doc."

"I'm no doctor."

"You're good as one."

"Thank you," said Monroe.

ALEX PAPPAS arrived at the nursing home on Layhill Road and found Miss Elaine Patterson in the group dining hall, not far from the reception desk where he had signed in. An orderly pointed to an old woman with thinning white hair and eyeglasses who was seated in a wheelchair at a round table with two other women her age and a woman who was spoon-feeding her. Alex had a seat, introduced himself, and got only eye contact in return. He had bought some carnations at a grocery store on the drive out, and he told her they were for her but kept them held across his lap.

Beyond pleasantries, he did not try to engage her in conversation. He did not want to speak about the incident in front of the caregiver, an African by the sound of her accent. He wanted her to enjoy her meal, as unappealing as it appeared to be. Also, there was much noise in the dining hall. Conversations repeated, orders and requests shouted at the employees, and the sound of one woman who was cursing like a rap artist and being ignored. In a room adjoining the hall, a woman played a piano and sang "One Love, One Heart" off-key.

Miss Elaine Patterson was in poor condition. One side of her face, collapsed and sunken by time, was obviously paralyzed, the left half of her mouth slack and heavy with drool. Her left hand was a claw, her left leg swollen and without muscle tone. Her speech was halting, with long silences between words, and slightly slurred. *She must have children and grandchildren*, thought Alex. *She is staying alive for them.*

After the last bit of applesauce was wiped from Miss Elaine's chin, Alex told the African orderly that he would wheel Miss Elaine to her room. The orderly asked Miss Elaine if that was all right with her, and she said that it was.

He pushed her down a long hall, past a nurses' station. Going by the residents' rooms, Alex heard game shows on televisions turned up way too loud. The smell of urine and excrement was faint but unmistakable.

Her room was private, with a view of the parking lot. He left her in her wheelchair beside the bed, and turned down the sound of her TV, which was showing a black-and-white movie on TCM. He substituted the carnations for a bunch of daisies whose edges were brown and wilted, and ran water into the vase. He replaced the vase on a stand where many photographs of middle-aged people, people in their twenties, and babies and children were on display. He pulled a chair beside her and repeated his name, which he had told her in the dining room. He told her why he was there and assured her that he would not stay long.

"Rodney . . . called me," she said, telling him to get on with it.

"Then you know that I was one of the boys who came into Heathrow Heights."

"Yes," she said, and pointed a finger of her working hand at his face. "Charles Baker."

"Right. I'm the boy who was beaten up." Alex looked away from her, then back into her black eyes, magnified by the thick lenses of her glasses. "I was on the ground, facedown. I didn't see the actual shooting."

"Neither . . . did I."

"But in court you related what you did see."

Miss Elaine nodded. She used her good hand to adjust the dead one in her lap.

"I saw you standing on the porch of the market," said Alex. "And then you went inside."

"Because . . . there was going to be . . . trouble."

"You watched from the window. And then you turned away to call the police."

"To tell . . . the owner."

"To tell him to call the police. But what did you see before you turned away from the window?"

Miss Elaine removed her glasses and wiped at her eyes with the back of her hand. She wasn't upset. She wasn't stonewalling him. She was thinking.

"I saw . . . the heavy white boy . . . get out of the car. I saw him get punched. The smaller white boy . . . *you* . . . tried to run. But you got kicked to the ground. One of the Monroe brothers had a gun . . . in his hand. The one with the gun . . ."

She stopped abruptly. Alex waited, but nothing came.

"Please, go on."

"He wore a T-shirt. . . . The number ten was written on it. Charles was yelling at the one with the gun. Charles was . . . always bad."

"What happened next?" said Alex, hearing a catch in his voice.

"I got Sal. . . . He called the police. I didn't see anything else. Next thing I heard . . . was the shot."

"You said all of this in court?"

"Yes. I testified. I didn't . . . want to. Those Monroe boys . . . The whole family . . . was good. I don't know why that boy did . . . what he did. It was . . . a tragedy. For all of you."

"Yes, ma'am," said Alex, looking down at his hands, balled into fists. He opened them and took a deep breath.

"Why?" said Miss Elaine.

Alex could not reply.

RAYMOND MONROE and Marcus returned from Park View Elementary, where they had been playing catch with a baseball on the weedy field alongside the school, at dusk. Marcus's mother, Kendall, was seated at the kitchen table, reading the *Post*, when they entered her house.

"Y'all have a good time?" she said.

"Kid's got an arm," said Raymond, his hand resting on the boy's shoulder.

"Go wash up," said Kendall, "and get your reading done before supper."

"It's Friday," said Marcus. "Why I gotta read?"

"You do it now," said Raymond, "and you got the whole weekend off to relax."

"Wizards playin tonight," said Marcus.

"You need to read before you watch the game," said Kendall.

"Gilbert got hurt, anyway," said Marcus.

"We still gonna root for 'em, right?" said Raymond. "I mean, would you turn down a chance to go see them play just 'cause Gilbert's not on the court?"

"To go to a game, for real? No!"

"Do your reading," said Raymond. "When you're done, come see me. I got a surprise for you, little man."

Marcus scampered off to his bedroom.

"You got the tickets?" said Kendall.

"Three," said Raymond. "Bring your binoculars, girl."

"Thank you, Ray."

Monroe washed his face and hands at the kitchen sink, then went upstairs to Kendall's bedroom, where he had a seat at her desk and clicked the Outlook icon on her computer. He hit Send and Receive in his personal box and watched as mail arrived. He felt his pulse quicken, seeing the subject head on one of the e-mails.

Monroe read the message. He read it a second time.

The cell phone in his pocket vibrated. He pulled it free, looked at the caller ID in the window, and answered.

"What's goin on, Alex?"

"Raymond. I'm glad I got you."

"Is this about Charles again? Look, man, I know it's a problem, but I'm gonna figure out a way to deal with it."

"It's not about Baker. Raymond, can I—"

"What?"

"I'd like to see you and James tonight. It's important."

"James is working, man. Gavin's got him on a late job."

"I'll meet you both there at the garage."

"I would need to call James and see if that's all right."

"It's important," repeated Alex.

"I'll get right back to you," said Monroe, and he ended the call.

He would call James in a minute. But first he needed to get downstairs and tell Kendall the news. Kenji was back at the Korengal Outpost after a long patrol. His son was alive.

TWENTY-SIX

TWO MEN sat in a gray Dodge Magnum that was facing east on Longfellow Street. They had chosen the spot because it was not under a streetlamp. The windows of the Dodge were tinted but not to a degree that would attract suspicion. They were from Maryland, but the car was a hack with D.C. plates. There were police on car patrol in the neighborhood, as the station was nearby, but the law would not bother with two men approaching middle age who were spending the early evening conversing in their vehicle. They looked unremarkable. They looked like they belonged here.

Their names were Elijah Morgan and Lex Proctor. They were in their late thirties, broad shouldered, strong, quick, and slightly overweight. They could have been road workers or hardware store clerks. Morgan had a squarish head, Asian eyes, and a close cap of pomaded hair. Proctor was dark, finely featured, and handsome until he smiled. His teeth were false, looked it, and were cheaply made. In their home neighborhood, in a section of Baltimore south of North Avenue and east of Broadway, they were known as Lijah and Lex.

Morgan sat under the wheel and stared through the windshield at an apartment house on Longfellow. It was a plain brick affair without balconies, its windows backed by blinds. Many of the units on the first and second floors had barred windows. Two stairwells served the building. A sign with white script letters mounted above one of the stairwell openings read Longfellow Terrace. Both of the men had already urinated once into plastic water bottles they had brought along. They had been here since sundown and were unhappy about it. Neither of them had any love for Washington, D.C.

"How we gonna know if it's him?" said Proctor.

"We'll say his name. If he react, it's him."

"I'm sayin, what's he look like?"

"Like a straight Bama," said Morgan. "He ain't been uptown all that long. Dresses like nineteen seventy-five. Got a long scar on his face."

"And the white boy?"

"You see many around here?"

"No."

"He's white. That's all you need to know."

"Why you gotta act the bitch?"

"Okay. The boy got a rack of pimples."

"On his face?"

"Nah, motherfucker, on his ass."

"See?" said Proctor. "You always tryin to be funny."

Proctor leaned forward off the passenger bucket. The thing that was holstered and hanging across his back under his cream-colored shirt was bothering him as it pressed against the seat. He hoped it would not be much longer before the old man or the white boy came outside.

"They got an alley behind this building," said Proctor, "right?"

"Every street in this city do," said Morgan.

"First one that comes out, we'll take him back *to* it."

"Okay," said Morgan, laughing deeply as a thought came into his head.

"Why you so amused?"

"On his face," said Morgan, shaking his head. "*Shit.*"

CHARLES BAKER was seated at the computer, struggling with the letter he was writing to Alex Pappas. He was trying to get the tone right. He was stuck on one line that did not sound correct.

" 'Give me what I ask for, and you won't never hear from me again.' Is that how you'd say it, Cody?"

"That's how you'd *say* it," said Cody Kruger. "But you'd write it out different."

"How?"

"Should be 'you *will* never hear from me again.' "

"Damn, you good," said Baker, tapping at the keyboard, fixing the mistake. "That's what I get for not finishin high school."

"Neither did I."

"How'd you know that, then?"

Kruger shrugged. He slipped into his lightweight Helly Hansen jacket and put two bagged ounces of weed into its inside pockets. He hadn't asked about the gauze bandage on Mr. Charles's neck or the bruise along his jawline. It was just another day of misfortune for him, Kruger supposed, and he didn't want to aggravate him any further by bringing the subject up.

"I gotta deliver these last two OZs," said Kruger.

"You hear from your boy Deon?"

"No."

"Now his mother ain't pickin up the phone. No matter. We don't need them anyway."

"But what're we gonna do? I'm sayin, Dominique and them haven't contacted us yet. Don't you think that's strange?"

"They just figurin on how to come to terms with us, is all. But see, I get this money from Pappas, we won't need to deal with no marijuana, anyhow. I don't even *like* that business, man. I'm thinkin, I get this money, we gonna share it. Not fifty-fifty or nothing like that, but I'll give you a taste. 'Cause you been loyal to me, Cody. You my boy."

"Thanks, Mr. Charles."

"You can just call me Charles. You earned that."

"All right, then," said Kruger. "I'm out."

Kruger left the apartment and walked onto the landing and down the steps, his chest swelling with pride. Okay, so Baker was a little bit silly and stupid with his schemes. Writing letters when he could just talk to the man face-to-face. Meeting lawyers for lunch. Trying to move in on the main weed dealer in the zip code. But Baker had thought enough of him, Cody Kruger, to call him an equal. Not fifty-fifty, but still. It meant something to be treated like a friend and a man.

You can just call me Charles. He'd never felt that kind of respect at his home or in school.

Cody stepped out of the stairwell of the building, into the night air. He went to the sidewalk and headed for his car. Two older dudes had come out of a station wagon thing and were walking toward him. They were big but looked to be minding their own. As they neared him, he saw a small gun emerge from one of their jackets.

Not tonight, thought Cody. His knees shook. He wanted to book but could not. They were up on him quick.

"Don't think about runnin." One man was in his face, the barrel of the gun pressed against Kruger's middle.

"Where your car at?" said the other man, who had moved behind him and was talking softly in his ear.

"Take us to it," said the man with the gun. He had a square head, Chinese eyes, and pomaded hair. "Open all the doors at the same time."

Kruger led them to the Honda, hoping to see someone else on the street, hoping, for once, that a police would drive by. But there was no one out, and he opened all four doors with the key fob he had retrieved from his jeans. He was directed to the driver's seat, and the gun was held on him as he settled into it. The man with the gun got into the backseat and the other one slipped in beside Kruger.

"Put your hands on the wheel and touch your forehead to it," said the man beside him.

Kruger did it. He farted involuntarily, and the man in the backseat chuckled.

The man beside Kruger gave the chuckling man an evil look, then frisked Kruger while he was in that forward position. He came away with a cell phone and two bags of weed. He told Kruger to sit back and returned his phone and his marijuana.

"Drive to the alley," said Elijah Morgan from the backseat. When Kruger did not move, Morgan said, "Hurry it up, boy. We just want to talk to you."

Kruger ignitioned the Honda and drove it behind the building. His teeth were chattering. He thought this only happened to frightened characters in cartoons.

"Keep drivin," said Proctor, sitting beside him. Kruger went slowly until they came to a spot in the alley where light was not bleeding out from the apartment windows. In this place it was close to full dark.

"Right here," said Proctor. "Cut it."

Kruger killed the engine.

"Which apartment you stay in?" said Morgan.

"Two ten."

"The old man up there now?"

Kruger nodded.

"Is he strapped?"

"No."

"Is he alone?"

"Yeah."

"Here's what I need you to do," said Morgan. "Call the old man from your cell. Tell him you forgot somethin and you comin back to the apartment to get it. Use your speaker so we can hear the conversation."

Kruger dialed up Baker's cell and activated the speaker.

"Yeah, boy," said Baker.

"I'm on my way back."

"So quick?"

"I ain't gone yet. I forgot my iPod."

"You and your gizmos."

"I'll be there soon, Mr. Charles."

"Thought I told you . . . All right, use the code."

"I will."

Kruger ended the call. Proctor took the cell phone from his hand and slipped it into his own jacket pocket.

"What code?" said Morgan from the backseat.

"He likes me to knock on the door a certain way when I come back home," said Kruger. "Before I turn the door key."

"Which key?"

Kruger took the keys out of the ignition and held out the one to the apartment. Proctor took the full ring.

"How does that code go, exactly?" said Morgan.

Kruger's lip quivered.

"Tell us," said Proctor gently. "What's gonna happen to him is gonna happen."

"Knock pause knock pause knock," said Kruger.

"Do it on top the dash," said Morgan.

Kruger rapped it out with his knuckles.

"Like Morris Code, Lijah," said Proctor, smiling at the man in the backseat.

Now one of them had said the other's name. Kruger knew what that meant. His bladder emptied into his boxers. Urine slowly darkened his jeans, and the smell of it saturated the interior of the car.

"Aw, shit," said Proctor.

"I won't tell nobody nothin," said Cody Kruger. "I won't."

Morgan lifted his Colt Woodsman and shot Kruger in the back of his neck. The .22 round shattered his C3 bone and sent him to darkness. He slumped to the side, and his head came to rest on the driver's-side window. There was little blood, and the small-caliber report had not carried far outside the vehicle. Kruger's Nike Dunks, trimmed in leather and hemp, drummed softly at the Honda's floorboards.

"Tool up," said Morgan.

"I'm good."

"I'll be in the hack, waitin on you," said Morgan. "Soon as I wipe this car down."

"Get there quick. I won't be long."

Proctor got out of the Honda and walked down the alley. Coming around to the front of the apartment building, he saw a Fourth District police cruiser coming down the block, its light bar flashing. After it had passed, Proctor pulled a pair of latex gloves from his jacket. As he neared the stairwell, he fitted the gloves onto his hands.

*   *   *

RAYMOND AND James Monroe stood in Gavin's Garage beside a white '78 Ford Courier. The hood of the minitruck was raised, and shop rags were spread on the quarter panel lip. A can of Pabst Blue Ribbon sat on one of the rags. James Monroe picked it up and took a long swig.

"Alex Pappas gonna be here soon," said Raymond. "Why don't you finish the job?"

"I'm close to done," said James. "What's he want with us, anyway?"

"He spoke to Miss Elaine. Least, I had Rodney point him that way."

"Why?"

"Because he did what I asked. Charles Baker threatened Alex's family, and he didn't call the law. He did that for *you*, James."

James scratched at his neck and had another pull of beer. "What should we do about Charles?"

"I already did it. I went to his group home and got up in his face. I don't know if he's smart enough to listen."

"I guess we'll see."

Raymond shifted his weight. "I almost killed him, James. I was carrying that screwdriver Daddy sharpened with the bench grinder he had."

"I remember it."

"I swear to God, I was close to pushing the screwdriver straight through his neck."

"But you didn't."

"No."

"'Cause you're not like that. You've got too many people counting on you. That little boy, and your own son, too. Not to mention all those soldiers you're workin on over there at the hospital."

"That's right. I got a lot of reasons to stay right."

"Charles don't need killin, anyway," said James. "He *been* dead."

Raymond nodded.

"Go on over there and fetch me a crescent wrench," said James. "While you're near the cooler, grab your big brother a cold beer."

"You're just as close to it as I am. Why don't *you?*"

"My hip."

Raymond Monroe walked to the workbench and did as he was told.

TWENTY-SEVEN

CHARLES BAKER read the letter he held in his hand. It was a good one. He hadn't addressed it to anyone in particular for security reasons, but it definitely was convincing. Baker had mentioned family several times in the space of two paragraphs. Not saying what he would do to them if he did not receive the money, but getting his message across nonetheless. Implying that the consequences would affect the Pappas family if he, Charles Baker, were to be ignored.

Baker had heard many times that "family was everything." He supposed that it could be true. Of course, it had been his personal experience that family, and loyalty in general, meant nothing.

Baker had no knowledge of his natural father. His mother, Carlotta, a brown-liquor alcoholic, had been a less than nurturing presence in his life. She had inherited her house, a two-bedroom structure of fallen wood shingles and exposed tar paper heated by an old woodstove. The roof leaked, and when windows got broke they stayed broke.

One time Ernest Monroe had come over with his sons, James and Raymond, and they had fixed the windows, using putty and little bits of metal that Mr. Monroe called glazier points, trying to teach Charles something. But Charles did not want to learn. The Monroe family thought they were doing something Christian, coming to his mother's house to fix the windows for free, but they were just trying to feel good about themselves, helping out the disadvantaged folks in the neighborhood, doing the work of God and all that. Charles never did like that family anyway. The boys showing off, handing their father his tools and shit, his putty knife and those stupid little points. The father with his job working on buses, wearing a uniform like it meant something, when he wasn't much more than a grease monkey. Charles didn't like them coming around to his house, acting superior. Seeing that shithole where he stayed at and feeling sorry for him. He didn't need their sympathy.

Charles had no father, but he had men around the house. One in particular, Eddie Offutt, who claimed he worked construction but slept off his hangovers till noontime. Offutt had been around for most of Baker's childhood. He liked to look at Charles across the dinner table with wet and knowing eyes. Charles Baker had listened to him and his mother laugh and drink at night, and he'd listened to them argue, and he heard the slaps across the face and his mother's sobbing, and he heard them fucking in his mother's bed. Sometimes Eddie Offutt would come into Charles's room at night and talk to him real soft with that smell of liquor on his breath, and he'd touch Charles's privates with his rough hands and put hisself into Charles's mouth. Telling Charles that it was all right but that others might not understand. Telling Charles that if he told, word would get out to the other boys in the neighborhood. Later on those same nights, Charles would lie on his mattress, listening to the dogs barking in the nearby yards, watching the black shadows of the tree branches, like claws trying to gain purchase on his bedroom walls. Charles's hands balled tight, dirt tracks on his face, as he thought, *Why was I not born in that house down the road with the fresh paint? Why don't I know the names of tools, the parts under the hoods of cars, the names of those players on the basketball teams? Why can't I be hugged by a man who loves me instead of touched by one like this?*

It wasn't just Offutt. Friends betrayed him, too. Larry Wilson had been his running partner when they were kids, his true boy. But Larry went into the air force while Charles was doing his first stay in prison, and by the time Charles had got out, Larry was working for the park service as some kind of ranger in West Virginia. Years later, when Larry Wilson was visiting Heathrow as a middle-aged man, he bum-rushed his family into their car when he saw Charles walking down the block. So went Larry. As for the Monroe brothers, shit, he'd stood tall and gone to jail behind them. Now they were turning their backs on him. Loyalty and friendship meant nothing to them. They didn't mean dick to Charles, either.

No matter. The second half of his life was going to be different. He'd be coming into money shortly. He had plans.

There was the sound of keys jingling outside the apartment's front door. Then a rap on the door: knock pause knock pause knock.

It wasn't the code.

Charles Baker got up out of his seat and walked back to the bedroom, to where Cody kept his gun.

LEX PROCTOR stood in the stairwell of the second floor, listening. He had knocked on the door in the manner that the white boy had said to do, and heard no response, only the scraping of a chair and footsteps.

Proctor reached into his inner jacket pocket and pulled free a .38 with electrical tape wrapped around its grip. He fitted the key to the lock, turned it, and stepped inside. He closed the door with his back, keeping his eyes ahead. He looked around the living room and the kitchen. No one was in sight. But he knew that the old man was here.

There was a hall. Proctor went along it with care.

He was pleasantly aware of the knife hanging in a holster under his shirt and against his back. He had paid dearly for it, and it was his prize possession. The blade was over twelve inches long and carried upon it the etching of a bird. Its five-inch handle was lacquered wood. Its pommel plate was thick and made of silver. It was a dagger, and it was weighted for throwing. It was not a hunting knife but a knife for close-in fighting. It was designed for the purpose of combat and killing men. One could stab with it or slash with it, as with a sword. The deep gash marks it left, due to its weight, mystified forensics units. One look at it panicked opponents. This was no bullshit Rambo knife. It was called an Arkansas toothpick, and it was a murder tool.

Proctor passed an open bathroom door and saw nothing. He continued down the hall, came to a closed door at the end of it, tried the handle, and found it locked. He knocked on the door and heard that it was hollow, then he stepped back, put his shoulder down, and charged forward.

CHARLES BAKER stood by the dresser, staring stupidly at a drawer holding boxer shorts and nothing else. Cody had got rid of his gun.

At least the white boy had tried to warn him by giving out the wrong code. Baker guessed that Cody had been murdered. Whoever had done the boy was now coming to kill him. Baker could hear footsteps in the hall.

He looked at the window. It was only a second-story drop to the alley. But the window had bars on it. No gun and no means of escape. A lifetime of fuckup and here he was. If Baker were the type to find humor in such things, he might have laughed.

There was a knock on the door. Baker turned to face it.

The door crashed open. A man stumbled into the room and stood straight. He was large and looked agile despite his weight. He held a gun loosely at his side.

"Who sent you?" said Baker.

The man said nothing.

"Say your name," said Baker, but the man merely shook his head.

Baker reached into the pocket of his black slacks and pulled his switch knife with the imitation-pearl handle. He pushed the button, and the blade sprang out of the hilt.

"You gonna do that thing from there?" said Baker. "Or are you gonna be a motherfuckin man and come *here?*"

Lex Proctor smiled. His teeth looked plastic and gray. He dropped the revolver back into his jacket pocket, reached behind him under his shirt, and pulled his long knife from its holster. Baker's eyes went wide. Instinctively, he raised his forearm to cover his face.

Proctor crossed the room very quickly. He brought the knife down like a sword, and its blade cut deeply into Baker's wrist. Baker dropped the switchblade, his arm useless, his hand swinging as if hinged. For a moment, Proctor studied his prey. He grunted as he swung the blade into Baker's neck. It cleaved flesh, muscle, and artery, and Proctor stepped into a crimson spray as he hacked at Baker again. He turned the hilt in his hand to alter his grip for power, and as Baker slumped against the wall, Proctor hammered the knife into his chest and twisted it in his heart. He stabbed like a blind butcher, diligently and repeatedly, long after the light had left Baker's eyes. Baker dropped to the wood floor.

Proctor stepped back to get his breath. The effort had tired him. He reholstered the knife and walked from the room. Leaving the apartment after checking the stairwell through the cracked-open door, he paused once more at the entrance-way to ensure that he would not be seen.

He crossed the short yard fronting the apartment house and got into the passenger side of the idling Magnum. Proctor peeled off his gloves and tossed them on the floorboard of the hack.

Elijah Morgan examined his partner. Proctor's shirt and jacket were slick with blood.

"Ain't you a mess," said Morgan.

"Man said to make it personal."

They drove out of town, finding a radio station they liked halfway up 295.

TWENTY-EIGHT

THREE MEN sat in an alley under the light of a security lamp and a crudely painted sign reading "Gavin's Garage." Two of them, Alex Pappas and Raymond Monroe, were on upended crates. The third, James Monroe, sat in a foldout sports spectator chair that Alex had brought from the back of his Jeep. All of them were drinking beer. James had his resting in a holder cut into the sailcloth arm of the chair.

Raymond had told Alex about Kenji's e-mail but was careful not to go on about it, mindful of the fate of Alex's own son.

"Kenji's got a long way to go before he comes home," said Raymond. "They'll be extending his tour, I expect."

"God protect him," said Alex, his usual comment when speaking of the young men and women serving overseas. Knowing, rationally, that God took no side in the human folly of war.

James took a pull of beer and wiped the excess from his chin. "This is nice and all that. Sitting out here in the fresh air, having a cold brew. But I've got to finish replacing the belts and hoses on that Courier."

"You said this was important," said Raymond to Alex, completing James's thought.

"Yes," said Alex.

"You got something you want to tell us?" said James.

"I'm sorry," said Alex. "That's the first thing I want to say. It occurred to me that I've never said those words to the two of you. I thought it was time."

"Why?" said Raymond.

"Funny," said Alex. "Miss Elaine asked me the same thing today. I wasn't sure what the question was, but I can guess. Why did we *do* it? Why did we have to drive into your neighborhood that day?"

"Well?"

"The simple answer is, we were all dumb kids. High on beer and pot on a summer day with nothing to do but find trouble. We didn't have anything against you guys. We didn't know you. You were the ones on the other side of town. It was like throwing a rock at a hornets' nest or something. We knew it was wrong and dangerous, but we didn't think it was going to hurt anyone."

"Not hurtful?" said James. "Your friend screamed *nigger* out the window of his car. It could have been directed at my mother or father. How is that not *hurting* anyone?"

"I know it. I *know*. Billy was . . ." Alex tried to find the word. "Billy was crippled, man. His father made him that way. It wasn't even hate, because he didn't have that kind of thing in him. He was a good friend. He was looking out for me, even at the end. I really believe that he would have turned out fine. If he had lived, if he had gotten out of that house and into the world, on his own, he would have been fine. He'd be sitting with us here today, having a beer. He *would*. If he had only lived through that day."

"What about you?" said James. "What's your story?"

"My brother's sayin, why were you with them?" said Raymond. "Because we've talked about it. And both of us remember that you were just sitting in the backseat. You didn't yell anything and you didn't throw anything. So why were you there?"

"I wasn't an active participant," said Alex. "That's true. But it doesn't absolve me. I could have been stronger and told Billy to stop what he was about to do. I could have gotten out of the car at that stoplight, up at the entrance to your neighborhood. If I had just done that and walked home, I wouldn't be carrying this goddamn scar. But I didn't. The truth is, I've always been a passenger, riding in the backseat. That's no excuse. I'm telling you, it's who I am."

James nodded, his eyes unreadable. Raymond stared down at the stones in the alley.

"What about you guys?" said Alex. "Anything you want to say?"

Raymond looked at James, imposing and implacable in his chair.

"Okay," said Alex. "I'll just keep going, then. You know the other night, when we were in the garage? The night I met you, James. You and your brother were revisiting your lifelong argument, the Earl Monroe versus Clyde Frazier thing. Raymond, you were talking about it, and I saw a shadow cross your face."

"That was just a tiny shadow," said James, forcing a smile. "That was the little man Gavin walking into the garage to give me hell. Man throws dark on all of our worlds, doesn't he, Ray?"

Raymond Monroe did not respond.

"That's what I thought, too," said Alex, "at the time. But then I got thinking further. I'm talking way back, to when I was a teenager. In the seventies, you couldn't buy replica jerseys like you can today. Maybe upper-class kids could, but I don't recall seeing any. We used to make our own, with Magic Markers. Put the name and numbers of our favorite players on the front and back of our white T-shirts, go to the courts, and play ball like we *were* those players. I know you guys did the same thing. I had one I made with Gail Goodrich's name on it. Small shooting guard for the Lakers."

"White boy out of UCLA," said James. "They called him Stumpy. Had a nice jumper, too."

"Yeah," said Alex. "Goodrich wore number twenty-five. I also made an Earl Monroe jersey. He was number fifteen when he played for the Knicks."

"We know that," said Raymond. "Why don't you tell us where this is going?"

"I got hold of the partial court transcripts from the trial," said Alex. "The transcript said that the shooter was wearing a T-shirt at the time of the murder."

"So?" said James. "I was wearing the shirt when I got arrested. That's no secret."

"I'm not finished," said Alex. "Miss Elaine told me that the boy with the gun was wearing a T-shirt had a number that was hand-printed across it. She has very good long-term memory, despite her stroke. She said that the number on the shirt was the number ten."

"Say what's on your mind," said Raymond.

"You might have been wearing that shirt when you were arrested, James. But there wasn't any way you would have put on a Clyde Frazier T-shirt when you got up that morning. You were an Earl Monroe man all the way. You *still* call him Jesus. I'm talking about Earl when he played for the Knicks and wore the number fifteen."

"Make your point," said James.

"You didn't shoot Billy Cachoris," said Alex. His eyes went to Raymond. "*You* did."

"That's right," said Raymond Monroe evenly. "It was me who killed your friend."

TWENTY-NINE

E VERYTHING HAPPENED quick," said James Monroe.

"James had this gun he'd bought hot," said Raymond. "I had just found it the night before. Charles tipped me off. That morning, I had put it in my dip, with the Frazier T-shirt hanging over the butt. A boy finds a gun, he's got to hold it. My father never kept one in the house for that very reason. He knew."

"When y'all came back up the block," said James, "and Charles knocked your friend's teeth out and then stomped you on the ground, Raymond's fever got up."

"I was young and hotheaded," said Raymond. "And being young, and a boy, I looked up to Baker. He was dangerous and slick, everything I wanted to be at that point in time. I pulled the gun out and pointed it at your friend. James didn't even know I had it. He pleaded for me to stop. But Charles kept pushing me, man. He won out, and I shot your boy in the back." Raymond chewed on his lower lip to stem the tears that had come to his eyes. "When I saw what I'd done, I got sick inside. James took the gun out of my hand and pulled me away. We ran back to my parents' house 'cause they were at work.

We got ourselves into our bedroom, and that's where we made a plan. I was outta my mind. . . ."

"*I* wasn't," said James. "I knew what had to be done. Raymond was too young to go to prison. I knew he couldn't jail, not even juvie hall. My father had charged me with looking after him, and I did. I wiped that gun down good and made sure my own prints were on it before I put it back in my drawer. I took that bloody T-shirt from Raymond and I put it on my own self. That's how the police found me when they came through the door."

"Charles Baker was in on it, too," said Alex.

"Sure," said James. "It turned out good for him. He flipped on me and made a deal with the prosecutors. Because of that, he only drew a year."

"That's why he thinks you owe him," said Alex. "That's why he keeps coming back."

"Like a penny you can't spend," said James.

"You went along with it," said Alex, looking at Raymond.

Raymond nodded, his eyes wet in the light.

"I was persuasive," said James. "The way an older brother can be."

"How did you all keep the secret?" said Alex.

"Wasn't hard," said James. "Miss Elaine was the only one who had seen Raymond holding the gun. But she couldn't say under oath who it was specifically. 'It was one of the Monroe brothers' is what she said on the stand. Back then, even with our three-year age difference, we damn near looked like twins. Same height. Even wore our hair in the same kind of blowout. She testified that the shooter's T-shirt had a number on it, but no one knew what the number meant except us."

"And your parents," said Alex.

"Yeah, they knew," said James. "When I was in holding, my

father and I discussed it deep. It hurt him to let it go to trial like that, but I convinced him that it was for the best." James looked at Raymond. "And it was, Ray. It *was*. I mean, look how you turned out."

"And look how it turned out for you," said Raymond.

"Don't put that on yourself," said James. "If I had handled my incarceration better, it might have been all right. I thought I'd do a couple of years and get bounced for good behavior. But prison, it even makes a clean man dirty. Those hard boys tried to take me for bad in there, and I felt I had to defend myself or die. One awful decision followed another, and when I came out I got mixed up with Baker again. I just made some real bad choices, I guess. Anyway, here I am. I can't change those things now."

"You're talking like it's over," said Alex.

"Not all the way," said James. "But I sure can see the finish line."

"Before all this happened," said Alex. "I'm sayin, when you were eighteen years old. Isn't there something you wanted to accomplish up the road?"

"You mean, like a goal?" said James. "There were things I had my sights on. But there ain't no point in talking about that now."

"So you got all this information," said Raymond. "What do you plan to do with it?"

"Nothing," said Alex. "We've all suffered enough."

A long-haired cat crossed through the shadows of the alley. James watched it as he drank off more of his beer.

"That's it?" said Raymond.

"Not quite," said Alex, turning to the big man in the chair. "You feel like going for a ride, James?"

"Where to?"

"I'll show you when we get there."

"A girl gonna jump out a birthday cake, somethin?"

"Better," said Alex. "Come on."

THEY STOOD in the empty space of the brick building off Piney Branch Road. Alex had turned on all the fluorescents inside and the spots out in the parking area. He was making comments and gesturing, talking more to James, letting James think on it, letting him see it.

"Here you go," said Alex, removing the Craftsman measuring tape that he had clipped to his belt, handing it to James. "Check it out yourself. It's wide enough to fit two cars with space for two guys to move around them and work."

"Two guys?" said James, taking the tape and going to the left wall, limping a little as he made his way. Raymond followed him, then held the end of the tape to where the concrete floor met the cinder blocks, so that James could walk the tape to the right wall.

"Right," said Alex. "You're gonna need help. An apprentice, like. You can't work on two cars at a time."

"Okay," said James to Raymond, after James had noted the width of the space. Raymond released the tape and joined his brother in the center of the room.

"We can install a couple of lifts," said Alex. "Beef up the electric service. Get you updated on tools. Get one of those, what do you call that, *diagnostic* machines they hook up to cars now."

"Like a computer, James," said Raymond. "I've seen mechanics use laptops now."

"I know what they do," said James, rubbing at his cheek. "But I don't know how to do all that stuff. All these rice burners out here, the German and Swedish cars, and I can't work on 'em. I don't have the experience."

"I'm going to send you to classes," said Alex. "You need to quit Gavin's and start preparing yourself. I'm transitioning myself out of the coffee shop, so there's going to be six months, a year maybe, before we can open up. I'll put you on a salary right away."

"What kinda salary?"

"We're gonna work it out," said Alex. "Whatever the going rate is for mechanics. And, oh yeah, music. I plan to bring in satellite radio. There's this station you're gonna like, it's called Soul Street. They play the good stuff you can't hear on the regular radio anymore. Bobby Bennett's the host."

"The Mighty Burner?" said James, his eyebrows raised.

"Him," said Alex.

"You don't mind my asking," said Raymond, "where is all the money coming from?"

"Don't worry, I have it," said Alex. "When my father died, he left me and my brother insurance money off a policy he had bought from a guy named Nick Kambanis. I put it in blue chips, like my dad would have done, and left it alone. My intention was to pass it on to my sons. Well, Gus was killed, and I just handed Johnny the business. So I'm going to draw from it for this."

"You said before *we* can open up," said Raymond. "What's your role gonna be in all this?"

"I don't know anything about cars," said Alex. "But I know how to market and run a small business. That's my specialty. I'm going to bring people through the front door, keep them coming back, and have them tell their friends, because of your good work, James, and because we'll be providing good service. I'll do flyers in the neighborhoods around here, place ads in the local papers to get us started, that kind of thing. My wife, Vicki, will be our accountant."

"But what's the arrangement going to be?" said Raymond.

"Forgive me for looking the gift horse straight in the mouth, but I'm thinking about the welfare of my brother."

"We're gonna be partners," said Alex. "You and me, James. I own the real estate; that's always going to belong to me and my family. But after your salary, any profits will be split even, fifty-fifty. The equity in the business will be shared the same way."

"You're comin off thirty-some-odd years in that diner," said Raymond.

"Why would you want to jump right back into something like this?" said James, completing his brother's thought.

"Because that was never mine," said Alex. "It was my father's, and I never had his passion for it. It was only a vehicle to provide for my family. I'm ready to take control of this and make it happen."

"Man does have fire," said Raymond to James.

"Come outside with me," said Alex.

Raymond and James exchanged a look before following Alex out into the lot lit by floodlamps in front of the building.

"We can stage cars out here," said Alex. "The guy who had this space before enlarged this for customer parking. And I was thinking we'll mount a basketball hoop up there. I always wanted one at my place of business."

"Do I look like I can ball with this hip?" said James.

"You could if you did your exercises like I told you," said Raymond.

"It's way past that and you know it," said James.

"You're gonna have health insurance now," said Alex. "Up the road, we get this thing going, maybe you can have that operation they do, to correct it."

"Ain't nobody gonna cut into my hip with a chain saw," said James.

"A surgeon does that procedure," said Raymond. "Not a landscape crew."

"And look," said Alex, hyped now, pointing to the space above the open bay door. "That's where we're going to mount the sign. I was thinking about the name of the business. You ready? *Monroe the Mechanic*."

"Does have a ring to it," said Raymond.

"That's 'cause it's got the double *M*'s," said James. "That's why it sings. It's called alliteration, Ray."

"I knew that," said Raymond. "Why you always have to school me?"

" 'Cause you're stupid."

"So what do you think?" said Alex.

James looked at the wall where the sign would be. He looked into the space through the bay door.

"I suppose you want a hug or something," said James.

The lines around his scar deepened as Alex grinned.

"Me and James need to talk a little," said Raymond, thanking Alex with a nod.

"Go right ahead," said Alex.

He watched them walk back into the building. They stood in the fluorescent light, bantering, arguing, touching each other on the shoulders and arms as they made their points.

"Man's got his head in the clouds," said James with a smile.

He's talking about me, thought Alex. John Pappas's son.

The dreamer.

The Writing Life
By George P. Pelecanos

Most of us, it seems, end up where we are supposed to be.

In the summer of 1968, two months after the riots, I went to work for my father at his lunch counter and carryout, The Jefferson Coffee Shop, on 19th Street between M and N. Every morning I took a D.C. Transit bus down Georgia Avenue, passing by charred storefronts on 7th Street, continuing on to F where I transferred to the cross-town line. The fires of April had crippled the city, but there had been a cleansing, too. It was obvious in the chin-high attitude, straight-up posture, and proud style of hair and dress of Washington's working class; obvious, even, to an eleven-year old boy. I found myself looking at these people on the bus, wanting to know more about their inner lives.

My father employed a skeletal, long-time staff. Through them I learned about struggle, friendship, hard triumphs, depression, alcoholism, loyalty and trust. Through our interaction with the suit-and-tie customers I learned about race and class. We worked to the sounds of gospel and soul stations WOOK ('K comes before L') and WOL. The old-school jams of that era, and the voice of DJ Bobby 'The Mighty Burner' Bennett, will be with me forever.

My job was to deliver food, on foot, to the offices in the Dupont Circle area. I listened closely to the rhythms of the speech and the unique slang of the street. I became familiar with every alley. On my runs I made up stories, serial-style, complete with music, to pass the time. I would space the stories out so that they would climax at the end of the week. I thought I was making movies, but I was writing my first books.

My teen years consisted of Rec-Department baseball, beer and fortified wine, girls, marijuana, pick-up basketball, musclecars, Marlboros, rock and funk concerts at Fort Reno and Carter Barron, and stock-boy positions at now-shuttered retailers like Sun Radio at Connecticut and Albemarle. Occasionally, I found trouble. When things threatened to spin out of control, I remained grounded by my family and a martial, Greek-American work ethic I had absorbed, by example, from my parents. It would be hypocritical now to rewrite my history or deny the elements of my former life. Yes, I wasted a lot of time. And yes, it was a whole lot of fun.

Meanwhile, my imagination continued to be ignited at the movies: *The Dirty Dozen* at the Town, *The Wild Bunch* at the Allen, spaghetti westerns and Bond at the RKO Keith's and the Loew's Palace, anything at the Circle, and blaxploitation and kung-fu wherever I could find it, from U Street to Hyattsville's Queens Chapel Drive-in.

And then, finally, in my last year of college at the University of Maryland, books. A teacher, Charles C. Misch, turned me on to the wonders of hardboiled crime fiction and its masters: Chandler, Hammett, Ross Macdonald and the rest. Peripherally, the stories were about crime; specifically, they dissected American society and human politics from the level of the street. In a reversal of the plot trajectory of most popular fiction, the protagonists in these novels rarely won. Noirists like David Goodis presented characters that stumbled and often fell, reaching for and sometimes grabbing a kind of tarnished, unbeautiful redemption. For the first time I knew, with the shock of recognition that only the most fortunate experience, what I wanted to 'do'.

How to get there was the question. Teachers had told me that I had a natural talent for writing, but I was clueless as to the mechanics. I had never taken a writing class. I wasn't connected. Novelists were other kinds of people, like pro athletes or movie stars. Writers had a certain pedigree and, as I had read many times on the back flaps of their books, 'divided their time between Manhattan and Martha's Vineyard'. How could any of this be for a guy like me?

Ten years passed. I fell in love with Emily Hawk and we were married. I continued to toil away at blue and gray-collar jobs. It was not as if I was putting on a literary pith helmet, going undercover among the masses to gather material for the books I was 'someday' going to write. I was simply working to pay my bills. I sold women's shoes. I hustled other kinds of salesfloors, washed dishes in kitchens and poured drinks in bars. All the while I read voraciously, amped by writers like James Crumley, Newton Thornburg and James Lee Burke, who were bringing a literary pedigree to the genre table and turning crime fiction on its head.

In 1989, inspired by the punk-rock movement, in which untrained musicians picked up guitars and played, I decided that I was ready to write a novel. I spent the next year in a dark room, writing in longhand, filling notebook after notebook, not knowing if I was writing for anyone other than myself.

My manuscript, *A Firing Offense*, was bought by the first publisher who looked at it. I was on my way. I took a job working in the local film industry, and in the next decade co-produced several independent features. I wrote a book a year, at night, as my family grew to five.

On an extended stay in Brazil, in the fall of 1993, I saw hungry children too weak to go on and children with murder in their eyes; it rocked my world and my world view. I began to write with more ambition. I chronicled the societal changes in Washington from 1933 to the present in four novels that have come to be known as the *D.C. Quartet*. Those books, the Derek Strange novels, and my most recent stand-alones, deal with local issues facing the working class: the endangerment of the city's youth, sub-par schools, racism, drugs, corruption, illegal guns, the importance of family, the responsibility of parenthood and the struggle to find some kind of spirituality in a violent world.

All of the novels, to some degree, attempt to humanize and illuminate the lives of people who are typically under-represented in American fiction. I mean to leave a record of this town, to entertain and to provoke discussion. My method is simple: to present the world as it is, rather than the way readers want it to be.

It is an unusual way to make a living. The work itself can be intense, solitary and socially retarding. When I'm writing a novel, I write seven days a week. On serious jags, I rarely leave the house. There are also long periods of inactivity, just sitting around thinking, bouncing a rubber ball on the hearth, listening to music, mind-navigating intricacies of plot and characters, dreaming. I've learned that this is part of my job, too.

When I speak to groups of students in public schools, I tell them that, twenty-five years ago, I was exactly where they are today. I want to demystify all of this, make them see that whatever they want in life is within their grasp. But they have to take the first steps. They have to try.

My life has accelerated to a different level these past couple of years. I travel extensively, both nationally and abroad, to promote the books. I've done readings in rowdy London pubs, drank Guinness and Irish whiskey in Dublin, eaten like a king in Athens, walked through Paris at Christmas time, and appeared on prime-time television shows overseas. I've been flown to foreign arts festivals to introduce and discuss my beloved westerns and film noirs. I ride in limousines, stay in first-class hotels, meet with rappers and actors on film projects, hear my voice on NPR and routinely see my face in magazines and newspapers.

And, honestly, I just laugh. I laugh because I know where I came from, and that's not me.

In the end, nothing has really changed. I'm still watching the people on the bus. I'm still walking the alleys, making up stories in my head. I'm where I'm supposed to be.

A version of this essay first appeared in the collection 'The Writing Life', published by Public Affairs in 2003.